SWEET JUSTICE

SWEET JUSTICE

Jerry Oster

1817
HARPER & ROW, PUBLISHERS, New York
Cambridge, Philadelphia, San Francisco, London
Mexico City, São Paulo, Singapore, Sydney

A HARPER NOVEL OF SUSPENSE

FIRST EDITION

Designer: Jane Weinberger

Library of Congress Cataloging in Publication Data

Oster, Jerry.
  Sweet justice.

  I. Title.
PS3565.S813S9   1985   813'.54   84-48186
  ISBN 0-06-015401-2

85 86 87 88 89 10 9 8 7 6 5 4 3 2 1

SWEET JUSTICE

Although this novel is set in what is recognizably New York City, none of its characters represents or is based on persons living there, or indeed anywhere, and all the incidents are imaginary.

ONE

Carlos drew his knife along the woman's thigh, bared to her hip by the slit in her long black dress.

The Prince shuddered and dipped, eyes clenched, dancing to the *salsa* blaring from the Panasonic he held in the crook of his arm, like a baby.

Zero undulated on a bench, sucking a joint.

With the stiletto point Carlos touched the space between the woman's breasts, her bare shoulders, the hollow at the base of her neck. Her green eyes studied him with contempt.

Zero laughed. "Yo, Carlos. You gonna *fuck* that broad?" As did all his efforts to be as one with Carlos, this one fell flat—flat on its face on the concrete subway platform.

Carlos traced with the knife point the underside of the woman's arm, bent into a hanger for a short white fur jacket slung over her shoulder.

The tracks clanked. A wind stirred in the tunnel.

"Train," Zero called, slithering off the bench, seeking redemption. He leaned over the edge of the platform, confirmed his prediction, and stood straight, tweaking the collar points of his nylon windbreaker. "I tolja. A train. 'Bout fuckin' time."

1

The Prince changed stations, twirling past commercials, news, talk, Mozart, Mantovani, searching for another song just like the other song, a shark needing to be ever in motion, sifting life from the music.

Carlos stepped back to see the woman altogether. Her left hip was shot and her left hand rested on her rump—rested lightly, not in place there but only passing over in a caress. Her skin was white: white against the black dress, white against her auburn hair, white against her crimson-painted lips, white against the short white fur jacket. On her left wrist was a gold bracelet, on her right ring finger a silver ring. She wore silver high-heeled sandals. She had been everywhere, done everything, and would again, as soon as there was something new to do; to run with her would be expensive.

The wind from the tunnel blew harder; it stank of the leftover heat of summer.

The poster was bigger than any other on the station walls; the woman was nearly life-size. She had been posed in front of a set that simulated Manhattan's skyline—lighted windows in buildings silhouetted against a night sky garnished with a crescent moon. The windows formed words: CHANNEL 3—THE PLACE TO BE. Above the window, in script the red of the woman's lipstick, was the invitation: *Stay Up Late with Chris Kaiser*. Below the woman's feet, in block capitals the silver of her sandals, was the exhortation: WATCH NEW YORK'S LATEST NEWS. MIDNIGHTS ON CHANNEL 3 WITH CHRIS KAISER . . . IT'S EXCITING!

The train's grumble became a roar.

Carlos wanted to be in her mouth, her ass, her cunt. He wanted to be pumped dry, sucked dry, pumped dry again. He put the point of the knife between her legs and pressed down hard, breaking the paper. He drew back his hand and stabbed at her crotch.

Zero laughed, slapping his thighs. "Stick her, man, *stick . . . her.* Yo, Prince. Check it *out.* Carlos is stickin' it to this *broad.*"

Carefully, Carlos slit her throat.

The train racketed into the station, swallowing the music, drenching the platform with heat and noise. Carlos stepped back from the poster, retracted the knife's blade, slipped it in the pocket of his camouflage jacket, then turned away.

The train stopped with a screech. The Prince's music bubbled up. "Yo, Carlos. Let's *go*, man." Zero stood in the middle door of the last car, holding the sliding panel open with his foot.

"Let go of the doors in the rear." The conductor's weary voice on the intercom droned through a blizzard of static.

Zero leaned out and gave the conductor the finger. He looked at Carlos for approbation.

Carlos put his hand on Zero's chest—it was soft, boneless—and pushed him into the car. "Come *on*, fuckhead. You heard the man." Carlos stayed at the door as the train strained into motion, looking back at the woman, who would no longer torment him. Then he moved to stand with his back against the pole in the center of the car, facing forward, his hands in the hip pockets of his jeans, knees loose to take the jolts, his eyes on the legs of a tiny Oriental woman in a nurse's uniform.

From its terminal at Two Hundred Forty-second Street in the Bronx to this stop, One Hundred Sixty-eighth Street in Manhattan, the southbound Broadway local had scraped only a few passengers off station platforms. They were out of sync with most of the rest of the world: workers getting off shifts or going on them, night people stepping out early, early risers slouching home late. And specialists: a bum who had made the train his flophouse for the night and was making his second round trip between the Bronx and the Battery; a graffiti writer who would change at Times Square for the Flushing line out to the yards in Queens—his studio—where he would spend the night decorating idle trains in Wild Style. The passengers sat flight distance apart, cloaked in fear, for any one of them might be a mugger—except the nurse, who could be only a victim.

The Prince turned the Panasonic up to hear the music over the noise of the train.

Zero inhaled the last of the joint and flicked the roach at an open window. It missed and fell on the seat beside a man in jeans and a corduroy jacket who read a paperback book. The man swept the roach off the seat with the book.

"Yo, *fuck*head. No litterin'." Zero laughed and looked at Carlos's back, his eyes begging him to turn and appreciate. When he looked

3

back, the man's eyes were on him, understanding his dependence. Zero read an ad poster over the man's head—or tried to; he had stopped going to school in the fifth grade.

Carlos undressed the nurse slowly in his mind, tossing aside the cap, the cape, pulling away layers of starched, sterile clothing until her tiny body lay spread out before him. He hissed through his teeth and smiled when she wouldn't look at him, for he knew she had heard. He sat across from her, his legs stretched out, his red Converse All-Stars nearly touching her miniature white shoes.

She drew her feet back.

No one got on or off at One Hundred Fifty-seventh Street.

Carlos moved to sit next to the nurse. She smelled clean. Her tiny hands held her pocketbook pressed against her pelvis. Her flat face was dull with fear. Her eyes were wide.

Carlos put a knuckle against her neck behind her ear and lifted a flap of her helmet of hair. "Hey, baby, you wanna have a good *time?*"

She shut her eyes and held her breath.

Carlos ran a fingernail under the lobe of her ear. "I gotta *big* dick."

The nurse got up and walked on stiff legs toward the door at the front of the car.

Carlos caught up with her and took her wrist and turned her around, pulling her close and ducking to kiss her mouth. She turned her head and he got a mouthful of hair.

Zero laughed, in spite of himself, then was at Carlos's side, a finger pointed between the nurse's eyes. "Yo, cunt. You don't like my *friend* or somethin'?"

Carlos took Zero by the collar and thrust him toward the door to the next car. "Don't let nobody *in* or out."

Zero, poor Zero—his given name was Roberto, after a baseball star, but he was ever Zero, not even a cipher—raised his hands and let them fall. "How'm I gonna do *that?*" He felt the eyes of the man in jeans and corduroy on him and wouldn't look at him.

Carlos slumped with despair. "You got a fuckin' *knife*, right?"

Delighted to be reminded, Zero took the knife from his jacket pocket and switched it open and sliced the air as he backed toward the door. "Nobody fuckin' *move*." He felt the man in jeans and corduroy shift on his seat.

4

The Prince, unbidden, was already at the rear door, his Panasonic on the floor between his feet, silent, holding his knife in both hands, a fighter.

Carlos held his knife in front of the nurse's face and sprung the blade. Though her eyes were shut, she started. He laughed. "Hey, baby. Don't be *scared*. I just wanna make *nice* with you."

The passengers sat numb and dumb, replicas of human beings, praying that it would end. All but the man in jeans and corduroy, who sat forward, his elbows on his thighs, the paperback book still open in his hands, like a missal, but not studying the text, watching everything.

The train went slower and slower until it crawled, checked by some inexplicable signal on the brink of the One Hundred Forty-fifth Street station.

Zero was sure someone had pulled an emergency cord, that the cops would swarm around the train, blinding them with flashlights, their bullhorns whining with feedback. "Yo, Carlos." He winced as Carlos flashed him a look of rebuke for naming him. "I . . . I just wanna know are we gonna get *off* here?"

Bumping his knees against her legs to make her walk, Carlos paraded the nurse down the aisle, stopping before each passenger, sneering as each looked away. "*Maricos.* Fuckin' cowards. Ain't you gonna *help* this chick? *Huevones. Hijos de puta.* Or maybe you want a piece of the action. That it, fuckheads? You wanna *fuck* this chick? Fuck *you*. Me and my friends here, we're gonna have a little *party.* The rest of you, you're gonna stay where you are. You're not gonna come after us. You're not pulling no emergency *cord.* You're not calling no fuckin' cops. You're gonna keep on going wherever you was going. You're gonna forget you saw *any*thing. You're not gonna remember *noth*ing. *Nada.* You *dig*? Don't worry about the chick here. We're not gonna hurt her. We're just gonna have a little party, me and my *friends* here." Carlos put the knife handle between his teeth and stroked the nurse's breasts, her mons, her buttocks.

Zero laughed, but he knew he wouldn't be able to get hard. He would go last, as he had the time Miguel's cousin from Santo Domingo had taken them all on; the thought of her, slick with their semen, made him sick to his stomach even now.

5

The train bucked, then began moving slowly into the station.

"Carlos." The man in jeans and corduroy stood in the aisle. He closed the paperback book and slipped it in a hip pocket.

Carlos took the knife from his mouth and held the point against the nurse's throat. "Sit the fuck *down*, man."

"Let her go," the man said, raising his voice only enough to be heard over the noise of the train. "Just get off here, like you said, but without her. Just get off here and everything'll be cool. No cops. Nothing. Now let her go."

He was lean, like a runner. He wore moccasins and a navy turtleneck sweater. He might have been a student, somewhat superannuated, or a precocious professor—of English or mathematics. He might have been a poet, or a banker out slumming.

"Let her go," he said again. It was a command—not a suggestion, not a plea.

Carlos heard the man's authority and sensed his quickness and his strength, but he was high on the danger; it was too far to come down. "*Coño de tu madre.*"

"*Carlos.*" Zero pressed against the door, ready to bolt. "We're *stop*ping."

The man took a step. "Let her go . . . Carlos." He smiled at the advantage—however slight—the name gave him.

Carlos dented the nurse's skin with the knife point. "Stay *there*, motherfucker."

The man kept coming, slowly, lithely.

The nurse opened her eyes. "No. Please. He'll kill me."

The man stopped. He ran a hand through his brown hair, combed straight back from his forehead. He turned abruptly and held the hand out toward the Prince, who had slunk closer. "Stay there."

The Prince smiled and moved his knife from hand to hand.

The man took a pistol from an inside pocket of his jacket and pointed it at the Prince's face, crouching slightly, feet spread, both hands aiming the gun. The Prince melted away.

The train stopped. The doors opened.

"Zero! Hold those fuckin' *doors*." Carlos backed toward the door, dragging the nurse with him.

6

Zero moaned at the loss of anonymity.

"Carlos!"

Crazily, Carlos peeked from behind his shield, compelled by the man's shout. They were more than adversaries; they were dancers in the same dance, and he must respond. The bullet hit him between the eyes.

Carlos's weight drove the nurse down over a metal seat arm, knocking her breath away. When she got it back, she screamed.

Passengers sprawled and cringed and screamed.

Zero ran. The Prince ran, forsaking his Panasonic.

The doors closed. The train ground into motion.

The man pulled Carlos's body off the nurse and flung it on the floor, as if it weighed nothing. He touched the nurse's shoulder until she looked up at him. He smiled, put a hand on her head, then went to the front of the car, opened the sliding door, and stepped out on the metal platform. He unslung the metal chain, stepped up on the conductor's footrests, opened the accordion gate, and jumped onto the platform, hands out, ready to fall, falling, rolling, coming to his feet, his pistol—put away as he jumped—drawn again, his feet spread, both hands supporting the weapon.

The platform was empty.

The man put the pistol away, brushed the platform's grime from his jeans and jacket, wetted a fingertip in his mouth and rubbed at a scrape on the soft side of his left hand, ran his hands through his hair, and walked to the exit.

The token clerk in his bulletproof redoubt only glanced up from his newspaper as the man went through the turnstile. The headline said:

VICTORY CLAIMED
OVER SUBWAY CRIME

TWO

DeWitt Strawberry unzipped his pants. He'd been hard for an hour, and his thing popped out like a jack-in-the-box. He fondled himself as he peered into the blackness, trying to make out the ebony paradise Ivory Snow Richardson had promised him.

"Ivory? Ivory, you there? Come *on*, girl, don't tease a man like that. I'm 'bout to pop."

There was no answer from the apartment on the top floor of the abandoned tenement where Ivory Snow had told DeWitt she would meet him and give him what he'd been after her for for weeks.

"Ivory Snow?"

DeWitt smiled as he heard a low moan from within the apartment. He got even harder, if that was possible, at the thought of Ivory Snow lying just inside the door on the mattress she said she'd done it on before—she didn't say who with—playing with herself as she waited for him.

"Ivory? What you doin' in there, girl? Tell DeWitt. You got your hand inside your pants, making yourself all nice and wet? Come on, tell DeWitt. . . . You tell me, I'll tell you what I'm doin', how I got my hand around my gigantic thing, so big I can't hardly fit my fingers around it, it getting all slick like with spit at the head, ready to slide into you like a greasy rod, a fuckin' tree limb. . . . Oh, come on, Ivory, tell DeWitt what you're doin'."

Another moan.

"Ivory? You got your hand on your tit?"

And another, which DeWitt was sure meant yes, yes. He took a step into the blackness, which hadn't gotten any more penetrable in the time he'd stood on the landing. DeWitt had stopped at the candy store on the way over and for fifty-nine cents had bought a miniature flashlight, just for the occasion. He felt for it in his back pocket, but he didn't take it out and switch it on. He would wait until he was

8

lying beside Ivory Snow, and by its light he would explore with his eyes her magnificent body.

DeWitt took another step and another.

"Ivory. I'm coming, girl. Your beautiful DeWitt is coming, and he's bringing along his best friend, and, girl, how you're gonna love his friend."

Another step brought his foot in contact with the mattress.

The moaning seemed to come from behind him, from a corner of the room, and DeWitt was momentarily startled. But he knew the tricks sound could play on you in these empty old buildings. He reached out and found a leg with his hand. "Ivory? Ivory, what'd you go and put pants on for? I told you to wear a dress, that red dress you look so fine in. Ivory?"

Still, perhaps they were those tight white slacks you could see the outline of Ivory's panties through. He would turn her over on her stomach and rub his thing against the space between her cheeks that those pants pressed together oh, so finely.

DeWitt knelt on the mattress and with a hand on each leg encouraged Ivory to roll over. "Come on, girl. I got a idea. I think you're going to like it just fine."

The legs were intractable. And not only that, their feet were shod in boots—big, heavy boots.

"Ivory, what're you doin', girl? You playing some kind of joke on DeWitt? *Ivory!*"

He shouted her name toward the corner, for there was no question that that was where the moan had come from. There was no answer.

Boots? Well, boots might be interesting. DeWitt thought about the women in the magazines at the back of the candy store, women who were sometimes photographed wearing boots—high leather boots, cowboy boots, construction worker boots, motorcycle boots—and nothing else. They looked just fine, and so would Ivory Snow Richardson. His ears were just playing tricks on him.

DeWitt lay on his side on the mattress, aching to have her touch him. He fumbled in his pocket for the flashlight and laid it between them, its head pointed toward the head of the mattress. "Ivory? I got something to show you. My friend I told you about? He's here. Come

9

on, girl, shake hands with him, tell him how glad you are to see him. Here, I'll switch on this light so you can get a look at his pretty black face."

With his right hand, DeWitt lifted her hand—her incredibly heavy hand—by the wrist and guided it to his cock. With his left, he switched on the light.

The light was surprisingly bright. It threw a dome of light around the mattress and revealed unmistakably that the individual on the mattress, the individual with a hand on DeWitt's cock, wasn't Ivory Snow Richardson at all but a man, a big man, a man wearing a blue track-suit top with white stripes down the sleeves, a man wearing black chino pants, a man with leather combat boots on his feet, a man with a shaved head and a thick drooping mustache, a man with a hole in the center of his forehead, a dead man.

The light also revealed Ivory Snow Richardson crouched in the corner in a pool of her own vomit, moaning.

DeWitt Strawberry vomited too, all over the dead man's chest.

THREE

All the men at the bar stared up at the television, like devotees before an altar.

The woman on the screen had auburn hair, white skin, red, red lips. Her eyes were green. She wore a lime green silk blouse above whose top button peeked a strip of dark green lace. "Hi. I'm Chris Kaiser. Welcome to New York's *latest* news program on Channel Three—the *only* place to be. . . . At the top of the news tonight: Mayor Berger and Transit Police Chief Nolan held a news conference this afternoon and asserted that the war on subway crime has been *won*. We'll have a report from Jim Giles in just a moment, but first . . ."

A beer commercial rolled.

"Yeah?" The bartender was a woman with disorganized red hair and a face that lacked symmetry.

"A beer," the man in the corduroy jacket said.

"Miller?" She flicked her head at the television. "It's Miller time."

"Ba Mi Ba," the man said. He rubbed the palm of his hand, where there was a red abrasion.

She put her hands on her hips. "Miller, Bud, Rheingold, Schafer, Schlitz, Lite, Heineken, Michelob, Coors, Bass Ale, Löwenbrau, Watney's, Rolling Rock. . . . You want me to keep going? I'm on till four."

"Bud."

"One Bud. Why is it whenever I tell people what beers we have they end up asking for Bud? If that's all the imagination they have why don't they ask for it in the first place?"

The man looked up at the television screen. Chris Kaiser sat in a white leather lounge chair, her long legs crossed, a white scimitar of thigh revealed by the slit in her gray skirt. She held her script in her lap. Her right arm was draped over the back of the chair, a gesture that molded the fabric of her blouse to her breasts.

"Like her?" the bartender said. "Lot of guys like her." She put a glass on a coaster and filled it and set the bottle on the bar. "Never met a guy who didn't like her. One-fifty."

The man paid with a five and sipped the beer and imagined that it was a Ba Mi Ba. But his hand didn't shake. The last time he had had a Ba Mi Ba his hand shook. The last time he had had a Ba Mi Ba he had just killed a man. To protect a woman. An Oriental woman. His hand had shaken then because he hadn't, in fact, protected her. He had arrived too late. All he could do was kill her attacker, perhaps to protect other innocents.

The bartender came toward him, wiping the bar with a towel. "Hurt your hand?" She took it in hers and gently touched the soft

11

flesh. "A bad scrape. You should wash it out. I'll get some hot water from the kitchen."

When she came back, with a bowl of hot water, a towel, and some soap, the man was gone, the beer unfinished, the change from his five on the counter.

"Oh, Linda. You've got the magic touch. And a big tipper, too."

FOUR

Chris Kaiser kicked off her shoes. It was her trademark gesture, a signal that the show was over, an invitation to her colleagues to come down from their podiums, set on risers above the well in which she sat, and stand in attendance around her white leather chair while the crawl ran out. To the audience at home the others were silhouettes; a single spot shone on Chris Kaiser.

She stretched her long body and put her hands behind her long white neck and flounced her auburn hair and smiled. But her voice was ice. "I don't ever want to be made a fool of like that again." To the audience at home she seemed to be talking shoptalk, enjoying the afterglow of a job well done.

Her colleagues bowed their heads, uncertain who of them had offended her by being imperfect.

David Dempsey, the weatherman, stuck his neck out. "There was no way around that forecast, Chris." Chris Kaiser's conviction was that the viewers believed that forecasters *made* the weather—how else could they know what it was going to be?—and that such bleak auguries as Dempsey's—he had predicted rain for the weekend—drove them to switch to other channels.

12

Chris held out her hand and invited Dempsey with a smile to take it. "David, darling. Don't be silly. Summer's over. People're glad to have an excuse to spend a quiet weekend at home."

At home, people wondered if they were lovers. They were always touching, smiling at each other.

Randy Peck, the sports editor, cleared his throat. "I, uh, hope you didn't mind the little joke." Reporting on an investigation by the Bronx County District Attorney into allegations that some local baseball players were doing cocaine, he had, *ad libitum*, called their club "The New York Junkies." Chris liked to make the jokes—or at least to know when they were coming from other quarters, that she might testify with her extravagant laugh to just how funny they were.

Chris retrieved her hand and granted Peck's a squeeze. "Randy . . . that was *fun*ny."

Ruby Tucker's lip trembled. She had sullied her own exclusive— that a settlement was imminent in a wildcat strike by public-school teachers—by saying that, "hopefully," classes would resume on Monday. When she took over as anchor, Chris had made it clear that no adverbs would dangle from her show.

But Chris Kaiser wasn't looking at Ruby, or at Kristen Richards, the entertainment editor, or at Tess Delaney, the New Jersey correspondent, in the studio to introduce a report on the gentrification of Weehawken. She was looking at Jim Giles, smiling a smile that people at home thought full of veneration. For Jim Giles was the doyen of New York television journalists, a man who had learned his craft from Edward R. Murrow and whom many considered to be the only repository of that giant's insight and grace. The anchor of Channel 3's six and ten o'clock news programs for fifteen years, Giles had been moved to the back benches when the station's management, hungry for a larger share of the audience, scrapped the six o'clock report altogether, replacing it with an hour of gossip and entertainment chitchat, and moved the late news to midnight, importing Chris Kaiser from Los Angeles to be its star.

"You screwed up, Jim," Chris Kaiser said, forgoing a more favored verb for one less likely to be lip-read by the people at home. "That transit story was a piece of shit." She smiled especially widely as she spoke the expletive, masking it. "I won't have pieces like that on my show. The viewers know it's a lie, and I won't have them thinking of me as a liar by association."

Giles put a hand in the pocket of his double-breasted blue blazer and fingered the tiny bottle of Dewar's he had emptied just before the show went on the air, while Chris and the others studied their scripts. "Just giving the facts, ma'am."

The camera lights went out and the studio lights came up. The crawl had ended; the show was off the air. The people at home watched a Potamkin Cadillac commercial.

"Facts?" Chris Kaiser screamed. "What facts? So the fucking mayor held a fucking news conference. So fucking what? It's an election year, for Christ's sake. What's he going to say—that he's losing the war on crime? Shit."

The crew, usually quick to leave, lingered in the shadows, enjoying what was becoming a regular epilogue to the show.

Giles took his hand from his pocket and touched the knot of his repp tie. "Aren't you forgetting something? This all started with our exclusive. *My* exclusive. The *Daily News* reported that felony arrests by transit cops were down. Berger got surprised with a question at a sidewalk news conference and admitted it was true. Everyone reported it the same way—Cops Helpless Against Subway Felons—everyone but us. I got the whole report that the *News* got only part of and found that felony arrests were down because *felonies* were down—because of more cops on patrol, more electronic surveillance, more citizens' patrols, more dogs—"

"Dogs," Chris Kaiser said contemptuously.

"Today's news conference confirmed our exclusive," Giles said. "It's a good story all around: The press goes off half cocked *and* things're getting better on the subways. But then, you know all this."

Chris Kaiser spread a hand on her chest, miming innocence. "Do you mean to say no one was mugged on the subway today, Jim?"

Giles reached into his pocket and stroked the smooth surface of the Dewar's bottle.

Chris Kaiser laughed. "Could you look that mugging victim in the face and tell him or her that the war on subway crime has been *won?*"

Giles turned away.

Chris Kaiser laughed again. "What we should've done—what we'll *do* the next time Berger tries to dazzle us with numbers—is send a crew down in the subway at the very *hour* he's holding his news conference. We'll find people who've just been mugged, who've had their purses snatched or their pockets picked. It won't be difficult. Felonies may be down, but they're not out. We'll ask those victims who's winning the war on subway crime. We'll get Berger up here live, face-to-face with those victims. That's what we should've done." She whirled on a production assistant. "Tell Cavanaugh to come out here."

"He's gone home," the p.a. said.

She put her hands on her hips. "Home? How the hell can the *producer* go home in the middle of the goddamn show? Get him on the phone."

"He won't be home *yet*," the p.a. said. "He just left. He lives in Yonkers."

Chris Kaiser rolled her eyes. "Yonkers." Slowly, loudly enough for everyone to hear, she said, "In the future, nobody goes home until I say so. No production staff, no writers, no technicians, no one in the booth, no *talent*." She looked deliberately at her colleagues, that they might know she was referring to them. "The time to talk about what's wrong with these shows is as soon as they're over, not the next afternoon. The next afternoon we should be concentrating on the next show. If we stay late enough, often enough, maybe we won't have so many things going wrong. Maybe we won't have to stay so late so often. Until that time, everybody stays. . . . Clear?" And she started up the ramp toward the door.

Jim Giles knew it was a hopeless cause, but it was a cause nonetheless, and he called after her. "What if we don't find any victims?"

Chris Kaiser stopped and turned slowly to face him. "What did you say?"

"What if we don't find anybody who's been mugged in the subway at the very *hour* the mayor's saying subway crime is down?"

Chris Kaiser put her head back and laughed. "Oh, God, Jim. You're such a bore. Such a . . . a gentleman. No wonder your show had such lousy ratings—a few thousand insomniacs hoping you'd lull them to sleep with a report on *interest* rates."

She walked back down the ramp to her chair and walked round and round it, one hand on the back, as she spoke. "There's never been a local news show in any time slot in any market with ratings as high as this one. But then, you know that. But I'm not sure you know why. It's not only because I'm sexy. Oh, I'm sexy; there's no doubt about that. But there's more to it than that. This show has the highest ratings of any show in any time slot in any market because I don't tell people what they don't want to hear. I don't tell them the city's a garden spot; I tell them it's a jungle. I don't tell them it's clean and sweet-smelling; I tell them it's a cesspool. I don't tell them it's a joy to be out and around in; I tell them the subways're full of killers and the roads full of drunks and the bridges're rotting and the highways falling down. I tell them, in a word, the truth. Call it bad news. Call them scare stories. I call it the truth. The only good news I'll allow on this show is the weather, which is why I don't like David talking about rain on the Fourth of July. The weather's the only thing that people have any hope about at all; I hate to deprive them of that. . . . You tell people the facts, Jim. You tell them about interest rates going up and felonies going down. But you don't tell them the truth. The truth is what exists in spite of the facts. The *fact* is, the unemployment rate's gone down; the *truth* is, people don't have jobs. The *fact* is, subway felonies're down; the *truth* is, people're getting mugged on the subway.

"Sex and violence: that's the formula, isn't it? The formula that sells a prime-time entertainment show, a movie. But it isn't just physical violence that sells; it's emotional violence, economic violence, environmental violence. You wouldn't tell people about that, Jim—which is why they didn't watch you. Oh, you think because you told them about *interest* rates you were telling them about economic violence. But *interest* rates aren't economic violence; economic violence is some poor sucker having his mortgage foreclosed and a padlock put on his front door. Now that's a story I could go for. Find me that man, Jim, and you'll have a good story.

"You asked me a question. You asked me what I'd do if I didn't find someone who got mugged on the subway while the mayor was holding a news conference claiming a victory over subway crime. I'd make up a victim, that's what I'd do. I find some guy and stand him in front of a camera and have him tell how he got mugged on the subway while the mayor was holding his news conference. And he'd do it. And he

16

wouldn't feel he was telling a lie. And I wouldn't feel I was making him tell a lie. He'd be telling the truth—the truth as he felt it. Because the truth is, people're terrified to ride the subway, whatever the facts say, and terrified people are victims."

Chris Kaiser stopped circling her chair and went directly to Jim Giles, stopping with her face just inches from his. "Drinking again, Jim? You know how I feel about that."

Giles gripped the Dewar's bottle so tightly he feared it would break—feared that, if it did, he would pull the shards from his pocket and slash Chris Kaiser's face.

"Which is one more reason, Jim," Chris Kaiser said, starting up the ramp again, "that and everything I just said, why I'm asking Cavanaugh to take you off the show altogether. My viewers want the truth, and I'm not going to be made a fool of by having people on my staff who won't tell it to them." She pushed open the soundproof door with a shoulder and was gone.

An hour later, the production assistant, whose name was Michael Magazine, heard a telephone ringing in Jim Giles's office and went in to answer it. Five tiny Scotch bottles stood in a row at the edge of the desk.

It was Giles's wife calling, and Michael Magazine told her her husband had just left, that there had been a staff meeting. She often called at this time and he always told her Giles had just left, even though Giles left quicker than even some of the crew members.

Michael Magazine dumped the tiny Scotch bottles in the wastebasket under Giles's desk, then thought better of it and retrieved them, finding, in the process, a small cardboard box that had contained a dozen .38 caliber bullets. The box was empty.

He took the bottles and the box to a trash bin in the hall and dropped them in, covering them with discarded wire service copy. He started down the hall, then turned back and retrieved the box and flattened it and put it in his pocket. He went to the newsroom.

Everyone had gone but the cute new p.a., who was jabbing at her permed hair with an Afro comb. She said she lived in Park Slope and hoped she wouldn't have to wait too long for the subway. He said he lived in Bay Ridge and had a car. "Like a ride?"

"For sure."

Michael Magazine tossed the box into a garbage can at the door to the parking garage.

FIVE

Jake Neuman studied the poster of Chris Kaiser, then tucked in his shirt. Even defaced, she made him feel untidy.

Bobby Redfield stood next to him. "Jesus."

"Somebody doesn't like her show, I guess," Neuman said.

"I was on it once, remember? Not *her* show, but a panel she moderated—'Killers, Cops, and the Courts.'"

"I missed it," Neuman said. "I was probably watching a ball game. These cuts're fresh."

Federici slipped in front of him and danced his fingers over the poster, a connoisseur. "Not a razor, but a thin blade. Maybe a shiv."

McGovern laughed. "*Maybe*, Sherlock?"

"A shiv like the DOA's," Federici said.

McGovern sat on a bench and lighted a Lucky. "Steve Federici, the Italian Scallion." He laughed. "Get it, loo? I mean, you ever see anybody so fucking skinny?"

Lieutenant Neuman stretched, trying to wring the last vestiges of sleepiness out of his body. "I've seen enough. Let's get out of here."

Here was the One Hundred Sixty-eighth Street subway station, where, the conductor had told the first cops on the scene, Carlos Pabon and two other Hispanic youths had boarded the southbound Broadway local at eleven twenty-six—if the train was right on time— the night before. The detectives had worked their way uptown from Ninety-sixth Street, where they took a look at the train, which had been routed onto a siding just north of the station; from One Hundred Thirty-seventh Street, where the conductor, alerted by passengers to the shooting, had summoned police; from One Hundred Forty-fifth Street, the scene, however momentary, of the crime—the place where the shooter, along with Pabon's pals, disembarked.

They were light on material evidence—not as light as on some homicides, but lighter than most. The subway car had given up little to Forensics: Pabon's body with a bullet in his brain; Pabon's blood; a switchblade with Pabon's prints, which were already enshrined in the memory of the National Crime Information Center's computer and on dozens of documents in the files of the New York City Police Department and the city and state Departments of Correction; the last half inch of a marijuana cigarette, with a partial print on the E-Z Wider paper; a Panasonic radio with a nice set of prints, but not one that rang any bells with the computer—in short, some spoor of the victim and his entourage, but no trace of the killer—except, perhaps, some partials on the accordion gate between the last two cars, through which he had jumped from the train.

That the killer had jumped they knew from Cecil Briggs, the graffiti writer, who was so far their best witness. A night worker—"Six, seven nights a week I go out to the yards. There's no more space, hardly, on the trains, so many new dudes're working these days, and I got a lot to say and I got to say it 'fore every train in town is filled up"—Briggs hadn't minded hanging around to talk to the cops long after the other passengers—those who hadn't fled when the train stopped at One Hundred Thirty-seventh Street—had pleaded exhaustion and headed for home, leaving behind phone numbers at which they could be contacted for further interviews. He had gladly forgone his art for one night to try his hand at a new medium. By the time the homicide detectives became his listeners, he had crafted a terse ballad.

"I'm sitting there *think*ing, man, laying out in my mind what I'm gonna do that night, and all of a sudden there's this spic with a *knife*, man, got this nurse around the *neck* and saying he's gonna get off the train and have his way with her, man, him and his friends, when this white dude stands up and says, 'Say *what*, motherfucker? You're gonna do *what*? You ain't gonna do shit, 'cept get *off* this motherfucking train, you and your motherfucking friends, but not with no *nurse*, you dig?'—"

"Is that what he said, Cecil," Neuman had interrupted, "or is that your artistic rendering?"

"Hunh? Oh. Shit, no, it's not what he said, I don't 'member what he said, not 'xactly. He said . . . shit, I don't 'member. But, yeah, I mean, yeah, that's like what he said."

"Go ahead," Neuman said.

"Where was I? . . . Okay. So. The spic with the 'Sonic, man, who's been down at the other *end*, he comes slipping up behind this white dude, man, and the white dude takes out this *piece*, man, and points it at the spic's *head* and the spic just fuckin' disap*pears*, man—I mean, like he was *there* and then he was *gone*. And the—"

"You know guns, Briggs?" Redfield interrupted.

"Hunh? No. Me? I'm an artist, man, not a fuckin' *kill*er."

"So you don't know whether it was a revolver or an automatic, or what caliber, or how big, or what color."

"Color? Sure, I know the color. It was black, man, blacker than me, and, yeah, it was an automatic. I mean, they're the ones that look like toy guns, water pistols almost, ain't they? And it wasn't big, not like Dirty Harry or something, but it wasn't small either. But what the fuck—you got a *bullet*, right?"

"Go ahead," Neuman said.

"Where was I? . . . Okay. So. The spic with the nurse, man, he starts backing toward the door—'cause the train's *stopped* now, you dig?—and the white dude yells out, 'Yo, Carlos,' which he knows is the spic's name 'cause the other spic—the little spic by the front door—called him that. The dumb fuck. Man, there is only one thing dumber than a spic, and that's two spics, and the only thing dumber than—"

"My wife's Hispanic," Neuman said.

"Say *what*? Oh, shit, hey, lieutenant, I didn't mean nothing. I'm just saying it was a pretty fuckin' dumb thing to do to—"

"Go ahead," Neuman said.

"Where was I? Okay. So. 'Yo, Carlos,' the white dude says, and Carlos kinda looks out from where he's holding the nurse in front of him, you know, and he *buys* it, man—I mean, one fuckin' shot in the middle of the fuckin' forehead, man. Well, you musta seen the stiff, you know what I mean. And the other two spics, man—sorry, lieutenant, the other two *Hispanics*—I mean, they *left*. And the doors close and the train starts up and the white dude, man, he picks up fuckin' Carlos—you see, Carlos fell on top of the nurse, man, after he bought it—picks him up and *throws* him on the fuckin' ground, man, like he's made of *air*, man—"

"On the ground, Briggs?" Redfield said. "Or on the floor of the subway car?"

"Hunh? Yeah, on the *ground*, man, I mean, on the floor."

"Go ahead," Neuman said.

"Where was I? Okay. So. The white dude, man, he goes over to the nurse, man, and gives her like this *smile*, man, and then he goes to the—"

"What kind of smile?" Neuman said. "Do you think he knew her?"

"Hunh? *No*. I mean, shit, I don't know. *Knew* her? No, he didn't know her. Least I don't think he knew her, I don't know."

"Go ahead."

"Where was I? Okay—"

"Briggs?" Redfield said.

"Yeah?"

"Could you please stop saying 'Where was I?' after every answer to every question?"

"Shit, sarge, I'm just—"

"Sergeant Redfield."

"Sergeant Redfield. I'm just trying to make sure I don't leave nothing out, you know. I mean, sometimes when I'm bombing trains I'll get distracted, you know, the cops'll come or one of them rent-a-cops, and when I get back I'll have to ask myself, 'Cecil, where was you?'—"

"So the male Caucasian smiled at the nurse, Cecil," Neuman said. "Did the nurse smile back?"

"Hunh? *No*. I mean, shit, I don't think—"

"Then what happened?"

"Then the white dude goes to the front of the car, man, and goes out the door and the next thing I see, man, he's rolling over and over on the platform, man. I mean, like the dude *jumped* off the fuckin'

21

train, man, just before we went into the tunnel. He rolled right up on his feet, man, like he'd done it a thousand times before. . . ."

"Go on," Neuman said.

"That's *it*, man. That's all she wrote. We went into the tunnel and everybody's screaming and yelling and this one dude, man, he wants to pull the emergency cord, but I popped him in the gut—not hard, man, just to get his attention, you know—and I say, 'Don't pull that cord, man, the whole fuckin' train'll—"

"What did the shooter look like?" Neuman said.

"Hunh? Shit, man, he was *white*. I can't tell one white man from the next."

"Cecil," Neuman said, "they've got this new thing for people they catch jumping turnstiles, painting graffiti, smoking in elevators, littering, and so forth. Quality-of-life crimes, they call them. They don't exactly incarcerate you, but they don't just slap your wrist, either. In your case, you'd get a month of weekends scrubbing graffiti off trains."

"Yo, lieutenant, now that's a fuckin' good idea, 'cause like I said, there ain't no more *room* to work anymore. I mean, I am the *king* of the graffiti artists, man, and I need more *room*. You should check out my work sometime, man. Sevens, E's, and F's, man."

"The only thing, Cecil," Neuman said, "is we're not talking about a quality-of-life crime in this case. We're talking about obstructing a murder investigation and about contempt if there's a grand jury and you have the same kind of trouble remembering, which means some nice clean walls for you to work on, only not on the subway, Cecil, in the joint."

"Tall," Briggs said. "Six-two, maybe. Brown hair. Not long, but not short, either. Light brown sport coat. Corduroy. Blue jeans. Old. I mean, washed a lot. Didn't notice his shoes, so they was probably just shoes. A sweater—like a dark blue turtleneck. I mean, shit, bro, what're you wasting your time for? The spic was axing for it, man—sorry, lieutenant—the Hispanic dude was axing for it; the white dude just gave him what he was axing for. The dude was *bad*, man. I mean, like fuckin' Dirty Harry, man."

"You said he didn't have a big weapon, Cecil," Redfield said.

"Hunh? *No*. No, he didn't. But I'm not talking about his *piece*, man, I'm talking about his *style*."

"So it wasn't just a lucky shot," Neuman said.

Briggs stared. "Lucky? Shee-it."

"How did he stand? Feet apart? Both hands on the gun?"

"Fuckin'-a right, he did."

Neuman looked at Redfield, who shook his head, meaning he didn't have any more questions.

"Anything else, Cecil?" Neuman said.

"Hunh? No. Well, yeah. The little spic—sorry, lieutenant—the little Hispanic guy . . ."

"What about him?"

"Carlos, man, called him Zero."

"Zero?"

"Zero."

"And the other one? The one with the radio? Anyone say his name?"

"No."

"Where'd you get on the train?" Neuman said.

"I *told* you, man—*Dyck*man Street."

"No, I don't think you did. So you rode a long way before the Hispanics got on. What about the shooter? Where'd he get on?"

"Don't know, bro. I told you, I was thinking."

"Laying out in your mind what you were going to do?"

"Right on."

"But you noticed when the Hispanics got on."

"I heard the fuckin' *radio*, man. And I smelled the joint. *Zero* was smoking a joint. He flicked it at the white dude, like, when he was finished tokin'."

"He flicked it *like*, or he flicked it?"

"You know, man—he *flicked* it. It landed next to the white dude. He swept it on the ground, like, with his *book*."

"Book?"

"You know, man—like a paperback."

"Did you notice the title?"

"What am I, man, a fuckin' libarian? I was thinking about my *work*, man. I wasn't noticing no *books*."

"That's why you're the king, I guess," Neuman said. "Concentration."

"That's why. . . . Listen, lieutenant, I'm sorry I said that about, you know, about the only thing dumber than one Hispanic being two Hispanics. But it's just, you know, man, you told me your name before, man, and you said it was Neuman, man, and I just figured, you know, man, I mean, if you were Jewish then your wife was probably Jewish, too. I mean, I didn't know if you had a wife, but if you did, well, you know, man, I mean, I didn't mean nothing by it."

"You can go home now, Cecil," Neuman said. "We'll be in touch if we need any more from you. You probably gave your number to one of the uniformed officers, but give it to Sergeant Redfield, too, just to be on the safe side."

"Hey." Briggs pointed at Redfield, then at Neuman. "Hey. I mean, holy shit. I mean, check it *out*, bro. Redfield. Neuman. It's like Redford and Newman, man. *Red*ford and *New*man. Butch Cassidy and the Sundance *Kid*. Far *out*, man. Far fucking out."

SIX

They had been known as Redford and Newman throughout the department for years and were known for handling the nuts that were toughest to crack. They didn't usually bother with nickel-and-dime homicides.

But the shooting of Carlos Pabon on the southbound Broadway local, although it had all the earmarks of a nickel-and-dime homicide, was being made into something more by the newspapers and radio stations—and would be made into something more than that by the television news programs that night.

One newspaper, the *Post*, had a headline calling the shooter THE

SAMARITAN KILLER. Another, the *Express*, likened him to the character played by Charles Bronson in *Death Wish* and *Death Wish II*, movies about a single-handed vigilante campaign mounted by a man whose wife was killed and daughter raped into catatonia by thugs. Furthermore, in a front-page open letter to the killer—it didn't call him that—the *Express* invited him to use its pages as a podium from which to tell his side of the story. Was he a man such as the man portrayed by Charles Bronson in the movies? Had he experienced some personal tragedy that left him embittered at the lawlessness that pervaded the city? Or had he acted spontaneously, moved by the plight of the helpless nurse to speak the only kind of language that a miscreant like Carlos Pabon would understand? The letter invoked, as well, Robin Hood and the Lone Ranger, other fictive defenders of the underdog.

The morning papers, which wouldn't go to press until that evening, were searching for wrinkles of their own. The story was the lead item on every radio newscast, and television crews were combing the story's various locales in search of anyone who had seen anything—or who merely had an opinion on what had happened.

In short, it was a "good" story—man bites dog, victim kills victimizer. And it was made even better by coming in the wake of the mayor's declaring a victory in the war against subway crime. It appeared, the *Post* editorialized, that not only had the war on subway crime not been won but it was up to the citizens to protect themselves against the criminals.

The mayor, understandably, wanted to put an end to such opinionating and dispel the circus atmosphere with which the media had surrounded the story. He wanted an arrest, and he wanted it fast. That was the message the mayor's deputy imparted to the Police Commissioner, who imparted it, in turn, to the Chief of Patrol, who imparted it to the Chief of Detectives, who imparted it to the inspector in charge of the Homicide Division, who imparted it to Deputy Chief Inspector Lou Klinger, head of Manhattan North Homicide, who imparted it to Captain Miles Easterly, who would supervise the investigation, who imparted it to Lieutenant Jacob Neuman, whom he awakened out of a sound sleep at six o'clock in the morning.

"Jake, I know it's your day off," Easterly began.

"It's my day off," Neuman said sleepily, trying to work his right arm out from under Maria's torso without waking her.

"And I know I promised you extra time off for the work you did on the Marcetti case," Easterly said.

"You promised me extra time off for the work I did on the Marcetti case," Neuman said, freeing his arm and smiling, for imprinted in the flesh of the underside of his forearm was an impression of Maria's right nipple.

"But—" Easterly said.

"Let me call you right back, Miles," Neuman said. "I want to make a pot of coffee and get my notebook. And I don't want to wake the missus."

"Give my best to Maria, Jake," Easterly said. "And tell her I'm sorry to drag you in on this. You can call me at the office. I'll be waiting."

"Must be important," Neuman said. "You in the office on a Saturday."

"It's political," Easterly said.

"Right," Neuman said.

The coffee made, bacon in the frying pan, two eggs scrambled in a bowl, toast in the toaster, a glass of orange juice in his stomach, Neuman called Easterly back and listened to what little he knew, making notes in his small leather-covered pocket notebook. When Easterly was through, and when he had made his breakfast and eaten it, Neuman called Bobby Redfield, to impart to him the message: "An arrest, one that'll stand up in court, by the numbers, but fast—above all, fast."

Neuman didn't bother to call Redfield's home number, for he knew that there was no chance Bobby would be there—not on a Saturday morning after a Friday night off. Where Bobby would be there was also no chance of knowing, for Bobby rarely saw the same woman more than a few times. He was making up, he told Neuman—whenever he wondered why Bobby seemed intent on sleeping with every reasonably young, reasonably attractive woman in town—for the six years he had spent in Vietnam; he wanted to make sure that the war hadn't destroyed his libido, as it had nearly destroyed his body and his soul. When he was sure, he said, he would be ready to settle down and have a family. Neuman didn't say that Bobby had been home from 'Nam for far more than six years; it wasn't really any of his business.

Neuman called the number that triggered the electronic beeper Redfield wore on his belt, along with his service revolver, Friday night off or no. Then he called the station house, where Redfield would check in to find out why he'd been beeped, and told the uniformed officer on the switchboard to have Redfield call him at home. Then he went into the bathroom to shave, for he knew that Bobby wouldn't just jump out of bed; he'd say a tender goodbye.

He was shaved and dressed when the phone rang. Before he could say anything into the receiver, Redfield said, "What the fuck, Jake?"

"Sorry, Bob," Neuman said. "But it comes from downtown. They've got a job for Redford and Newman."

They looked nothing like Redford and Newman—that was part of the pleasure of nicknaming them thus. Neuman weighed two hundred fifty if he weighed a pound (Maria tipped the scales at two hundred, and during their lovemaking they slapped together like happy whales), he had dark curly hair that no matter how long it was or how short always looked to be the same length—and never looked styled, no matter how much he spent for a haircut—and wore clothes that clashed more often than matched: bright plaids, bold checks, shirts of yellows and blues and pinks that can only be achieved in entirely synthetic fabrics. He had two hats, a straw snap-brim for spring and summer, a brown felt snap-brim for fall and winter.

Redfield looked, if anything, like Al Pacino. He was small and dark, with carefully styled hair, carefully tailored clothes—he favored sport coats over Fred Perry tennis shirts in the summer, a sheepskin coat over a wool turtleneck sweater in the winter, and, as now, in the fall, tweed sport coats over cotton turtlenecks—and a careful way of never letting his face show what he was feeling until he was sure it was the feeling for the situation. If Neuman was sometimes ramshackle in the way he proceeded with an investigation, Redfield was over-scrupulous. Though this was never something textbooks would recommend, it was a perfect mesh of styles, and the results of that meshing were impressive: more arrests—and, more importantly, more convictions per arrest (nearly 75 percent)—than any other pair of homicide detectives in the city.

So successful were they that they had been freed as much as possible from routine. They made their own hours, worked their own work weeks, and, although they operated out of the 25th Precinct Station House in Harlem, were by no means tied to the precinct's boundaries. They were free-lancers, floaters, and they went where they were needed. This might have bred jealousies, caused rivalries, among the homicide squads in other precincts, but Neuman and Redfield were never pushy, never stepped on toes or got in the way of long-established routines and rituals. They tried to function not as chiefs but as braves with special skills.

Their mere presence on an investigation was enough to inspire other detectives—especially younger detectives—to try harder. For example, even after Newman said he'd seen enough at the One Hundred Sixty-eighth Street subway station, Steve Federici, pumped up by adrenaline at having been assigned to work with Redford and Newman, suddenly swooped under a bench—the bench on which Matt McGovern sat smoking—and came up with a burnt paper match. "This yours, Matt?" Federici said.

McGovern, who was a fat, lazy cop incapable of being inspired by anything but the approach of his lunch hour or the end of his shift, rolled his eyes. "What're you going to do, Steve, bust me for smoking in the subway?"

"It's warm, so it's yours," Federici said, and tossed the match aside. Then, like a magician, he showed that he'd been palming a second match. "But this one's cold. . . . Let's just say, lieutenant"—he held the match up so Neuman could see it but kept his fingers over the stem of the match—"let's just say that the kid smoking the joint— Zero, Briggs the graffiti king said his name was—let's just say he lighted up here."

Neuman smiled. "We know they got on here, Steve. The conductor's sure and so are a number of the passengers, including Briggs."

"Which is no big surprise," McGovern said, "seeing as how the DOA lived two blocks away."

Federici tested the roll of his shirt collar. When it felt right, he said,

"But the DOA can't tell us anything about the shooter. The guys who were with him can. This match has lettering on it." And it did; it was a wide cardboard match with an advertising slogan on it: THREE ZS MARKET. FT. WASH. AVE.

"Federici, for Christ's sake," McGovern said.

Neuman felt Federici tense, so he moved between the two and nudged Federici away from the bench. He had been as enthusiastic once, scraping for every piece of the jigsaw when only the center had to be assembled. "We'll find Carlos's buddies, Steve. We know the one's nickname; we've got the other's radio. We'll talk to Carlos's family; we'll ask around the neighborhood. We'll get them. Whether it'll help us get the shooter or not, I don't know, but we'll get them. . . . What you're doing—it's good work, but it's off the mark. It'd be on the mark if we knew nothing: no nicknames, no radio, nothing. Then the Three Zs Market'd be a damned good place to check out."

Neuman ran his fingers under the lapels of Federici's expensive glen plaid suit coat, like a salesman. Time was, all plainclothes cops shopped at Robert Hall, which made them easy marks; nowadays, they dressed like record producers, or gigolos.

"McGovern'll ride you about this for a long time. Let him. All it means is you're working too fine, trying too hard. I'd rather have you doing that than doing what he does, which is collect a paycheck. Redfield'll ride you too, but for a different reason. He'll ride you 'cause he wants you to keep working that hard, but doing it where it really counts, and when. When Redfield ignores you altogether, then you'll know you're fucking up—that you're either so wide of the mark he'll tell me you're a space cadet, or you're missing what's right in front of your face, in which case he'll tell me you're a fuck-up. So ignore McGovern riding you, and be glad when Redfield does."

Federici opened his hand and closed it quickly, like a boy caught by his teacher with a frog. "I should just throw this away, then?"

"You found it, you keep it," Neuman said. "I wouldn't bag it and label it evidence, but I'd keep it in mind. It's not what you found I'm criticizing; it's the time you spent looking. In this case, it was no time at all, so nothing's lost, but it's the principle I'm talking about. Understand?"

"Yeah. Yes, I do, lieutenant. Thanks."

Neuman joined Redfield, who was studying the poster of Chris Kaiser. "Think this means anything, Jake?"

Neuman started to say no, then he said "Well . . . ," then he closed his eyes for a moment, trying to see what might have happened. "Let's say Carlos cut this poster—maybe it was one of the others, but probably Carlos. He was standing around waiting for a train, he saw the poster, he was provoked by it. It's provocative, right? It made him mad. She's not a woman he could have, but she's a woman any man would want. So he cuts the poster, then gets on the train and sees a pretty young nurse. He's wired up, he's horny, he goes over the edge—"

"He gets blown away," Redfield said.

Neuman crossed his arms over his stomach. "Yeah. And by who?" It was so much easier to speculate about what Carlos had done and why he'd done it than to speculate about the shooter. He turned away from the poster, rubbing his hands together, ready for action. "Matty, get the names of all the token clerks working last night between here and Two Forty-two. Just southbound. I don't think we have to bother with northbound. Call them up, ask them did they see anybody who looked like what the shooter's supposed to look like. Where'd he get on? He ever get on there before? Like that. Especially ask the guy who was working at One Forty-five. If he saw Zero and the other guy tear-assing out of there, and then a white guy on their tail, there's a good chance he did more than glance at the white guy. I mean, isn't that the way you see it, Bobby? Don't you figure the shooter went after the other two, too, so they wouldn't I-D him?"

Redfield shook his head. "I-D-ing him indicts them. I think the shooter knows that. I think he let them get away. He had to get off the train, but he probably just got on a bus or in a cab. Or walked away."

Neuman sucked in his cheeks, tasting the notion. He made a face that said it didn't taste badly. "So, Matt, go up on the street at One Forty-five. Ask around. Are there any stores that were open late last night? Anybody hanging around on the street, playing dominoes, drinking beer from bags—it's that kind of neighborhood. Did they see Zero and the other guy leaving the station? Where'd they go? Did they go together or split up? What about the shooter? Anybody see him? Where did he go? Did he get on a bus, in a cab, walk? If he walked, where'd he walk? If he got on a bus, check the schedules, find the drivers working those routes last night. If he got in a cab, check the trip sheets—"

"Trip sheets?" McGovern said with a groan. "Loo, for Christ's sake it was a Friday night. You know how many cabs're out on a Friday night?"

"No," Neuman said, "but when you're through checking trip sheets you'll tell me. And I'm not telling you go do all this legwork yourself, you dumb fuck, I gave you five guys and all the patrolmen you need, so use them." Neuman turned to Federici, who was enjoying watching McGovern take orders. "Steve, you got the list of eyewitnesses, right? Except for Briggs the graffiti king, who I don't exactly trust, not entirely, seeing as how he doesn't exactly love his Hispanic neighbors, everybody else split after they talked to the cops who filed the unusual. So go find them and talk to them some more. Ask them especially did they notice where the shooter got on, if they ride the train regular at that hour did they ever see him get on before, and if they did did they notice where he got off if he got off before they did? Like that. And don't do all the legwork yourself, either; use the guys I gave you. Sergeant Redfield and I'll go talk to the DOA's family and to Miss Koo, the nurse, who I understand is at St. Luke's, which reminds me, Matt, did you call Forensics like I asked you and see if they made that slug yet?"

"A twenty-two. An automatic. They don't know the make yet, but probably a Smith."

Neuman put his hands on his hips. "Any reason you didn't tell me about that when you found out about it?"

McGovern shrugged. "You know. . . ."

"No, I don't know," Neuman said. "Now get the fuck out of here and get to work. You too, Steve. And stay in touch, both of you. Thing like this, we have to be ready to move fast."

Redfield was sitting on the bench, now, and Neuman sat next to him. "So speak to me, Roberto, 'cause I got a feeling you're thinking what I'm thinking."

Redfield rubbed the back of his neck. "I'm thinking I have to do something about this stiff neck."

Neuman smiled. "Rough night last night?"

"The night wasn't so rough, it was the phone call at six in the morning."

"Six fifteen," Neuman said. "Anybody I know?"

Redfield laughed. "You know me, Jake, a different starlet every night."

"I've been meaning to ask you, Bobby. Do you take—you know, drugs or something to keep the equipment going night after night?"

Redfield laughed. "Haven't needed to. You know how it is, you get on a roll. . . . Why? You having a mid-life crisis or something?"

"I won't see mid-life again, Bobby," Neuman said, "and no, everything's great in that department, but—well, being with Maria, it's kind of like having roast beef every couple of nights, or whatever your favorite food happens to be. In your case, you change your diet so often, it's a wonder to me you get enough vitamins and minerals."

Redfield laughed again. "You want to know what I'm thinking, Jake?"

"Yeah. I guess I do."

"I'm thinking, twenty-two-caliber automatic. Small, light, accurate, deadly. A professional's weapon."

Neuman nodded. "Just what I was thinking."

"Briggs the graffiti king said the shooter fired like a trained marksman," Redfield said.

"I remember him saying that," Neuman said.

"So maybe what we have here is more than meets the eye," Redfield said. "Maybe what we have here is a pro on his way to or from a contract. He's riding the train and three punks get on and start giving the nurse a hard time. Maybe he doesn't like punks, maybe he's got a thing for nurses, but he tries to talk them out of it, according to Briggs the graffiti king, but they won't listen. So he does the only thing he knows how to do when someone won't do what he wants."

"Just what I was thinking," Neuman said.

"So," Redfield said, "it might be worth our while to get on the radio and let it be known we're interested in any twenty-two-caliber homi-

32

cides last night—on the chance he was coming back from a job—or early this morning—on the chance he was going to a job."

"And not just last night or early this morning, either," Neuman said, "but maybe any time yesterday and even any time today, or even tomorrow, 'cause for all we know the shooter couldn't keep his appointment on account of what happened on the train and he's still looking to keep it."

"Just what I was thinking," Redfield said.

"Of course, there is another possibility," Neuman said.

"Yeah, I know," Redfield said. "The shooter might not be a pro at all; he might be a cop. And he walked 'cause he didn't want to explain why he was carrying an against-the-regs piece."

Neuman nodded. "I hope to Christ he's not a cop."

Redfield laughed. "If he's not a cop—if he's a pro—it's going to rain on the parade of the reporters who're trying to make him look like a cross between Lancelot and St. Ives."

"Who's St. Ives?" Neuman said.

"Isn't he the guy Charles Bronson played in the movie about the guy who kills the punks who killed his wife?" Redfield said.

"That was another movie," Neuman said. "I didn't see it, but I remember reading about it—a movie where Bronson plays a detective named St. Ives. I didn't see it, so I don't know if he had a shield or was a private. I don't know what Bronson's name was in the other picture. I didn't see it, either."

Redfield nodded over and over, as if Neuman had said something terribly profound. Then he said, "There's only one thing that makes me think the shooter isn't a pro."

"He was carrying a book," Neuman said.

"Right. You ever hear of a pro who reads books?"

After a while, Neuman said, "Gaetano Polazzi."

"Who?"

"He was the hit man in the Meisel rubout. Moonlighted as a pastry chef at Zampieri Brothers."

Redfield laughed. "Not *cook*books, you fat fuck. Let's get out of here. We hang around any longer we're liable to get mugged. The war on subway crime may be over, but there're a lot of stragglers around who didn't get the word."

SEVEN

The Prince put it succinctly. "We split, man, or we go to the joint. I ain't never going to the joint, so I'm splitting. I got an uncle in Detroit." As if he were already there, experiencing a Michigan winter, he hugged his jacket about him.

Zero stared out over the gray, greasy Hudson River. Overhead, the George Washington Bridge made its perfect gesture. His head ached; he was cold; he needed to sleep. Yet he could appreciate the elegance of their dilemma: to say anything was to say they'd been there. Unless . . .

Zero slapped the Prince's shoulder with the back of his hand. "Yo, Prince. I *got* it, man. We don't tell the cops we was *with* Carlos. We tell them we was just on the train—you know, going *out* or something."

The Prince got up in one motion from the rock on the riverbank. He looked naked without his radio—and felt naked. "The *nurse*, man. The other fuckin' *pass*engers. They gonna say we was just passengers *too*? Shit."

"Well, then, no. Hey, whoa, Prince. Listen. We'll *call* 'em. We'll call the cops on the *phone* and tell 'em what the cat looked like who wasted Carlos, man."

The Prince climbed up the slope to the verge of the highway running along the river, traveled only lightly on a Saturday. "They got my radio, man. You know? I paid cash for that, man. Filled out the fuckin' guarantee and everything. They're gonna find me, man. Maybe they won't find you—I ain't gonna tell them—but they're gonna find me, man. And I'm going to the *joint*. Unless I split, man, so I'm splitting. *Adiós*, man. *Adiós, hermano*."

And Zero knew that the Prince, if caught, would turn him in. "Yo, Prince. Wait. Your uncle . . . you think . . . ?"

The Prince shrugged. "¿ *Quién sabe*, man?"

Zero stood up. The bridge made him feel infinitesimal. And yet it arched away from here. Did buses to Detroit leave from the bridge terminal, or would they have to go downtown to the Port of Authority? And how much was a ticket to Detroit? The Prince had a pocketful of money—he worked in a sporting goods store on One Hundred Twenty-fifth Street and had been paid on Friday—enough money, he said, to pay his fare. Zero had a couple of dollars. He knew how to make quite a few more dollars in not very long. He had done it before, giving blow jobs to sweaty gray men in toilet stalls at the Port of Authority. He nearly gagged at the thought. He wanted to go and say goodbye to his mother. He wanted his mother to hold him in her arms. "Yo, Prince."

But the Prince had trotted across the southbound lanes and was standing on the concrete divider, waiting for a break in the northbound traffic.

How simple, Zero thought, for the Prince to jump in front of a speeding car, bringing everything to a conclusion, obliterating the anxiety of being a fugitive. How simple to push the Prince.

But the Prince didn't jump in front of a car; he waited until the way was clear, then jumped down to the roadway, trotted across the three lanes, and went up onto the grass alongside the road. And when Zero stood on the concrete divider, waiting to follow after the Prince, he understood that it wasn't simple to jump in front of a car. It would be more difficult than anything he had ever done, for it would require that he act on his own. And there was no one to push him—no one except the man in jeans and corduroy with the knowing eyes.

EIGHT

Linda Walsh stood very still, her eyes closed, trying to see the future. She couldn't, but nonetheless she turned and ran up Broadway after the man in jeans and corduroy jacket, who had his head in a newspaper as he passed her. She caught up to him and got in front of him and walked backwards. "Hi. Remember me?"

He stopped and folded the newspaper and tucked it under his arm. In his gray eyes were glints of recognition—not of her but of her need.

To Linda the look was as familiar as her own face in the mirror. "Right. The Gold Rail. Last night. Come by again sometime and I'll buy you that beer you didn't finish. How's your hand? My name's Linda Walsh."

He smiled. He had to; he liked her. "Ray." The name sounded strange to his ear—not counterfeit but . . . antique.

Linda put her hands in the back pockets of her moleskin slacks, brand new, just arrived by mail from L. L. Bean, a gift from herself. Who else would give her a gift? She had to tip her head back to look into his eyes, and the sun shone full on her face. She felt sybaritic. "Ray what?"

"Howell." He passed his hand over his mouth as he said it, shaping it into an approximation of the truth.

Nice name. Nice eyes. Nice face. Nicely dressed—casually, as she liked men to dress. He wore a faded blue work shirt instead of the navy turtleneck, for which the day was too warm. Linda felt like a character in a good movie, like a woman in a favorite song—by Bonnie Raitt or Juice Newton. "You live around here, I guess."

"No."

He would say where he lived when he wanted her to know. She was getting to know him.

He wanted her to know something. "I'm from out of town. Here on business. I came up to see the Columbia campus. And last night to see the Gold Rail. A friend of mine went to Columbia, drank at the

36

Gold Rail. He talked about it a lot. It was an important time in his life, the late sixties. I wanted to see it."

Men were like that—loyal to dead friends (he said his friend *talked* about Columbia, about the Gold Rail)—in a way women weren't. Or maybe it was that men were ever nostalgic, missing their games, their pals, their puppy lovers, in a way women, whose capacity to give birth gave them the ability to grow, did not. "And where were you? In the late sixties, I mean." Linda shrugged. "It's not such a silly question. People always ask what you do, where you live, where you're from. They never ask anything that would really tell them something about you—like where you were in the late sixties. I mean, I'm a bartender, right? So you think you know everything about me. But what if I told you that in the late sixties I managed a children's theater company? Plays *for* children, not with children in them."

Ray smiled. "Sounds interesting."

"If you like working with actors," Linda said. "Actors're worse than children. It's 'I, I, I,' 'me, me, me,' all day long. But that's not why I gave it up. I'd still be doing it if it weren't for the economy. We lost our funding. People drink no matter what the economy's like, though, so I went to bartending school. I can make drinks you've never heard of. Not that you'd order one; you'd order a Bud. Look—how about lunch? We don't have to stand out here in the hot sun."

Ray glanced over his shoulder at the sun and was surprised that it shone so brightly, for it wasn't warming him, wasn't driving out the chill between his shoulder blades. Maybe it would be just the thing to have lunch with a woman. When had he last had lunch with a woman? In the late sixties? He nearly smiled, for it had been then.

On June 2, 1968, to be precise, he had had lunch with Leila, red-haired—like this Linda Walsh—slim and pale and beautiful. A picnic lunch beside a stream outside Atascadero. They only nibbled at the cheese and cold cuts. They tried making love behind a scrim of cattails, but their ardor was crushed by the weight of their uncertainty, for that afternoon he was to go by bus to San Francisco, by plane from there directly to Vietnam. They sat on a scratchy blanket and held cold hands and were consumed by dread. It was he they imagined would die; it was she who died, asserted by a syringe on a naked mattress in a cheap hotel just a stagger away from the Greyhound bus station in Los Angeles.

Linda took Ray's arm. "Let's go to the Green Tree. I bet your friend ate there. It's Hungarian—goulash and stuff. Very cheap. I'll buy." She lifted his hand in hers and probed at it gently. "Swelling's down. What were you doing, karate or something?"

Ray smiled and resisted her pull. He had told her nothing, yet he needed to tell her everything, yet there wasn't time and wouldn't be. "I won't be in New York long. When I go, I won't be coming back."

Linda smiled. "An honest man. . . . So it'll be brief, then. Brief is better than not at all. I live right across from the Green Tree. We can take a nap after lunch."

As he let himself get in step with her, he tossed the newspaper in a trash can.

"Hey," Linda said. "I wanted to read that—about the murder on the subway. I heard something on the radio."

Ray wouldn't let her go back. "It's just what you heard on the radio. Nothing to read before lunch."

NINE

Michael Magazine started when the elevator door opened, for Chris Kaiser stood before him, wearing a long black evening dress, carrying a short white fur jacket slung over her shoulder.

Michael smiled when he registered that it was not Chris Kaiser in the flesh but a photograph, like the ones on subway platforms and billboards and bus shelters all over town. It was framed in a white frame and hung on the wall of the foyer outside the door of Chris Kaiser's apartment—the only apartment on the twenty-second floor of

Essex Towers, one of the most exclusive apartment buildings on Central Park West. The floor of the foyer was carpeted in white. The walls and the apartment door were painted white. When the elevator door slid shut, Michael saw that it, too, was white.

Michael stood aside while the superintendent fitted a key into the top lock. He turned it, then selected another key from the dozens on his key ring and fitted it into the bottom lock. Before turning it, he looked over his shoulder at Michael.

"You sure nothing's wrong?" the superintendent said. He was gray: he had gray hair, gray skin, wore gray work pants and a T-shirt gone gray with age; only his shoes were black, but they were covered with a gray dust.

"Absolutely," Michael Magazine said. "Miss Kaiser asked me to come by and pick up some things for her show. She's too busy to get them herself."

The superintendent shook his head, as if that were the wrong answer. "I told you, she ain't been out this morning. The night doorman checked her in at one A.M.—we got a list of tenants and we check them in and out whenever they come and go, for security purposes— but the day doorman ain't checked her out, which means she didn't go out."

Michael didn't say that he had come in through the lobby door unchallenged and had gone all the way to the superintendent's apartment at the rear of the ground floor without a doorman or anyone else asking him what his business was. He just said, "I showed you Miss Kaiser's note. Can we just get the things?" He wanted to be done with this errand as quickly as possible, for he was sure something was wrong.

No one at Channel 3 had been able to understand why Chris Kaiser wasn't at the station first thing in the morning, even though it was a Saturday, her day off, to coordinate the coverage of the killing on the southbound Broadway local.

Ted Cavanaugh, Chris Kaiser's producer, wasn't able to understand it because he had gotten a phone call from her at one thirty in the morning; she had heard the first sketchy reports of the shooting on the radio on getting home and was nearly beside herself with glee.

"Ted, listen," she had said. "Turn on WINS. There's been a murder on the subway. You remember the subway—there was a war on crime down there, but it's over. I want a crew on the scene. I want them there now, not in the morning. One of our crews, not a week-end crew. I want them to shoot everything that moves. Call Art Albert. I know he's on vacation, but he's in town; he's working on his new apartment. Tell him to get up there. Now. Not in the morning. I know he's new, but he's hungry. I want a hungry reporter on this story. I don't care what the weekend news says, this is our story—my story. We'll devote the whole show to it if that's what it takes to tell it. Tell Art I want eyewitnesses. I want cops. I want police brass, TA brass. I want the fucking mayor and I want him good. If he won't talk, send a crew to stake out Gracie Mansion until he shows his cute little bald head. Don't put Albert on the stakeout. Keep him on the move. I want him on live from location at midnight—from wherever the latest developments're taking place. You stay on top of everything. Get every one of our people in you can find. Fuck the weekend people; tell them to take the weekend off. And if any of our people say they won't come in because it's a weekend, tell them not to come in on Monday. And once they're in, nobody goes home. Call a caterer; get meals sent in. Get pillows and blankets. Get lots of coffee. And cigarettes. I don't want anyone sneaking out on a so-called cigarette run and not coming back."

"Anything else?" Cavanaugh had said.

"Yes. I want Jim Giles off the show. Immediately."

"Let's talk about it Monday, Chris. Okay?"

"I'll still want him off on Monday. I'm not backing down on this. He walks or I walk. Okay?"

"I take it you don't want me to call Giles in for weekend duty," Cavanaugh said.

"Everybody but Giles," Chris Kaiser had said.

And everybody but Jim Giles was either in the station on Saturday morning or out on the street working on the story—everybody, that is, but Chris Kaiser.

Cavanaugh assigned Michael Magazine to call Chris Kaiser's home number every fifteen minutes. Each time Michael called he got Chris's answering machine. Finally, at eleven fifteen, Cavanaugh went to Chris Kaiser's office, got a piece of her personalized note-paper, and typed a note to the superintendent of her building saying that she had left behind a few things she needed for the show. Would he please let Michael Magazine in so he could get them and bring them to her? Cavanaugh signed Chris Kaiser's name, trying for, but only approximating, her large, loopy handwriting.

"What if the super asks me why she didn't give me her own keys?" Michael Magazine asked Cavanaugh.

"Tell him she doesn't trust you," Cavanaugh said. "Tell him she wants him to keep an eye on you."

That hurt Michael a little, even though it was just a story, because Michael had a crush on Chris Kaiser—a crush that even the cute new p.a. hadn't been able to distract him from. Sure, he had given her a ride home, just on the chance that she was as interesting as Chris. She wasn't, of course, and it had caused him no pain to simply say good night and drive on home, pleased that he was able to remain faithful to Chris.

The superintendent turned the bottom lock and pushed open the apartment door.

"Chain's not on," Michael said. "She must be out."

"If she went out," the superintendent said, "the doorman would've checked her out."

Michael sighed. "Can I go in?"

The superintendent stepped aside to let him in, but just as Michael stepped over the threshold, he put a hand on his arm. "Say, how come Miss Kaiser didn't give you her own keys? How come she gave you this note to give to me?"

"She doesn't trust me," Michael said, unable to look the superintendent in the eyes. "She wants you to keep an eye on me."

The superintendent laughed and let Michael pass through the door.

He had a surge of vertigo as he entered, for the windows were closer to the door than he anticipated, and he felt as though he were step-ping out into space. The windows rose from floor to ceiling and gave onto a panorama of Central Park, of the East Side of Manhattan, even of Long Island, on the other side of the East River.

Except for the gleaming parquet floor, everything was white: white

41

banquettes, white leather chairs, white area rugs, white metal floor lamps with white shades, white cylindrical end tables, and a white Parsons coffee table. On the white walls were paintings: an abstract, white swirls on white, and a life-size female nude, seen from the back, painted in a shade of white against a white background. The telephone on one of the end tables was white—a Princess.

Chris Kaiser's nude body was white, too. Her hair, of course, was auburn—and so was her pubic hair. Her nails were polished with silver. She had a deep brown mole on her right hip and a bullet hole in her left breast. The blood had stopped pouring from her long ago and formed a sticky red lake on the parquet floor.

TEN

Susannah Keyes spent Saturday morning going into every bookstore in midtown Manhattan, making sure that each had received ample copies of her book and was displaying them prominently.

Even when there were plenty of copies and the location was choice, Susannah asked to speak to the manager—asked loudly enough so that customers would be sure to hear her give her name.

Inevitably, when she had thanked the manager for taking care to see that the book was where people would see it—or chiding them gently for not having done so—someone would come up to her, a copy of the book in hand, and ask her to autograph it. Susannah took care to date the autograph, explaining as she did so that an autograph with a date would be more valuable, in time, than one without. Inevitably, again, they would thank her, and thank her again for putting into words what they—they were all women—felt but had never been able to express.

Susannah's publisher had planned an extensive publicity tour to promote her book, but it wasn't set to begin for another two weeks, around the time of the official publication date. But she knew that most stores put the books on the shelves when they received the shipments and that some personal publicity now was vital. She also knew that it was one thing to stand on line to meet an author who sat at a table behind velvet ropes autographing books, and another to stand face-to-face with that author in the aisle of a bookstore. Susannah wanted her readers to think of her as a friend—and as a lover.

That was the message of Susannah's book, which was called *Womanlove* and which had already been touted in the trade press as one of the most interesting and most controversial books in years. That message, simply, was that the feminist movement had utterly failed to make a single male convert; that men, no matter how eloquent the lip service they paid to feminism, were steadfastly resistant to its basic tenets; that it was time for women to turn their backs on men once and for all and get friendship and love exclusively from other women.

Susannah Keyes was not, she stressed in the introduction to *Womanlove*, a lesbian by inclination; she was a heterosexual for whom heterosexuality had ceased to be viable. Nor, she stressed, was she suggesting that women abdicate their role as bearers of children, but scientific advances had cast that role in a new light. Semen was necessary to reproduction, but men were not.

After leaving the Doubleday Book Shop on Fifth Avenue and Fifty-third Street, Susannah hailed a cab and returned to her apartment on West Twelfth Street between Sixth and Seventh avenues. Although it was Saturday, she wanted to work for a few hours on her next book, a novel based on her own experiences. She was nearly finished with the second draft and was anxious to deliver the manuscript to her publisher before the exhausting publicity tour began.

She nearly passed the mailbox without opening it, for she didn't want to be distracted by bills or letters—or by some juicy catalogue from Neiman-Marcus or Lands' End that she could curl up all afternoon with. But she was curious to know if Martha had gotten her letter, and what she had to say about it if she had, so she opened the box and removed the mail.

There was surprisingly little: a Con Ed bill, a fund-raising letter from Channel 13, a notice from *Psychology Today* saying her subscription was about to expire, a catalogue from Brookstone—usually a favorite, but she was on their mailing list twice and had already read this one—and a letter in a note-size envelope with no return address. Nothing from Martha, nothing about how she would feel about Susannah's staying with her when she was in San Francisco.

Susannah put the Con Ed bill in the pocket of her navy blue blazer, dropped the Channel 13 letter, the *Psychology Today* notice (her subscription, in fact, had expired six months ago, but they still sent her the magazine) and the catalogue in the wastebasket her landlord had thoughtfully placed next to the mailboxes, and opened the letter.

It contained a slip of inexpensive paper, folded in thirds, with two typewritten words on it:

Your next

"Your next what?" Susannah said out loud, and balled up the paper and envelope and tossed them in the wastebasket. She climbed the stairs to her second-floor-rear apartment, thinking that maybe she would call Martha—not now, but when she had finished writing. It would be afternoon in California by then, and Martha, a late riser, would be sure to be up.

ELEVEN

Iris Pabon spat dryly at a photograph of her brother. It was years old, and in it Carlos wore a communion suit and a half smile; his eyes warned the photographer not to try and coax anything more from him. "Good riddance. My brother was an animal. . . . How easy it is for me to talk of him in the past tense."

44

"Yeah, well," Neuman said. "But the fact is, Miss Pabon, somebody killed him, which is against the law, animal or not."

She snorted, then jerked her head toward the dining room door, behind which her mother, some neighbors, and a priest moaned antiphonally. "You should join them. To them, the crime is that Carlos died without Extreme Unction. God, what a world: a man helps an innocent woman; he rids the world of a vermin—or worse, of the droppings of a vermin—and you're trying to punish him."

"Just arrest him," Redfield said. "We don't do punishment."

"Nevertheless, it is a waste of your time and the taxpayers' money."

"Yeah, well," Neuman said, "maybe so, but the thing is we have an idea—it's just an idea; we don't know for sure—that the man who killed your brother is a professional killer. Not that this was a professional killing—we don't think that. It was just one of those things where an individual engaged in the commission of a felony doesn't get away with it on account of another individual acting even more feloniously."

Iris Pabon laughed a coloratura's laugh, spreading a hand over her high breasts. "Will you please be a guest of my class one day, lieutenant? I teach a class in English composition at a community college. My students write essays on all sorts of subjects. They read them, too—and a particular favorite of theirs is one by George Orwell called 'Politics and the English Language.' Orwell perceived long before others the odiousness of using a word like 'pacification' to describe the murder of innocent civilians and the destruction of their homes. He also describes a tendency to choose, instead of words with vivid meanings, phrases without any meaning—phrases like 'an individual engaged in the commission of a felony' when what you mean is a lowlife scum rapist pig."

Neuman looked away from a crèche by which he had been distracted while Iris Pabon spoke. Someone had inked a mustache on the Christ Child, altogether altering the spirit of the tableau; the magi looked like mafiosi coming to call on a diminutive godfather. "Miss Pabon . . . Iris"—he pronounced her name as she did, the Spanish way, and noted in her wide brown eyes a look that wondered if he were mocking her—"I know what you're talking about: 'A mass of

Latin words falls upon the facts like soft snow, blurring the outlines and covering up all the details.'"

Her eyes had panic in them now, and she leaned forward in her chair to see Neuman better around a lampshade.

"I read Orwell's essay in college," Neuman said. "I had my nose rubbed in it by an English teacher. I knew a lot of big words, and I used to like to sprinkle them on my essays. My teacher once made me copy out Orwell's essay. Along the way, I memorized bits and pieces. . . . In the kind of work Sergeant Redfield and I do, we see a lot of ugliness. To call it like we see it all the time is monotonous and tiring. So sometimes we use big words—what do they call them?—euphemisms. It keeps us sane. Orwell said insincerity was the greatest enemy of clear language. But we're not insincere; we're just over-worked. We see rat shit, as you didn't quite put it, like your brother every day. Sometimes we call it rat shit and sometimes we call it an individual engaged in the commission of a felony, because sometimes it's hard to face up to the fact, at the end of a long day, that you spend so much of your time up to your asshole in rat shit."

Iris Pabon fought a smile and lost. Redfield smiled too. She laughed, and so did Redfield. Neuman joined in, and the three of them cackled like drunks. The dining room door opened a crack, and a red eye sent out a beam of censure.

"So," Neuman said when the hysteria had passed, "the man who killed Carlos has some of the markings of a professional killer—the kind of gun he used, the way he fired it, the fact that he fired so accurately. We're just guessing, but we think he may have been coming from a contract killing, or was on his way to one. In any case, we think he's a man who's killed before and will again, and we'd like to put a stop to his killing. You don't have to think of it as justice, as revenge, as anything at all, but it would help us if you'd tell us something about your brother's friends, 'cause maybe they can tell us something about the man who shot him. In particular, about a friend called Zero, and another friend who carried around a big portable radio—a Panasonic."

Iris Pabon fingered the gold cross on a chain around her neck. "They won't come to you themselves, will they? They are guilty of something themselves, are they not? Attempted rape, or—"

46

"Nobody's guilty of anything until they plead guilty or a judge or jury convicts them," Redfield said. "But, yes, they could be charged with assault, with weapons violations, maybe with attempted rape."

"But you would lighten their sentences if they tell you about the man who killed Carlos?" Iris Pabon said.

"As the sergeant said before, we don't punish," Neuman said. "But if what you're asking is would I make a deal to get their charges reduced in exchange for what they know about the killer, the answer is, I'd recommend to the assistant DA that he make such a deal."

Again, she mimed spitting—not at the photograph of her brother but at the idea of his fugitive friends. "I *want* them to go to jail."

"They keep on hanging around with rat shit like your brother, you can count on it," Neuman said.

His artlessness seemed to offend her, but she relaxed, after a moment, and tapped a thumbnail against her teeth. "I only meant . . . I do not think they should suffer less for terrorizing an innocent woman just because they give you the name of my brother's killer. I am a Hispanic woman, and I believe that machismo is the greatest evil in the world. I suffer for this poor woman. All women do."

"Yeah, well," Neuman said, "my wife's Hispanic, too"—again, the look that wondered if he were making fun of her—"honest. From San Juan. I met her there when I was at a police convention—about a hundred years ago. Haven't learned much Spanish, I'm afraid. Maria—my wife; *mi mujer*—has an English mother—English from England, that is—and she spoke it from scratch—English, that is—so I haven't had much call to speak Spanish, but I know about machismo; Maria's old man has a bad case of it—or had; he's dead now, about five years—and I think you're probably right; it's not such a good thing.

"Anyway, I doubt if it'll be the killer's name Carlos's friends'll give us. We don't think they or your brother knew the guy. A good description of him is the best we're hoping for. The other passengers feel the way you do, you see; they think the killer should be allowed to get away with it; they're having trouble remembering what he looked like. Your brother's friends, though, they looked down the wrong end of that gun the same way your brother did. Chances are they'll remember pretty good what the guy looked like who was pointing it at them."

Without turning her head, Iris Pabon looked toward the dining room door and put up a finger that said she thought they were being eavesdropped on. Neuman thought her posture at once cute and erotic; her mouth was a small O, like a cartoon character's; her fingernail glistened as if wet. Her dark hair and caramel skin conjured up the feel of Maria's body against his. He got so absorbed in her that it wasn't until Redfield shifted in his chair—Redfield's taking the back seat was s.o.p.; it had nothing to do with rank, but only one of them steered a course of questioning at a time—that he realized Redfield had been watching him watch her. He blushed.

The moaning resumed.

"Zero," Iris Pabon said, "is the name they call Roberto Andujar. He lives in this building, on the third floor, with only his mother. The other, the one with the radio, could be any one of a number, but it is probably Javier Prinz, whom they call the Prince. He lives nearby, on Fort Washington Avenue. I don't know the address, but it is above a market on the corner—"

"The Three Zs?" Neuman said.

She nodded, without remarking that he knew the neighborhood as well as Orwell. But Redfield gave Neuman a look. Neuman just smiled.

"You are here so soon," Zero's mother said.

"Uh . . . how do you mean?" Redfield said.

"My son is missing. I just telephoned the police to say my son is missing and here you are so soon."

"Uh, let's go inside and talk about it, please, ma'am," Redfield said.

Neuman rang the Prinzes' bell and stepped back on the sidewalk and looked up at the second-story window.

A man in a singlet put his head out the window. "¿Sí?"

"Javier Prinz?" Neuman said.

The man jerked a thumb at his chest.

"Your son. Uh . . . hijo. Su hijo."

The man shrugged and spoke rapid-fire.

Neuman took out his shield and held it up and put it away.

The man retreated, and his place was taken by a woman in a slip. "You want Javier?"

"*Sí*," Neuman said.

The woman didn't know where he was. He hadn't come home the night before, but that wasn't unusual—it was a Friday. But he hadn't gone to work that morning, which was unusual. He loved working in a sporting goods store and hoped one day to have one of his own. The manager had called at ten to ask where Javier was, and again at noon to say he still hadn't come in.

"*Gracias*," Neuman said.

Nancy Koo was so slight that she scarcely ruffled the sheets of her hospital bed. She spoke so softly that Neuman had to sit on the edge of his chair, like a chamber musician. "I'm very frightened. Can't you understand that?"

Neuman put a hand on the sheet and looked at it lovingly, as if it were a toy animal he had brought to cheer her up. "Sure we do, Nancy, which is why we got a cop outside the door. But those two punks—there's nothing to be afraid of. We've got their houses staked out; they've got to come home sometime, and when they do we'll nail them. And even if they don't come home, we got an alarm out on the street. We know their names, sweetheart; we're not on a fishing expedition."

She turned her head away. "I don't want to know their names."

Neuman moved his hand a little closer. "Nancy . . . the guy who shot Carlos . . . you must've got a good look at his face."

She kept her head averted. "No. I had my eyes closed"—she closed them now, as if by way of demonstration—"I was so frightened. He was . . . a man. That's all I'm sure of." She peeked from between her eyelids to see how they were taking this.

Neuman's hand retreated some. "Yeah, well. I can understand why you don't want to finger him, Nancy, but the thing is we're not so sure this was just one of those things that happens now and then in, you know, the naked city. We're not so sure this guy doesn't go around killing people for a living—"

"No!" Her shout propelled her upright so that her face was just

49

inches from Neuman's. She shouted again. "No! You fucking lying cop!"

Neuman sat back in his chair, wondering if a day would come when everyone hated everyone.

Redfield, standing on the other side of the bed, moved closer and put a hand on her shoulder, tentatively, ready to withdraw it if she snapped at it. "We wouldn't lie to you, Nance. Honest. There're people we'd lie to to get them to tell us something they didn't want to, but you're not one of them. Christ, I mean, I feel the way you do: a hundred years ago, the guy'd get a medal or something; if this was Dodge City or something they'd make him sheriff or something. But look at it this way, Nance. If he was really such a good guy, such a hero, like the newspapers're trying to make him, why'd he run away? If he has a license to carry that gun, if he doesn't have a criminal record, if he's totally on the up-and-up, then there's not a judge or a jury outside of maybe Mars that's going to find him guilty of anything. So why did he run away? Unless it's 'cause he doesn't have a license, he does have a record, he's not on the up-and-up, which is what we have reason to believe he isn't." He took his hand off her shoulder and stepped back, looking at Neuman to say it was his turn again.

But Neuman didn't think she could be coaxed—not just yet. He got out a card and wrote their home numbers on it and put it on the bedside table. "Call us if there's anything you think we should know, Miss Koo. Call us day or night. The hospital'll keep us abreast of your condition. When you're feeling a little stronger, we're going to ask you to look at some photographs. We'll also ask you to spend some time with a police artist, who'll try to put together a portrait of the . . . of the man who shot your attacker. In the meantime, get some rest. If there's anything you want that the hospital can't give you, just ask the officer outside your room. He and his relief men have instructions to do whatever's reasonable to make you comfortable."

She was lying back now and wouldn't look at them as they left. Her silence infected them, and they didn't speak as they waited for the elevator. They were weary of talking. Why didn't they find witnesses who talked as much as they did? The only witnesses who talked as much as they did were witnesses like Briggs the graffiti king, who talked to hear the sound of his own voice.

50

When they reached the lobby, Neuman said, "So what do you think?"

"I think Nancy's in love," Redfield said.

Neuman nodded. "The thing of it is, this guy turns out to be a pro, she's not going to want to I-D him then any more than she does now, for different reasons. The same with Briggs the graffiti king. The same with all the passengers. The son-of-a-bitch may just walk."

"Lunch," Redfield said.

"Yeah, all right."

"There's a place down the block I got to like when I was on that Pospisil stakeout."

"Popsicle?"

"Pospisil. The Columbia prof who was selling drugs to students. The Green Tree."

"That the name of some new drug?" Neuman said.

Redfield laughed. "That's the name of the restaurant."

Neuman sniffed at the name. "Not one of those organic places, is it?"

"Hungarian," Redfield said. "Meat and potatoes."

Neuman patted his stomach cautiously. "I don't know. Maybe I should just have something light. We had paella last night."

"I thought you didn't know any Spanish," Redfield said. "Speaking of which, you kind of took a liking to Ee-*reese*—is that how you say it?—didn't you?"

"Yeah, well, if I were a hundred pounds lighter and twenty years younger and single . . . I thought you were kind of interested in Nancy."

"Just curious," Redfield said. "You know, to this day I can't look at an Oriental woman without wondering if she's packing a grenade, going to pull the pin when I turn my back."

"Jesus. And it's been—what?—ten years since you were in 'Nam?"

"Ten years, eleven months, and sixteen days," Redfield said, "but who's counting?"

TWELVE

The dragon had red eyes rimmed with gold. A red tongue flicked from between its golden fangs, teasing Ray's left nipple. The body, green with blue scales, undulated over his shoulder. The tail curled down below his left shoulder blade.

Linda walked her fingers along the dragon's spines. "Didn't it hurt?"

"Probably. I was real drunk when I had it done."

"It must've taken a long time."

"I stayed drunk a long time in those days."

"When? Where?"

"Oh, a long time ago, real far away."

"Like a fairy tale," Linda said, and didn't push him, lest, as in a fairy tale, he disappear or be transformed. "I thought about getting a tattoo once. A flower or something in some secret place where only somebody special would discover it. Then I decided that was backwards—that I should find somebody special first, then surprise him."

"And?"

Linda laughed. "I should've gotten a tattoo. At least the tattooist might've been turned on."

Ray pulled her head down to him and kissed her mouth. "I have to go out for a while."

"Sure." She turned to face the window, golden with grime. If he stayed around awhile, she might wash the windows. She might get the rug cleaned and have her rocking chair re-caned. She might cut her hair differently, less pathetically. She might lose some weight. But he had an airline ticket envelope in an inside pocket of his corduroy jacket; she saw it there when he hung the jacket over the back of the bentwood chair beside the bed. A man who carried an airline ticket around with him wasn't planning on staying long at all—not long enough to be worth a renaissance.

He came around to her side of the bed, dressed now in his jeans and blue work shirt, and sat on the edge. "Linda—"

"I know, I know, you have things to do. It's Saturday, though—that's all. I don't have to work tonight. I thought we could . . . I don't know—go to a museum, to the park, to a movie. I thought we could—"

"Get out of bed?"

"Well, yes. Not that it hasn't been lovely. It's been lovely. But—"

"But there're other things in life?"

"You keep finishing my sentences with questions," Linda said. "Aren't you sure? Do you think maybe we shouldn't get out of bed? Do you think there aren't other things in life?"

Ray spread his hand on the sheet and studied its topography.

"Not for us, hey?" Linda said. "Is that what you're thinking—for us there's only fucking?"

Not for me. For me, there shouldn't be even that. Not until . . . "I won't be long. A couple of hours. Then we can do whatever we like."

"In a couple of hours," Linda said, "I'll probably want to fuck again."

Ray smiled and kissed her forehead and got up and went into the bathroom.

She was out of bed as soon as the door closed, lifting the ticket envelope from the inside pocket, holding it between the sides of her fingers, remembering some movie about pickpockets. She turned her back to the window, to read by its light.

There was no ticket in the envelope, just a receipt for a flight from Detroit to La Guardia. Three days ago. Coach. Paid for with cash. Issued to Paul Howell.

Paul? Why give only half an alias?

As she slipped the envelope back in the pocket Linda saw that there was handwriting on the back. She removed the envelope again and read:

Stearns 650 W. 175
Smith 9 Powell Drive, Mineola
Redfield E. 72

The toilet flushed.

Linda returned the envelope to the pocket. It caught on something and wouldn't go all the way in. She left it that way and dived onto the bed.

Ray came out of the bathroom and lifted the jacket from the chair by the loop sewn in its neck. He slipped it on and gave a tug to the lapels and with a fingertip lightly touched the pockets to see if the contents were in place. He reached inside and adjusted the ticket envelope.

Linda ignored him exaggeratedly.

"I'll see you in a couple of hours." He had a paperback book in his hand, extracted from some pocket somewhere.

"What're you reading?"

He showed her the cover.

She sat up to see it better, although she recognized it. "I don't believe it. *Pilgrim at Tinker Creek*. It's my favorite book. It changed my life; it taught me how to see—not how, but that I must. I wrote her a letter—Annie Dillard. I told her I especially loved the stuff about baseball. I told her I've always thought the world would be inherited by those who love baseball. Do you love baseball?"

Ray smiled and nodded. Over all these years, over all the distance, he had somehow always managed to find out who had won the World Series.

"You see? I knew we had more in common than just liking to fuck. Annie Dillard and baseball. She wrote me back, Annie Dillard, from someplace out west. On yellow paper with her name engraved on it, but so delicately you could barely read it. She said she was playing baseball there, too—with cowpies for bases on a field that slanted uphill. I'll find the letter. It's in my copy of the book, in the living room. I read it first in paperback, then bought the hardcover. I wanted to have it forever."

Ray bent to kiss her forehead again. "A couple of hours."

When he was gone, Linda got up and put on a sweatshirt and jeans and went to the window. She saw him come out the front door and walk down the street toward Broadway—away from the Green Tree.

She wondered about the man who had come into the Green Tree as she and Ray were leaving: a small wiry man with dark hair and stylish clothes, a man who looked a little like—she closed her eyes to try to recapture his face—Al Pacino. He was with another man: short, round, dressed in a hideous combination of stripes and plaids. The two men had stood in the doorway for a moment, letting their eyes adjust from the brightness of the street to the dimness of the restaurant.

Ray and Linda had just left their table—they had split the check—and were heading for the door, Linda in front. She had heard a small intake of breath from Ray, the sound one makes when one has forgotten something or seen something or someone one didn't expect to see. He had put his hand on the small of her back to encourage her forward, but when she opened the door, having slipped between the two men, smiling an *excuse me* at each of them, getting smiles in return, she saw that Ray hadn't followed. He had gone to a wall phone to the left of the two men and was standing with his back to them, the receiver to his ear.

The two men had taken seats at a table near the door, and the small wiry man had gone to the men's room. When he had, Ray had hung up the phone—there was no sound of money being swallowed or returned, and Linda knew that he hadn't been talking to anyone—and walked toward the door to join her, taking a long look at the short round man sitting at the table. The short round man hadn't noticed, being absorbed in the menu.

Linda wondered if the small wiry man was Stearns or Smith or Redfield—or someone else. She wondered who Paul Howell was and what Ray's last name was and if his Christian name was really Ray. She wondered what she was doing, looking forward to his return.

THIRTEEN

"Silverman, Emanuel," McGovern said, "is the token clerk at One Forty-five, southbound. Says he didn't hear a shot, which makes sense 'cause the shot was fired inside the train—right?—and the booth's down at the other end of the station. Says he saw two male Hispanics, mid to late twenties, leave the station, moving real fast. One of them, the tall one, hopped over the turnstile, which Silverman says made him laugh 'cause usually they hop it going the other way. Says the male Caucasian came out a few minutes after them—maybe two minutes—just walking slow, like nothing was on his mind. I mean, not like he was chasing the perpetrators, loo—"

"*He* was the perpetrator," Neuman said.

"Right. Well. Anyway, he wasn't chasing them, according to Silverman, he was just walking normal-like. Didn't get a good look at him—Silverman. He was reading the paper—"

"The perpetrator?" Redfield said.

"No, sarge, the clerk, Silverman. He had to laugh when I told him what the perp'd allegedly done, 'cause he was reading the story about Berger and Nolan saying there was no more crime in the subways." McGovern laughed, but no one else did, so he turned it into a cough. "Anyway, I showed him the picture the artist came up with after talking with Briggs the graffiti king, and he said, yeah, it might've been the guy he saw, but it might've been a hundred other guys too, 'cause the guy he saw didn't have anything unusual about him; he was just a guy, male, Caucasian, twenty-five to thirty-five, tall—maybe six feet, maybe more—"

"We know all this already, Mac," Neuman said. "If Silverman didn't add anything, there's no need to run it down."

"Right. Well. I went back up the line, like you said: One Fifty-seven, One Sixty-eight, One Eighty-one, One Ninety-one, Dyckman, Two—"

"And?" Neuman said.

"Zip, loo. I mean, nobody noticed anybody looking like the shooter getting on. 'Course, at that hour, a lot of those stations aren't manned. They just have, you know, those big turnstiles: Two-oh-seven, Two Fifteen, Two—"

"Mac, don't tell us where you've been," Neuman said. "Just tell us what you've got—if you've got anything."

"Castillo, Raul," McGovern said, "owns the bodega at One Forty-five and Broadway, southwest corner, by the subway exit. Didn't see anything himself, *but* one of his customers, Lopez, Abel, was standing outside with some of his buddies, drinking beer from bags like you said, loo, and saw the kids come up the stairs, moving fast, and head west on One Forty-five, toward Riverside. They weren't neighborhood kids; he'd never seen them before. Couple of minutes later, maybe two, the male Caucasian comes up, hails a cab, gets in, heads downtown. I got Wyman checking trip sheets, loo; it's a bitch of a job. You know how many cab companies there are, how many cabs're out on a Friday night?"

"Mac, this isn't the *Guinness Book of Records* we're working on here, it's a fucking homicide," Neuman said, "so just tell me what you've got and spare me the fucking statistics."

"Right. Well. I asked Lopez—"

"Who?" Redfield said.

"The guy outside the bodega."

"Right," Redfield said.

"I asked him and he said he thought maybe, he wasn't sure, but maybe the cab was off duty—you know, had his off-duty lights on. If that's so, loo, and the cabby was heading home, he might not've logged the trip, just did it, you know, off the meter and pocketed the fare himself. When Grace and I were, you know, having that trouble, and I was moonlighting driving a cab to pay the extra rent 'cause I had my own apartment for a while along with the house, I used to do that now and then, you know, on my last trip of the night."

"Don't tell me things like that, Mac," Neuman said. "Don't tell me felonies you have perpetrated. Someday I might have to tell the IRS, 'Yes, he did mention to me once that he took fares off the meter.' Anything else?"

McGovern flipped through his notebook. "That's it so far, I guess."

"You guess, or that's it?"

"That's it."

"Steve?"

Federici made a point of putting his notebook away. He crossed his legs and locked his fingers over one knee. "The passengers who saw anything didn't see anything much, lieutenant—or they're not telling if they did. The descriptions they gave of the shooter match what we have so far, with maybe one or two details. One guy—I can tell you his name if you want, but it isn't important—says the shooter was wearing a corduroy sport coat and a navy-blue turtleneck sweater. One woman says he was wearing blue jeans—not designer jeans, but, like,

Levi's—and brown shoes, except not really shoes, more like moccasins—Topsiders, she called them, which is a brand name: Sperry Topsiders. I remembered an ad for them in a magazine and cut it out and gave it to the artist. He'll give it back when he's done. . . . The same woman—her name's Angela Ruocco, which I mention 'cause I think she's our best witness, or the best I talked to so far; I haven't talked to everybody—she was visiting her sister up by Baker Field. She's a teller at a Citicorp branch on Fifth Avenue—"

"Her sister?" Redfield said.

"No. Angie."

McGovern laughed. "Angie. The Italian Scallion scores again."

Federici blushed. "Angie made the book the shooter was reading. She read it herself, so she knew what it was from the cover when she saw him reading it. It's called *Pilgrim at Tinker Creek*. It's by Annie Dillard and it won some awards. It's about a time she spent living in this cabin—"

"Do you really think we need to know what it's about, Steve?" Neuman said. "I mean, okay, so it's a nice touch knowing what the book is. Maybe it'll help us somewhere along the line, like if we bust down this guy's door and he's sitting there reading this book and we'll know he's the guy we're after—maybe. But what the fuck're we supposed to do in the meantime, go to bookstores asking have they sold a copy recently and do they happen to know the name and address of the individual who bought it 'cause we'd like to arrest him and it'd save us a lot of time if they'd help us out?"

McGovern laughed.

Federici adjusted the roll of his shirt collar. "The only reason I mention it, lieutenant, is—well, Angie said it so I don't have to say it—it's the kind of book a guy would read if he was, you know, an intellectual. I mean, it's not a novel or anything. It's . . . I don't know exactly how to put it, but, well, it's a mystical book. It's about nature, about the weather, about spiritual things, about God. It's, well, an unusual book for a professional killer to be reading."

"You read it, I guess," Neuman said.

Federici nodded.

McGovern rolled his eyes.

"Well, then, I guess you would know. . . . So tell me, Steve-O, did your friend Angie, since she noticed this guy was reading this intellectual book, happen to notice anything else about him we might want to know?"

Federici looked at the floor. "Her description jibes with what we've got so far, lieutenant. Except . . . well, she said he was very handsome."

McGovern cackled.

"Handsome," Neuman said. "Somehow I don't think I can add that to the alarm we got out. I mean, I can't ask all units to be on the lookout for a handsome male Caucasian, can I? I mean, Christ, they'll start arresting each other—or the white guys anyway. . . . Anything else, Steve?"

"That's it for now, lieutenant," Federici said.

The phone rang.

"Maybe that's the shooter," Neuman said, "saying he's sorry he led us such a merry chase but now he's decided to give himself up."

Redfield answered the phone and listened and said, "Yeah?" and "Oh, yeah?" and "How about now?" and "How about the Blarney Rose?" and "We're on our way," and hung up.

"Was I right?" Neuman said. "He's going to turn himself in at the Blarney Rose?"

"That was Nick Cariello," Redfield said. "He's got something we might be interested in—a twenty-two-caliber DOA in Harlem. Died last night or early this morning."

"Speaking of DOAs," McGovern said. "You guys hear about Chris Kaiser?"

"She wants us to be on her show?" Neuman said. "Telling the viewers how even as we speak the forces of justice're closing in on the—what'd the papers call him?—the Samaritan Killer?"

"She bought it, loo," McGovern said. "In her apartment. A thirty-eight, I think somebody said, last night or early this morning. McIver and Bloomfield have it. No sign of B and E, no rape. Just, well, somebody said it looked like a professional hit."

Neuman looked at Redfield, who was filling a cup at the water cooler.

"The poster in the subway," Redfield said.

"You don't think . . ." Neuman said.

"Probably just a coincidence," Redfield said.

"Still," Neuman said.

"Yeah," Redfield said.

Cariello sang in an amateur opera company and enlightened them in recitative:

"Jake, how are you, Bobby, Rudy says to say hello I don't have a lot of time I know you don't either so here it is, about two months ago I heard from a snitch there was some new blood in town a guy called Detroit, not like Nathan I mean that wasn't his name it was where he's from. Michigan. Pretty well-connected for a free-lance, had a lot of merchandise to move and moved it without too much trouble even though he was trying to cut himself a piece of turf out of turf belonging to some businessmen of long standing. Old-timers. Heavies. We let him operate 'cause we were interested in finding out where he got it, the merchandise, horse mostly and a little blow, was it local or was he getting it from back home, Detroit, and in that case was any of it coming through Canada? Detroit's right next to Canada, practically, which I never knew until somebody showed me on a map, maybe that's why they used to have such good hockey teams remember Howe, Delvecchio, Red Kelly? Not just us but the Feds and the Mounties are interested, too, there really are Mounties, but they don't wear those red coats and those what-do-you-call-them pants, they dress like us. . . .

"About three weeks ago we nailed a dealer we'd been trying to nail for a long time caught him with twenty-four pounds of H in one of those hotels by the park, I can never keep them straight, you must've read about it in the papers, Felix Mazza, Felix the Cat they call him, a black guy despite the guinea name, no offense but then there aren't any guineas here except me are there, you still working with Federici, Jake? a good kid, Steve, smart he'll go far. Looking at eight to twelve, Felix started singing and one of the songs he sang was that Detroit, the guy not the town, was about to unload a major score and some of the heavies I mentioned weren't too happy about it since he was from out of town, Detroit I mean not Felix.

"I had one of my men set up a buy, Rich Pursinger, you know him, Pursesnatcher we call him, he was supposed to meet Detroit at six

A.M. in the morning Saturday, that's today isn't it, is it still Saturday, I don't know, I haven't slept since Thursday, meet him on the footpath by the FDR near the Wards Island bridge, but he didn't show, Detroit I mean. Reason he didn't show, 'cept we didn't know it at the time 'cause the goddamn motherfucking cocksucking computer went on the blink, the one that's supposed to tell you when a subject under investigation turns up on the unusual of some other unit 'cept it can't if it's on the blink, can it, which it seems to be about half the motherfucking time—reason he didn't show, Detroit, I mean, is that he was dead.

"A white-top answered a nine-one-one call just after midnight Saturday, that's Friday midnight, I mean, but it was Saturday morning. A couple, a man and a woman, kids really—you're going to love their names, Jake, Bobby, get this, DeWitt Strawberry and Ivory Snow Richardson, that's right, Ivory Snow—went to this abandoned tenement on West One Seven-five for a little recreational humping, how the fuck anybody can even get it up in one of those places with the fucking rats and junkies and all I don't know but they were planning to, or DeWitt anyway, and who do they find lying on the very mattress they were going to do their humping on but Detroit, the guy not the town, DOA, a bullet hole in his head, execution-style, a twenty-two, Smith and Wesson, according to Forensics. Naturally, we thought it was the work of the heavies I mentioned, a way of telling Detroit that's where he should've stayed, but then I was reading through the six-oh-fives and there was one from you guys, Jake, Bobby, asking does anybody happen to know if there're any DOAs lying around with twenty-two-caliber holes in their heads, a Smith, so I thought I should let you know, I already saved you the trouble, Forensics says it was the same piece."

When he was sure Cariello was through, Neuman said, "Nice of you to take the trouble, Nick. Any chance of getting Detroit's real name?"

"Maybe, maybe not, the cops there, Detroit, 've been informed so to speak but you can't exactly blame them for not falling all over themselves 'cause he's our stiff isn't he and good riddance to bad rubbish. Here's a picture"—he took an eight-by-ten glossy, folded down the center, from his coat pocket and tossed it on the bar—"ugly fuck ain't he this doesn't show it but he's got a tattoo on his shoulder, left, a dragon, like, very fancy, goes halfway down his back, Pursesnatcher was in 'Nam—so were you, Bobby, right?—says it looks like something might've been done there so I sent his prints to the Pentagon for whatever that's worth, anyway I got to go so if I hear anything more I'll let you know, you do likewise okay, so I'll see you, Jake, Bobby, you buying? okay, I accept, I'll get it next time, thanks for the beer."

"Say hello to Rudy," Neuman said.

"Rudy's got the day off he just got a new car, Accord, ten grand with interest rates the way they are it'll cost him twenty, it's got this thing where you hit a switch and it keeps on going the speed you're going even if you take your foot off the gas, Cruise Control or something, he just had to have it I don't know why, he can't work in it, it stands out like a spade in Scarsdale, he's hanging on to his old car, Citation, I guess he's just going to drive it on weekends we must be doing something wrong, hunh?"

"So long, Nick," Neuman said, "and thanks." He turned to Redfield, but Redfield wasn't there. He came out of the men's room a few minutes later, looking pale and haggard.

"Threw up," Redfield said.

"Nick can do that to you," Neuman said. "Christ, what a talker."

"Must've been that Hungarian food," Redfield said.

"Yeah? I'm feeling okay."

"I'm feeling better."

"You sure?"

"Yeah."

"Let's call it a night, hunh? Get some rest."

"Yeah."

"That's good 'cause we got a long day tomorrow the captain'll want to give us some more troops I'm hoping we're going to need them since we're not just looking at the Samaritan Killer anymore so much for him we're looking at a crime wave. Listen to me, I'm starting to talk like Cariello and I'm not even in Narcotics, just Homicide, where before you can get too close to the bad guys first you have to find them. You sure you're all right, Bobby?"

"Yeah."

"You look like you've seen a ghost."

"Not a ghost," Redfield said. "Just goulash."

Neuman laughed.

FOURTEEN

The phone woke Neuman from a dream he couldn't remember but was glad to forget.

"Yeah?" The digital clock by the bed said five fifty-nine.

"Neuman Klinger."

That wasn't his name. Or was it? Was it the caller's name? A strange name. He decided to start over. "Hello?"

"Are you awake, Jake? It's Lou Klinger."

Ah. So he'd said Neuman *comma* Klinger—Deputy Chief Inspector Lou Klinger, head of Manhattan North Homicide. "Hello, inspector. Yeah, I'm awake."

"Good, Jake, 'cause I'm pulling you off the subway thing, no hard feelings, you were doing a helluva job, I heard about the connection with the drug rubout in Harlem and now we want to get the guy more than ever; but downtown they want you on this TV thing, you heard about it, right, Chris Kaiser?"

Klinger talked like Cariello too. But then, he had been in Narcotics as well. Or did they all talk like that, as disorderly as the city they policed? "I only heard a little, inspector."

"McIver'll fill you in," Klinger said. "He'll be at the *Express*."

What express? Express as opposed to local? What line? What station? Which platform? What the fuck was he talking about? "He'll be where, inspector? I've got a bad connection."

"The *Express*, the New York *Express*, the newspaper, where the killer sent the letter."

Maria stirred and said something in Spanish, the language she dreamed in. More than anything in the world, Neuman wanted to hang up the phone, turn on his side, and fasten his body to the contours of hers. Less than anything in the world, he wanted to ask the inspector what killer, what letter. "Which killer is that, inspector? And what letter?"

"McIver'll fill you in, Jake," Klinger said. "Get a move on. Oh, and, uh, I want Redfield on this too, I've told Easterly to put McGovern in charge of the subway thing."

Neuman sat up and swung his feet over the edge of the bed. The floor looked to be about forty stories down. "With all due respect, inspector, McGovern's not good enough. I suggest you put Steve Federici in charge. I know he's only a second-grade, sir, but he's smart, he'll do a good job."

After a moment, Klinger said, "Did I ask you, Jake?"

"No, sir."

"Get a move on, Jake. This is a bad one. We've got a psycho on our hands."

A psycho, Neuman thought, will be easy to find. There're ten million of them within spitting distance.

Tim McIver didn't talk like Cariello. He talked like a writer of primers.

"Chris Kaiser's show is on from twelve to twelve thirty. After the show she chewed out the staff. She was upset about their piece on subway crime. The piece was prepared by Jim Giles. Giles was the station's star before Chris Kaiser came along. She told Giles she was going to get him fired. Giles drinks. A production assistant went into Giles's office after the argument. He heard the phone ringing and went to answer it. It was Giles's wife. She wondered why he wasn't home yet. Giles goes on benders regularly. The production assistant's name is Michael Magazine. He found some empty Scotch bottles in Giles's office. They were the miniature kind they serve on airplanes. He also found an empty box of thirty-eight-caliber bullets. It was in a trash can under Giles's desk. He took it out of the trash can and threw it away later. He threw the bottles in a trash bin in the hallway. He liked Giles and was afraid someone would find them and that it would mean trouble for Giles.

"Chris Kaiser got home at one o'clock, according to the doorman's log in her apartment building. The doormen log tenants in and out so the next shift will know who's at home and who isn't. It's a good system. Trouble is, it's only as good as the doormen. Several tenants told us the doormen are often away from their posts, watching television in the basement. The tenants have keys for when the doorman's away, but the door's on a slow hinge and someone hanging around the building could get to the door before it closed after a tenant. That's our best guess as to how the killer got in. The ME put the time of death at right around one, so he must've been waiting there for her, either in the apartment or on a stairway, when she arrived.

"She was nude. We don't know what to make of that. Her clothes were in the bedroom, folded neatly on a chair. There were no bullet holes or powder burns on them, so it doesn't look as though the killer undressed her after he shot her. There's no indication she was molested. She certainly wasn't raped. Then what was she doing naked in her living room? Okay, it was her apartment and she could be naked if she wanted to. It's on a high floor and the only way to see in is from clear across the park, on Fifth Avenue. We're checking to see if there're any known peeps in any of those buildings.

"The door was double-locked, meaning the killer had a key or took one of hers. She had a ring of keys in her pocketbook, and the ones for the door were on the ring. If there're others missing we don't know about it. It looks like the killer used keys to get in as well as out, since there's no sign the locks were picked or jimmied or forced. I think she knew the guy, Jake. I can't be sure it was a guy, of course, but I think it was someone she knew, a boyfriend who had keys. It would explain her being nude. She was expecting him, she was planning a little roll in the hay, she decided to save time by taking her clothes off. He opened the door, or maybe she opened it for him—her prints are on the inside knob, along with some others, but none we've made—and he popped her.

"Only trouble with that theory is that according to the people at the station she didn't have any boyfriends. She's only been in town since last spring. She's a workaholic—or was. When she goes out—or went—it was to big parties, opening nights, benefits, like that. When she was with a guy it was some big shot—a politician, a lawyer, a diplomat—and she was never with the same guy twice in a row. The doormen say a lot of guys brought her home—in limos, in cabs; one guy brought her in one of those Central Park horse carriages—but nobody ever went upstairs with her, not unless she had a whole bunch of people going up along with them. The doormen started wondering if she was, you know, gay, but she didn't have any girlfriends either—at least none that they ever saw her with.

"That leaves Giles. Giles hated her guts, and vice versa. Giles owns a thirty-eight—it's registered. Giles is missing and unaccounted for; he hasn't been seen or heard from since after the show on Friday night, Saturday morning. Maybe Giles followed her home. Maybe he got there ahead of her. Maybe he let himself in with a key he took from her pocketbook at the station. Like I said, getting past the doorman wouldn't've been all that hard. Let's say he got there first. He lets himself in, locks the door, and hides somewhere. It's a big place. She comes home, goes into the bedroom, takes off her clothes. Maybe she's going to take a shower. Maybe she sleeps in the nude—or slept. Giles appears. She runs from him. He catches her at the door, spins her around, pops her in the chest. He goes out, locks the door, walks down the stairs probably, waits till the doorman's fucking off, and walks out.

"Let's say Giles got there second. She's in the bedroom, undressing, and hears the key in the door. She starts for it, maybe thinking to put the chain on, but he's already inside. She sees the gun, freezes, maybe, or maybe makes a rush for it, but he pops her. He goes out, locks the door, and so on.

"Only trouble with that theory is the letter. I know you know the *Express* made an offer to the subway killer to print his side of the story. Well, Chris Kaiser's killer decided to try and get them to tell his story, too. He delivered his letter—or somebody did—to their offices sometime after midnight this morning. They don't publish on Sunday, so there was no one around but a watchman. The watchman heard the night bell around two A.M. while he was on his rounds on the seventh floor, the editorial offices. He took a look at the TV monitor at the reception desk on that floor but didn't see anybody, so he didn't go downstairs. Around three thirty he went down and outside for some air and found the letter pushed under the front door. It didn't have any address on it, no name or anything; it just said 'Urgent. Open Immediately.' He did. Not that that's his job or anything, but he says he had a sense it might have something to do with the subway killing. Here it is, Jake. It's been dusted—it's clean as a whistle, except for the watchman's prints; he was pretty careful about handling it, though."

Neuman took the envelope from the glassine evidence bag. It was a cheap white business envelope. The message had been typewritten on its face on what looked like a manual typewriter, pica type. The gummed flap was still ʻsealed, for the envelope had been slit open at one end. "The watchman cut this, I guess. With a knife or something?"

"A pocketknife, Jake," McIver said. "Sorry I didn't mention that."

"You mentioned everything else, Tim," Neuman said. "You guys did a hell of a job." He put the envelope down on the desk in front of him; they were in the offices of the *Express*'s managing editor. "Listen, before we go any further, I just want to say I know it's tough to have an investigation taken away from you like this. But Bobby and I— Bobby'll be here in a little while; he wasn't feeling so good when I left him last night so I let him get an extra hour in the rack—Bobby and I don't look at it that way. I mean, the way we always work, when we make a collar it's your collar. I know it sometimes goes down in the books as our collar, but as far as the press and everybody in the department's concerned, it's yours. The second thing is, we don't Monday-morning quarterback what you've already done, since nine times out of ten it's what we would've done anyway if we'd handled things from the start. Sometimes we'll see something you didn't do, but we don't rub your face in it 'cause we know how it is, sometimes when you're on the scene from the start it's hard to see things as clearly as when you walk in off a night's sleep and a good meal—not that I slept all that much, and all I had was some cold cereal and some warmed-over coffee—but you know what I mean."

"I appreciate that, Jake," McIver said. "By the way, Bloomfield went over to Grand Central—there's an all-night deli—for some coffee and egg sandwiches. I told him to get a couple apiece for you and

Bobby. Scrambled on a roll, I told him. I don't know if that's up your alley, but I figured I'd give it a shot."

"Scrambled on a roll'll be just fine, Tim," Neuman said. "And I'll pay the tab and don't give me any argument about it. . . . Now, let's see what we got here." Neuman tapped the letter from the envelope and spread it on the desk. It was typed on cheap white business-size paper, sixteen pounds, probably, and it said:

To the New York Express,

I read with interest your offer to the man you have christened "the Samaritan Killer" to use your pages to explain why he killed a cheap punk on the subway late Friday night. I know you want to sell papers, but this killing is really small potatoes, don't you think?

Perhaps you would be more interested in another murder, committed just a few hours after that of Carlos Pabon. I'm referring to the murder of Chris Kaiser, the cunt-bitch star of Channel 3's midnight news. Perhaps you would like to know why she died.

I can tell you because I killed her. I killed her because she deserved to die. She deserved to die because she is a murderer herself. She murders men—castrates them. She cradles their balls in her hands, then chops them off, chews them up, spits them out. Night after night, while millions of people watch. For this she is paid half a million dollars a year. For this she is called a star—a journalist.

She's not the only cunt-bitch of her kind. Not by a long shot. The world is full of them. With their plunging necklines, their slitted skirts, their suggestive mannerisms. They are killers—man-killers. Ball-breakers. Castraters. They suck the life out of men—and suck the spirit. They call themselves feminists, but all they are is killers.

I killed Chris Kaiser and I am going to kill more of them until there are no more of them left. Your pages will be full of my exploits. So forget about the Samaritan Killer. He only did what any of us would have done. Print this instead. Why not call me

The Cunt-Bitch Killer

"Nice fellow," Neuman said, refolding the letter, returning it to the envelope and returning the envelope to the evidence bag. "I guess Forensics'll try to make this typewriter."

"When they get up, Jake," McIver said. "They don't come to work till ten on Sundays."

"That's a job I could go for," Neuman said. "Anybody from the *Express*—other than the watchman—know about this letter?"

"Klinger called Tremaine, the publisher. Tremaine called Lucas, the managing editor. This is his office we're sitting in. He's down the hall, waiting to talk to you. He wants to print the letter—cleaned up a little. Want me to get him?"

"You talk to him, Tim. Tell him—he's got to know this, unless he's a fucking bimbo—tell him he not only can't print the letter, he can't even mention the letter. Tell him I know that means we owe him a favor. Tell him I've got one ready and waiting. Tell him the Samaritan Killer popped a drug dealer in Harlem before he got on the subway the other night. Tell him to have one of his reporters call Nick Cariello in Narcotics for the scoop. Tell him nobody else has it and nobody else will till he comes out with it. Tell him if he goes easy on the Chris Kaiser follow-up we'll give him anything else good we get before we give it to anybody else. Don't tell him anything about Giles."

"You think it's Giles, Jake?" McIver said. "You think he wrote the letter to throw us off his trail?"

"That's what you think, I guess, Tim," Neuman said. "Well, it's a good thought, but I don't know. Giles is a drunk, not a killer. And if he's the kind of drunk I think he is, he doesn't get meaner the drunker he gets, he gets meeker, until there's nothing left of him but skin and bone, not even any muscle, and not enough gumption to pull a trigger, not even if the gun barrel was in his mouth. My old man was that way, so I know a little about what I'm talking about."

"Mine too," McIver said.

"Well, it's a small world, Tim, I guess," Neuman said. "And just to prove it, here's Bobby Redfield himself, looking a hell of a lot better than he did a couple of hours ago. You see what I mean, Bob? Sleeping by yourself isn't such a bad idea now and then."

McIver laughed. Redfield blushed. McIver went out to talk to the managing editor of the *Express*. Redfield sat where McIver had been sitting.

"I'll fill you in on all this in a while, Bob. You are feeling better, aren't you?"

"A lot better, Jake. Thanks."

"I'll fill you in on this later, but for starters I'd like to know what you think about Chris Kaiser. I mean, seeing as how you met her and all, on that TV show you told me about."

"I didn't really meet her, Jake. We were introduced before the show, but she was the kind that looks right through you unless you've got something she wants. And there were a lot of other people around—technicians, her staff, the other panelists: there was an assistant DA, a Legal Services lawyer, a Criminal Court judge, a reporter, from the *Times*, I think. After the show she continued a debate that started while we were on the air—with the DA and the judge—about whether they were too soft on career criminals, made too many deals. Nobody'd paid much attention to me during the show, and nobody did afterwards, either, so I just kind of left."

"Never saw her again, hey?" Neuman said.

"Only on TV," Redfield said.

"You watched her show? Christ, when did you get the time? I thought you were in the saddle every night around midnight."

Redfield blushed again. "Only on my nights off, Jake. Other nights, if I'm up, I watch the news."

Neuman showed Redfield the letter and, when he'd read it, said, "Well?"

"I can see how she'd do that to a guy," Redfield said. "A guy who wasn't too sure of himself, a guy who was getting passed over by women at work—it happens a lot these days; in the department, even—a guy who wasn't getting it from his wife, his girlfriend. Chris Kaiser was sexy; she . . . well, she flaunted it. I can see where she'd get a guy mad. Like the guy says, she was getting half a million a year for teasing his cock. That's enough to piss anybody off."

"Trouble is," Neuman said, "the kind of guy you're talking about isn't the kind of guy who goes out and gets a gun—he's not the kind of guy who has one lying around at home, either—works out a very careful MO, gets himself a set of keys to someone's apartment, and pops her. And he's not the kind of guy who says he's going to pop other women who rub him the wrong way in the same way, which is what this guy says he's going to do. And who should walk in the door as I'm saying that, speaking of gentlemen and scholars, but Nate Bloomfield himself, bearing scrambled eggs on rolls and cups of cof-

70

fee—it's got to be lousy coffee, coming from an all-night deli in Grand Central, but thanks anyway, Nate. I told Tim it's on me, so let me see that check, will you? Nine ninety-five, not bad at all for breakfast for four, not bad at all."

"Nothing for me, Jake," Redfield said. "I had some juice and coffee before I left the house."

"I thought you said you were feeling okay," Neuman said.

"I'm feeling okay. I just think I'll give the old stomach a rest today."

"In that case," Neuman said, "you won't mind if I take a bite out of this sandwich that has your name on it."

"I don't mind at all, Jake."

FIFTEEN

Mineola Auto Body, on Mineola Avenue, in Mineola, was what you'd expect—a gray cinderblock building amid gray cinderblock buildings strung along a ribbon of concrete that, if you drove on it, would take you from nowhere to nowhere else, and take you forever to get there.

But it was unaccountably busy for a late Sunday night. Ray counted nine cars in forty minutes—a red Chevy wagon, a black Jeep Cherokee, a blue Dodge Charger, a green Volvo, a blue Chrysler Imperial, a white Corvette, a gray Plymouth Horizon, another red Chevy wagon, slightly newer, and a black import whose make he didn't recognize. The drivers all stayed five or ten minutes, then left in cars other than the ones they'd come in.

At last, no more cars came, and the driver of the black import had left in a Dodge van.

Ray waited another half hour, until the lights in the shop were turned off and only those in the office in the rear burned. He moved from shadow to shadow.

The sliding door was locked from the inside and so was the smaller door alongside it. The only other door led directly into the office. Ray stood alongside it, waited until he heard the sound of an adding machine—the occupant would have his head down, preoccupied with figures—and took a quick look through the filthy glass.

Sitting at a metal desk, his back to Ray, was a man with a bald head and a fringe of hair that he had let grow too long, by way of compensation. At his right hand was the adding machine, at his left a stack of papers. A single light in a cone-shaped metal shade hung above him, making his bald spot glisten.

Ray faced the door, put his hand on the knob, braced the door with his other hand, and slowly turned. He could feel the rust and decay in the mechanism and cautioned himself to turn the knob even more slowly. It took a full minute before he had completed half a turn and felt the latch slip free.

He took a long breath, made sure that the bald man was still busy, then carefully pushed against the door. It stuck, as he had known it would. Running his eyes along the edge of the door, he saw from the light leaks where the sticking point was, just about at his eye level. Keeping his grip on the knob, he moved his left hand up on the door until it was even with his eyes. By lifting up on the knob and pushing against the door, he opened it without a sound.

The man got up suddenly, muttering a curse, and went to a metal filing cabinet at the other end of the room. He pulled open a drawer, then another, then another until he found what he was looking for. He pulled a thick wad of paper from the drawer, closed it noisily, and returned to the desk.

Ray stayed as he was, the door held open just a crack, knowing the man couldn't make him out in the dark through the dirty panes—even if he were to look up, which he didn't.

The man sat, coaxed a cigarette out of a pack in his shirt pocket, lighted it with a disposable lighter, took two puffs, and balanced the cigarette on the edge of the desk.

Ray pushed the door open, slipped inside, closed the door, applying pressure on the opposite side from where he'd pushed before, and

72

carefully let the latch slip back into place. He pressed down on the push-button lock and turned to face the man's back.

He hadn't heard a thing.

The phone on the desk rang and the man answered it, after deliberately letting it ring three times. He tucked the phone under his ear, stuck the cigarette in his mouth, and kept on working the adding machine as he spoke.

"Yeah? . . . I wondered when the fuck you were going to call. I wanna get out of here. . . . Yeah, a fucking great day. I tolja, a nice day like today, people go out to the parks, for a drive, they leave their cars for hours, man, hours. Lot of the time they forget their keys, forget to lock them. Even when they do lock them, nobody thinks anything of seeing a guy trying to jimmy the door open, they think he locked himself out. Sixteen fucking cars today, man. Two fucking Volvos. A fucking Volvo dis*tribu*tor goes for a hundred bucks, man. . . . I know, man. They'll be fucking scrap by noon tomorrow. I got three guys coming in at six. They're fucking maniacs, man, they can tear a car down in an hour and a half. . . . I know, man—that was last week, this is this week. Last week, I tolja, it fucking rained, people stayed home. This is this week, man. . . . About six o'clock is good—and, man? Bring the fucking cash with you this time. None of this 'I'll pay you when my connection pays me.' . . . Up yours, too, you slimy wop bastard. . . . See you at six."

Ray had worked his way around the perimeter of the room, taking care to avoid the piles of junk that were scattered everywhere. When the man hung up, Ray stepped into the pool of light cast by the single lamp. "So business is good, Joey."

"What the fuck? Hey. Who the fuck? Hey." Joey shoved his chair back from the desk and stood upright. The lamp blocked his view of Ray's face, and he leaned to one side to try and make him out. "You got a delivery? I don't know you. Who the fuck are you, man?"

"Yeah, I've got a delivery, Joey," Ray said. "And you do know me."

Joey stepped back to the desk, his fingers dancing on the top. He looked like a bad pianist, showing off by playing standing up.

"If you've got a gun in that drawer, Joey, you'll be making a big mistake by going for it"—Ray moved his hand into the light to show the twenty-two-caliber pistol in it—"unless you'd rather die right now, get it over with. I was planning on enjoying watching you squirm for a while, the way I did with Clarence."

"Clarence? Who the fuck is Clarence?" Sweat glistened on Joey's bald head and ran into his eyes and down his nose.

"Clarence was a pretty successful businessman too, Joey," Ray said. "Narcotics. Funny, isn't it? It was in 'Nam that he started dealing dope, and it was in 'Nam that you started playing around in the black market. The black market's not too different from what you're doing now, is it? Ripping off cars, stripping them down, selling the parts. Funny, isn't it? Everybody always says we didn't learn anything in 'Nam, that we went over there untrained to fight a war nobody wanted to fight in the first place, that we came back—those of us lucky enough to get out alive—unable to find a place in the society that hadn't wanted us to fight that war. But it's not true, is it? Clarence learned to deal, you learned to steal, I learned to survive."

Joey was quivering now. The sweat poured down his face like rain. "R-Ré?"

*   *   *

Nha Trang.

Oh, baby, check it *out.* Bobby, look at the one in the red, man. She likes you, man. She wants you. Go to her, Bobby, save her life, man. Show her what she's been missing.

Yo, Clarence, there's one for you. You gotta go with her, man. She's fucking *blond.* I don't care if it's a fucking wig, man. Fuck it. You don't want her, I'll take her. Hello, baby. What's your name? Mine's Joey. Joe Smith. Honest to God.

Hey, Ré. André. Where the fuck you going? Ain't you gonna get yourself some pussy?

You go ahead, Clarence. You go ahead, Miguel. I'll catch you guys later. At the Enlisted Men's Club, all right? In like two hours.

Shit, Ré. What're you gonna do, write another fucking letter to your fucking girlfriend? This is live action, baby. Real meat. U.S. prime, man. This ain't no fucking *let*ter.

I'll catch you later, Clarence.

Hey, Joey, Joey. Get five more beers.

I gotta take a leak, man. I'm gonna fucking pop. That fucking whore did something to my insides, man.

Bring them on the way back, you fucking asshole.

Just piss into five bottles. We won't know the difference.

Shee-it. You hear that, Bobby? Fucking Ré is loosening up. Just piss into five bottles. We won't know the fucking difference.

See this bottle? Clarence, see this bottle? Ré? Bobby? Joey? This bottle is motherfucking cocksucking asslicking Phelps. Whomp! Off with his fucking head. How do you like that, you goddamn gringo slime?

Hey, Miguel, you stupid spic. Break the fucking bottles we already drank from, okay? Not the fucking ones we didn't fucking drink from, okay?

That is fucking right, Miguel. Listen fucking up. Don't fucking break the fucking bottles we didn't fucking drink from yet. Fucking break the fucking ones we fucking finished. 'Cause if you fucking break the fucking ones we didn't fucking drink from yet, how the fuck're we gonna fucking drink from them? Whereas—

Shee-it. Listen. Whereaaas.

No, man. This is great, man. Fucking Ré is getting fucking loose. Hey, Ré, you wanna go back and get a whore now, man? I'm telling you, man, this fucking Nha Trang nooky is something fucking else. You wanna, Ré, hunh?

What I wanna do is I want fucking Miguel to stop fucking breaking the fucking bottles we didn't fucking drink from yet.

Shit, man, this is fanfuckingtastic, fucking straight-arrow Ré is fucking looped. Hey, Ré, you don't wanna fuck, whaddaya wanna do?

Tattoo.

Tattoo?

Tattoo.

Tattoo.

Tattoo, tattoo.

Tattoo, tattoo, tattoo. How 'bout our names, man, on our fucking chests?

Fuck that shit, Joey. How 'bout the outfit?

The outfit, man. All right. Fucking Bravo.

Fucking Bravo Ballbusters.

How 'bout this, man? Check it out, Joey, Clarence, Bobby, Ré. How about Fuck Phelps?

Shit, man, you gonna go around for the rest of your fucking life with a fucking tattoo that says Fuck Phelps?

I hate the son-of-a-bitch, man.

So frag him, you fucking coward.

I thought you were gonna frag him. The other day. At the LZ. Fucking bigmouth Redfield.

The l-t was right behind me, man. How the fuck was I supposed to? Fucking *hijo de puta*.

You wanna step outside, Miguel, you fucking wetback?

Hey!

Fuck you too, Ré.

Hey! What about the fucking tattoos?

Right on, man. What about the fucking tattoos?

Tattoo, tattoo.

Tattoo, tattoo, tattoo.

Dragons.

Say what, Ré?

Dragons, man. Big fucking dragons crawling all over our fucking bodies, man.

Phelps-eating dragons.

All right. No fucking dragon's afraid of fucking Phelps.

I ain't afraid of fucking Phelps.

Hey, nobody's afraid of fucking Phelps, man. Fucking Phelps is a big fucking bag of wind.

A bag of shit.

A bag of rat shit.

A bag of VC shit.

NVA shit.

ARVN shit.

Right on, man. Dragons. Fucking dragons.

Firebase Enid.

Smith?

Sir.

Stearns?

Sir.

Chavez?

Sir.

Redfield?

Sir.

Keller?

Sir.

Five fucking scumbags. Isn't that right, Smith?

Yes, sir.

Isn't that *right*, Smith?

Yes, sir!

You're a scumbag, aren't you, Smith?

Yes, sir.

Louder!

Yes, sir!

Say it, Smith. Say I am a scumbag, sir.

You are a scumbag, sir.

Who . . . said . . . that?

I did, sir.

Keller?

Yes, sir.

I know you said it, Keller. What the fuck do you think I am, deaf?

No, sir. I know you're not deaf, sir. I know it as surely as I know you're a scumbag. For example—

Lieu*ten*ant!

Sir!

—for example, only a scumbag would threaten to discipline his men for getting tattoos, when the right to be tattooed is an inalienable right—

Lieutenant, arrest this man.

A-arrest him, captain?

Are *you* deaf, lieutenant?

No, sir, but—

Then arrest him, pretty fucking quick.

—and only a scumbag would've taken us through the terrain you did this morning—with no reconn, no air support, no artillery—so we could—what?—take prisoner two mama-sans, a baby, two dogs, and six chickens. VC cadres, shit—

He spat at Phelps's feet.

—innocent, scared, helpless fucking civilians.

Lieu*ten*ant.

Captain, we don't have a brig set up here. The only thing is the tent with the civilians.

VC, lieutenant. The tent with the VC.

That's right, captain. That's the only place to put this man.

Then put him there, goddamn it. Get him out of my sight. Oh, and Keller? It was your idea, wasn't it, getting these tattoos?

—and only a scumbag would try to spend the night at this firebase. With no Claymores, no wire, no water, no food, no insect repellent. We're undersupplied, Phelps, you moron. Get us fucking out of here.

Phelps struck him across the mouth with the back of his hand. As he reeled off-balance, Phelps kicked him in the groin. As he lay doubled over on the ground, Phelps kicked him in the face.

One of the mama-sans was ancient, the other nearly still a girl.

"Your mother?" Ré said, indicating the old woman. He was one of the few GIs who bothered to learn Vietnamese.

"My grandmother," the young woman said. "My mother was killed by American planes four years ago. My father, too—and my brother and sister. The Americans have always believed that our village is a Viet Cong village, but that is not so."

"I'm sorry," Ré said, and his heart ached—because his people had killed hers and because she was beautiful, like a doll, with a bright flat face, black black eyes, and long hair that fell about her face like an elegant scarf.

"And your baby?" Ré said. "What's his name?"

"I have not given him a name," she said. "I would rather, when he dies, that he not have had a name."

"He won't die," Ré said. "They'll let you go tomorrow, probably, when they realize you're not VC. You can go back to your village. The war will end soon. Everyone says that."

"He will die," the woman said, and turned her back to him.

That night, on Phelps's orders, the prisoners were given only water.

Miguel Chavez, who was on guard duty, slipped Ré a tin of C rations, and he divided them among the two women, the baby, and himself. Miguel brought a bottle of Ba Mi Ba beer, too, which Ré put under the tent flap for later. When they had finished eating, he buried the tin in a corner of the tent. The old woman bowed her thanks to Ré and the young woman looked at him coolly, evenly, holding the sleeping child easily in her arms.

After a long time, she said, "Do you have a wife, in America?"

Ré wanted to lie, to say no, no wife, no girlfriend. He wanted to say, Come with me to America, you and your baby and your grandmother. I'll make it up to you—repay the lives you have lost. But he said, "I have a fiancée. I'll marry her when I get home."

"But you are not going home," she said. "You are a prisoner."

Ré looked away, understanding for the first time the enormity of his insubordination. It didn't matter that Phelps was a martinet, a tyrant, an incompetent; he was an officer, and his word was law. When he looked back, the young woman was asleep, her head fallen forward on her chest. The old woman slept too, and, in time, so did Ré.

He woke at the baby's cry. It lay writhing in a corner of the tent, like some discarded thing gotten suddenly animate. The old woman cowered near it but was too frightened to pick it up. Phelps knelt between the young woman's legs, stroking her thighs, the barrel of his pistol touching her lips.

"Suck me, sweetheart, or you're gonna suck this gun and it'll be your last blow job. What do you think, Keller? You think these VC give good head?"

Ré sat on his haunches, trying to get the young woman to look at him, trying to make her understand that he would help her.

Phelps took a flask from the hip pocket of his fatigues, opened it with his teeth, and held it to the young woman's lips. "Come on, honey, have a shot of Jim Beam. Nothing like a little drink before a blow job. Oils the old throat."

The young woman spat into the flask.

Phelps hit her in the mouth with the butt of the pistol.

"Guard!" Ré called.

Phelps laughed. "You stupid fuck. There's no guard. _I_ relieved Chavez. _I'm_ the guard. You stupid fuck. You see, Keller, I got to thinking. I thought, I bet that son-of-a-bitch Keller is trying to put the make on that pretty little mama-san. Everybody knows he speaks fucking Slope. He's probably up there sweet-talking her into slipping off her drawers and giving him a little VC nooky. I thought, I better get up there and make sure that what I'm thinking ain't happening. Plus, it'll give the men some extra time in the rack. No sense tiring my men out guarding a couple of VC and a motherfucking mutineer. Oh, didn't I tell you, Keller? I talked to headquarters tonight and told them I had a goddamn mutiny on my hands. Told them I took care of it, but the ringleader's in the brig and as soon as they can get a chopper in here they're going to fly you out and put your ass through the wringer.

"Or maybe they won't. Maybe when the MPs get here they'll find you're in no condition to face a court-martial, seeing as how you're dead and buried. You see, Keller, I know what you're thinking. You're thinking I don't have a snowball's chance in hell of making charges against you stick. And maybe you're right. The fucking brass, man, you never know how their minds're going to work. But I got a charge against you that'll stick, Keller, and the charge is the rape and murder of an innocent civilian woman and the murders of her mother and baby—"

"Grandmother," Ré said. In Vietnamese, he said, "Tell your grandmother to pick up the baby."

Phelps pointed the pistol at Ré. "You shut the fuck up, you hear, or I'll blow your fucking head off right here and now."

Ré stood. "Go ahead, asshole." In Vietnamese, he said, "When I start moving toward you, he'll stand up. When he does, as quick as you can, get up and get the baby and get him and your grandmother out of the tent." He took a step.

Phelps rose. "Goddamn it, Keller."

The young woman scrambled up before Phelps could stop her and scooped up the bawling baby. She tried to get her grandmother to her feet, but the old woman was frozen in a crouch.

Phelps pointed the pistol at the young woman. "Stop it, there. You stop it."

Ré dived for the pistol just as Phelps fired. The bullet drove into the floor of the tent.

With Phelps's wrist in his hand, Ré stuck out a hip, pivoted, and tossed Phelps over his head. He landed flat on his back and screamed with pain. Ré kicked him in the face, then kicked the pistol from his hand.

Ré picked up the pistol, felt its heft for a moment, then stepped over Phelps and shot him in the face. He stepped back and aimed at Phelps's crotch. A hand grabbed his arm and he whirled, the pistol ready.

The young woman had her hand up in a gesture of surrender. In her other arm, the baby stared. "Come with us."

Ré shook his head and pointed to the door of the tent. "Go. Now. *Di di mau.* Go quickly."

The woman stepped up to him and touched his chest. She stood on tiptoe as if to kiss him, then thought otherwise, and was suddenly gone, urging her grandmother before her.

Redfield was the first to arrive at the tent. "Holy shit, Ré. What the fuck . . . ?

"Get the l-t, Bobby," Ré said.

"Get the l-t, man? Shit, the l-t bought it, man. On patrol, man, about two hours ago. Fire in the hole, man. Ryder bought it, too, man, and Esposito got his fucking leg blown all to shit. Fucking Phelps, man, he just laughed. He said, Now you motherfuckers got nobody anybody's going to believe over me. Now you mother-fuckers're up the fucking creek without a paddle. . . . What the fuck happened here, man? Where're the VC?"

"Bobby, for Christ's sake. They weren't VC."

"Phelps was on the horn, man, to HQ."

Chavez was at the door, and Stearns and Smith.

"What the fuck, man . . . ?"

"Fucking Phelps. Oh, no, oh, no."

Ré drew them inside and shut the flap of the tent. "Listen to me. Phelps is dead, the l-t is dead. Clarence, that means you're in command. Get on the horn to HQ, man, and tell them to get us the fuck out of here."

"What do I tell them about Phelps, Ré? What do I tell them about Phelps?"

"Yeah, Ré. I mean, shit, you killed him, right?"

"Oh, no, oh, no."

"Listen to me, for Christ's sake. Phelps tried to rape the girl. He was going to kill her and the old woman and the baby, then kill me, saying I killed them."

"He *said* that, man?"

"No, but . . . *Yes*, he said it."

"No? Yes? Come on, Ré."

"*You* come on, for Christ's sake. Don't you believe me?"

"Phelps was a *cap*tain, man. A fucking captain."

Ré grabbed a handful of Redfield's shirt. "Bobby, it's me—Ré. You've got to believe me."

"I don't know, man. Phelps called the MPs, man. They'll be here in the morning. They'll be here for you."

Ré shoved Redfield away and went to the others in turn. "Clarence, Miguel, Joey, what the fuck . . . ? You don't think . . . ?"

One by one, they looked away. One by one, they moved toward the door of the tent. One by one, they went out. Chavez went last. "I believe you, Ré."

"Thanks a fucking lot, Miguel."

"It's just . . . you know . . . Phelps was a captain, man."

"Miguel?"

"Yeah, Ré?"

"I need my rifle, my pack, four canteens, two belts of ammo, four grenades, my helmet, and my knife."

"Shit, Ré. The others'll—"

"Don't bring them here. Leave them by the LZ, the northwest corner. Do it now, before the others come looking for you. They'll come looking for you because they've got to get their fucking stories straight and they'll want you in on it. So hurry, Miguel. Now."

"Ré?"

"Now, Miguel."

"It's just . . . you know . . . a captain, man. I mean, who's going to believe us, man?"

"Now, Miguel." When Chavez had gone, Ré drank the Ba Mi Ba.

* * *

"I mean, Phelps was a captain, Ré," Joey, raining sweat, said for the dozenth time. Then he changed his tack and cocked his head curiously. "Where've you been all this time, Ré? We thought you must be . . . you know." Then again:

"Ré, listen. You probably need a job, right? You probably need some cash. Let me give you five hundred—a thousand, even." The thought of giving away a thousand dollars, for whatever the reason, made him sweat more. "Not as a loan. Call it an advance—an advance against your first paycheck. I could use a guy like you in this business. Hell, I could use you so much I won't even make it an advance. I'll make it a bonus. A bonus in advance. Ha ha ha. This is a hell of a good business, Ré. People always need parts for their cars, right? But where're they going to get them? Ford, Chevy—they don't make parts for their older models anymore. So people get them from me. Nobody loses. The guys whose cars I steal, they collect insurance, right? So they get a new car, and the guy who needs parts gets the parts. So what's the big deal? I mean, it's ecology, right? Recycling. Come on, Ré, let's have a drink and talk about going into business together."

As he babbled, Joey moved away from the desk toward a locker in the shadows along the wall.

"And you can tell me what you been doing. Where you been. Christ, it's been a long time, Ré. You know, Ré, it was Redfield who talked us into it—telling the MPs the story he made up, I mean. It was the same story Phelps was going to tell, I guess you know. Redfield and Phelps were buddies, did you know that? I didn't either, until then. Nobody did. Clarence thought maybe they were, you know, faggots. I don't know. Hey, Clarence—you said you saw Clarence, right? How is the big coon? Christ, we should get together, you, me. . . . Where the fuck is that bottle? I had a bottle of Scotch in here. The fucking help took it, probably. That's the thing about this business, Ré, you can't trust nobody. That's why I like the idea of working with you. You I can trust. You motherfucking scumbag."

With that, Joey swung around the shotgun he'd squirreled in the back of the locker. But he never pulled the trigger. The bullet from Ré's pistol struck him in the chest and he fell backward into the locker.

SIXTEEN

Whores, pimps, junkies, runaways, con artists, deadbeats, and lost souls were the clientele of the Cairo Hotel, just a lurch away from Times Square. The night manager had spotted Jim Giles as one of the last, although he had been wearing a necktie, and hadn't been surprised that he'd registered as Mr. Jones. It was only when he got around to reading the Sunday paper—he always saved it for late Sunday night, the slowest of slow times—that he realized that Mr. Jones was a murder suspect.

"Four-oh-six," the night manager said. "It's all the way in the back."

"And you're sure he's still there?" Neuman said. "According to this"—he spun the register around to face the night manager—"he checked in at three o'clock yesterday morning. And you say he hasn't left since?"

"I don't exactly say it," the night manager said. "I say some of it; the other part I *hear*say, if you know what I mean. I say he didn't leave between three o'clock Saturday, when he checked in, and eight o'clock Saturday, when I got off. And I say he didn't leave between midnight Saturday, when I came to work, and eight o'clock Sunday, when I got off. And I say he hasn't left since—"

"We get the picture," Redfield said. "And the day shift and the night shift say the same thing: that he didn't leave during their tours, right?"

"Right. There were the liquor store deliveries, is all. He brought his own in with him when he checked in. Dewar's—I saw the bottles. Two of them. He had another delivery Saturday afternoon. I didn't see it; Murray saw it, the day guy. Didn't say how many bottles, or what kind. He had *another* delivery just before midnight Saturday. He couldn't've drunk all that in that time, but he must've figured the store'd be closed on Sunday, he better stock up. The kid was leaving just as I came on duty. Two more Dewar's. I didn't see them, I asked the kid."

Neuman couldn't move. He was addicted to talk. He couldn't get enough of it. It was all people did. They'd stopped living, acting, moving; all they did was sit and talk. All he did was sit—sometimes he stood, as now—and listen. That day alone he'd listened to Michael Magazine, the Channel 3 production assistant who'd found Chris Kaiser's body; to the superintendent of Chris Kaiser's building, who'd found the body along with Michael Magazine; to Ted Cavanaugh, the producer of Channel 3's Midnight News; to David Dempsey, Randy Peck, Ruby Tucker, Kristen Richards, and Tess Delaney, all part of the supporting cast of Channel 3's Midnight News and therefore among the last to see Chris Kaiser alive; to Jaime Ortega, a driver for the Star Cab Company, who remembered driving Chris Kaiser from Channel 3's studios to her apartment house; to Rafael Ortega (no relation), the overnight doorman at Chris Kaiser's apartment house, who, except for her killer, seemed likely to have been *the* last to see Chris Kaiser alive; to Donna Giles, the wife of Jim Giles, who, for want of a better one, seemed the best candidate to be that killer.

Talk, talk, talk. He knew more about the television news business, the taxi driving business, the overnight doorman business, the business of being the wife of a drunken has-been than he cared to know. He knew about ratings and sweeps and audience response tests and how much people were paid and how much a station charged for commercials; he knew about trip sheets and dispatchers and radio calls and taxi stands and the shortage of decent places to eat since the Belmore closed and shocks and points and bulletproof panels and medallions and what the drivers thought of the Taxi and Limousine Commission and, by extension, the mayor, the City Council, the borough presidents, the governor, two senators, several congressmen, and the president; he knew about night bells and tenants' habits and elevators and intercoms; he knew that being the wife of a drunken has-been hadn't changed much since his mother had been one.

All he didn't know was who killed Chris Kaiser, and how he got close enough to her to do it, and why.

There was one other thing he didn't know, and that was what was on Bobby Redfield's mind. Bobby had listened to every bit of talk Jake Neuman had, but he hadn't listened to it as Neuman had—with the knowledge that it was inevitable and that somewhere within it might be lurking something they wanted to know. Bobby had listened to it without hearing it, his eyes focused somewhere over the speakers' heads, his mind's eye staring fixedly but glazedly at Neuman knew not what. He could have asked Bobby, of course, but just as it wasn't his style to ask what Redfield thought about a case—he knew Redfield would tell him what he thought when he felt like telling him—so it wasn't his style to ask Redfield what he thought about life, love, politics, the price of swordfish, or the prospect that it would be a warm winter. He knew that Redfield would tell him what he thought when he felt like telling him, if he felt like telling him.

It wasn't that Redfield was altogether out of it. In fact, he was more impatient than usual—impatient to be moving instead of sitting or standing and listening. Now, for example, although Neuman could have stood and listened for an hour to talk about the night hotel management business, Redfield stepped up to the desk, held his hand out, and said, "The key."

The night manager stepped to the key rack, put his hand on the key to room 406, but didn't take it down from its hook. "So this guy— *Jones*—is really Jim Giles, hunh? The TV guy? You know, before I worked these hours, I used to watch his show. His show was on earlier then, and I used to work days, over at the Collingwood. Well, not days, exactly; I used to work from two till ten. His show—Giles's— was on at ten, and I used to go into a bar on Lexington—not the Collingwood's bar, but another bar; never drink where you work, I always say—and have a beer before going down into the tunnel of terror. Hey, the cops catch that Sumarian Killer yet, the guy who—"

"The key," Redfield said. "And if you say another fucking word— anything—I'll come over the top of this counter and fix it so it's the last word you'll ever say."

Maybe, Neuman thought, it was simply that Bobby had come to the realization that police work was ninety-nine percent shitwork and that the other one percent wasn't all that much more exciting. Neuman had been a cop three times as long as Redfield, and he had come to the same realization around the time he'd been in the department as long as Redfield had. He would have thought it would take Redfield a little longer to come to that realization, if only because there were far more police shows on television than there had been in the old

86

days, and they held out, if nothing else, the prospect that police work was exciting—driving fast in unmarked cars with the siren stuck on the roof, kicking down doors and shouting at suspects to get their hands up, tackling purse snatchers and slamming them in the face with a handy garbage can, blowing holdup men through plate-glass windows, slipping into bed on your lunch hour with a slinky public defender. In Neuman's nonage, the only TV show had been *Dragnet*, which, in its way, had been true to the shitwork, although it had been guilty of an overdose of luck. Luck, in Neuman's experience, was something that reared its head when you had done ninety-nine percent of the ninety-nine percent that was shitwork. Then, because a suspect wasn't home when you didn't want him to be or was when you did, or some such, you considered yourself lucky, overlooking the fact that you'd done all that shitwork in order to know that the suspect was a suspect in the first place.

The night manager, without a word, without so much as a sound, surrendered the key, and Neuman and Redfield took the elevator up to the fourth floor, walked all the way to the back, and found room 406, by a window looking out on an airshaft.

This not being television, and kicking down doors being a lot harder than it looks, Neuman knocked. The only sound was the sound of pigeons cooing in the airshaft.

Neuman stepped aside so that Redfield could slip the key in the door. Before he could, Neuman put a hand on his arm and with the other hand, tried the doorknob. It turned all the way. He held the door closed, drew his revolver from his shoulder holster, and motioned with his chin for Redfield to do the same. Then, just like on television, he threw the door open and they went in with their guns braced in both hands, Neuman left, Redfield right. They panned the room in search of their adversary.

He was asleep on the bed in the corner by the window, which looked out on the back of another hotel. In a room across the way, lighted by a bare light bulb, a black woman, in a robe that might have been silk or might have been synthetic, stood before an easel painting a seascape—from memory, or from her imagination?—in water-colors.

Neuman put his gun away, went to the window, drew the shade—

at this hour of the night he could cope with only so much irony—
went to the bed, and shook Jim Giles by the ankle. Giles held a bottle
of Dewar's in his arms like a baby; strewn about the room were half a
dozen other bottles. The room smelled like the john of an Irish saloon
on St. Patrick's Day night.

Giles stirred but clutched the bottle tighter. He had a dusting of
gray beard on his chin and cheeks, but his upper lip, somehow, was
clean-shaven. His necktie was pulled loose and askew, his shirt was
wrinkled and stained with sweat, the crotch of his beige pants was
dappled with urine stains.

Neuman looked at Redfield, who nodded, put his gun away, and
went into the bathroom and turned on the shower. He came back,
leaned down to slip his arms under Giles's shoulders, and nodded to
Neuman to grab his feet.

As they lifted, they saw the gun barrel protruding from under the
pillow. They kept on going into the bathroom, maneuvered through
the door, and lowered Giles into the tub, Dewar's bottle and all.

Giles blinked as the water spattered his face.

Neuman went back into the bedroom, took a handkerchief from his
pocket, shook it out, and used it to lift the gun by its barrel. A .38
caliber Smith & Wesson. He dropped it in an evidence bag, tagged it,
and put it in the pocket of his jacket. When he went back into the
bathroom, Giles was awake, sitting up and sputtering. He hadn't located the source of the moisture yet and was screwing on the cap of
the Dewar's bottle, as if it were champagne gone amok.

Neuman turned off the water, took the bottle from Giles, put it on
the floor beside the tub, then thought it would be more like television
to pour it down the sink and did, used a towel to dry his hands, and
sat on the closed toilet seat, his elbows on his knees, facing the man
he knew as well as he knew his own name had not killed Chris Kaiser,
ready to listen to yet more talk. And to talk.

"My name's Neuman. Lieutenant Neuman, Manhattan North
Homicide. This is Sergeant Redfield. We're investigating the murder
of Chris Kaiser. We came here to arrest you as a prime suspect. If we
were going to arrest you, I'd read you your rights. But we're not going
to arrest you, so I'm going to save my breath. The desk clerks say you
haven't left this room since three A.M. Saturday morning. From the

88

look and the smell of it—and you—I'd say they know what they're talking about. And anyway I'm not especially interested in what you've been doing since three A.M. Saturday. I want to know what you were doing between quarter to one, which was the last time anybody saw you around the Channel 3 studio, and the time you checked in here."

Giles continued to blink water from his eyes. His hands, which he might have used to wipe them, were still curled in a mime of holding the bottle. "Redford and Newman. The famous Redford and Newman."

"Where were you, Giles?" Neuman said.

Giles stared suddenly, having registered what Neuman had said. "Chris is dead?"

Someday, somewhere, Neuman thought, someone, on being told that someone else is dead, will not say, *Dead?* Until then, a lot of unnecessary talking will have to be done.

"Dead," Neuman said. "Dead, dead, dead. Somebody shot her in the left tit with a thirty-eight-caliber Swiss and— Oh, fuck. See? See how tired I fucking am? A thirty-eight-caliber *Smith* and Wesson semiautomatic pistol. Like yours. In her apartment. Between one and two Saturday morning. Did you do it, Giles? Just say yes or no. No— wait. Don't say yes or no. Don't say anything. 'Cause if you say yes, I won't have read you your rights and nothing you say'll be any fucking good to me. But I don't want to read you your rights, I don't want to arrest you, I don't want to do the fucking paperwork, I just want you to tell me where you were between quarter to one Saturday morning and three A.M. Saturday morning, the time you checked in here, and I want you to tell me the name of someone who saw you there, and then I want you to go home to your wife, who's worried sick about you, you dumb fuck, why the hell can't you leave that stuff alone and straighten up and fly right?" *Oh, daddy, daddy, daddy.* Neuman got up off the toilet seat and went out to the bedroom.

Redfield took over. "Where'd you go when you left the studio, Giles?"

"Hurley's."

"On Sixth Avenue? By Radio City?"

"Yes."

Neuman shut his mind to it. He went to the window, drew up the shade, and stood with one hand against the frame, the other tucked into his belt.

The black woman in the room across the way heard the shade and turned to look at him. She smiled.

He smiled back. "Evening."

She rinsed a brush in a plastic jar filled with water, rested it on her palette, and came to her window. She held her robe closed, but not so closed that he couldn't admire the wide space between her big breasts, couldn't enjoy the red lace heart that decorated her pink silk panties. "You want to have a good time, honey?"

He shook his head. "I'm afraid I'm having about the best time I could be having under the circumstances."

She shrugged. "Up to you, honey. I wasn't going to work tonight, but when I saw you standing there looking beat I couldn't help but think you could use a good time and that Valentine's the girl to show it to you."

"Valentine? Oh, yeah. The heart."

He thought she blushed. He couldn't be sure, for her skin was the brown of polished oak. She had corn-rowed hair; on a dummy on a dresser was her working hair, a teased blond wig.

"You're a cop, ain't you?" Valentine said.

"I'm a cop."

She sighed. "I guess that means he did it, hunh? I'm kind of surprised. I thought he changed his mind. And I didn't hear no shot."

"'It'?" Neuman said.

"Killed hisself," Valentine said. "He had that gun in his mouth two or three times the past couple of days."

He didn't ask her why she hadn't done something, called the manager of the Cairo, called the police. He knew she would say it was none of her business, and he knew that it wasn't. "He didn't kill himself, Val. We got here in time."

She brightened a little, seemingly glad. "He done something else, then? That why you come looking for him?"

"You didn't see him any time before he checked in here, did you, Val?" Neuman said. "Any time between midnight and three on Saturday, for example."

She pulled her robe closer. "I ain't going to testify."

"I'm not asking you to testify, Val. It's just between the two of us. If you care at all about him, and I think you do, or you wouldn't've been concerned that he'd eaten his gun, if you care at all about him it'll save him a lot of grief if you can say where he was between midnight and three on Saturday."

She pulled her robe closer still, turned sideways to him, and, as if it hurt her to say it, muttered, "Arizona."

Neuman wanted to shout at her not to fuck with him, that he would run her in so fast her hair would straighten—she had solicited him, after all. Then he remembered that the Arizona, wildly, was the bar in the ground floor of the Cairo—east and west, the meeting of the twain. He smiled. "Thanks, Val. . . . Oh, and Val?"

"Yeah?"

He pointed toward the easel. "That someplace you've been?"

Again, possibly, a blush. "Someplace I'm going."

Neuman nodded. "I hope it's soon, Val." He waved, pulled down the shade, and went back into the bathroom.

Giles sat on the toilet seat, looking clearer-headed but in every other way more disreputable.

Redfield stood against the wall, his arms folded on his chest. He shook his head. "Memory problems, Jake. He remembers going to Hurley's. Had just one drink 'cause there were people he knew there and he didn't feel like talking. After that, zilch."

Neuman motioned Redfield out into the bedroom and spoke softly. "There's a place downstairs. The Arizona. Check it out. He was there Saturday morning."

Redfield pulled back a little. "Who says?"

"What the fuck difference does it make, Bobby? Just check it out. I want to get Giles home, then I want to go home myself. I'm fucking beat."

Redfield frowned. "What the fuck's the matter with you, Jake?"

"Nothing's the matter with me. What's the matter with you? You've been walking around all fucking day in a fucking fog. You still sick? Tell me, and I'll send you home. I don't need you getting sicker. You got something on your mind? Don't tell me what it is if you don't want to, but tell me if you do. I can deal with it. I can pick up some of the slack. But don't slack off and pretend you're not. You've been

91

no more fucking use to me than a fucking probationary patrolman. I'd rather be leading fucking McGovern around than having you do this number on me. What's the matter with *me*? Nothing's the matter with me. What's the matter with *you*?" It had come out all wrong; he hadn't been going to say anything, and now he had, and it had come out all wrong. Maybe there *was* something the matter with him— something like one too many murders, far too many conversations with people who had nothing to tell him, far too few ideas as to who the murderer was.

Redfield had turned his back and was poking with a toe of a shoe at the threadbare carpet. "I'm sorry, Jake."

"Yeah. I'm sorry too."

Redfield turned. "All day long, listening to people tell us about Giles, about Chris Kaiser, about their rivalry, all that shit about the station, the news show, the ratings, I knew we were wasting our time. Just now, talking to Giles about where he's been, I knew I was wasting my time. And yet, I didn't want it to be a waste of time. I wanted him to be our man. I wanted to nail him and put him on ice and just walk away from it. His gun probably hasn't been fired, has it? Well, I wanted to fire it; I wanted to doctor the ballistics to make it look like it was the gun that killed Chris Kaiser. I wanted to take advantage of his not being able to remember anything. I wanted to frame him, Jake, just so we could say it was over and done with."

Neuman had felt that way many times. Life was full of compromises, wasn't it? Weren't you always settling for the next best thing? Well, why not settle for the next best suspect? What difference did it make if he hadn't pulled the trigger? He had a motive, didn't he? So what if he hadn't quite had the motivation? People were always complaining that cops didn't prevent crime, they only reacted to it. Well, wasn't it prevention to put someone on ice who had a motive even if he hadn't quite had the motivation? Why wait until he got his shit together, got motivated, got up the courage to kill? *That* would be reaction, not prevention.

He put his hands on Redfield's shoulders. "Go home. Get some sleep. I don't want to see you till noon tomorrow. Try and get your mind off it. Go to a movie. Watch TV. Call a girlfriend. *Call* a girlfriend. Don't go see her, don't ask her over, just talk to her awhile.

92

This is going to be a rough case. We got shit. It's even worse coming on top of the subway thing. We had shit there, too. I wish they'd left us on it, just for continuity's sake. I understand why they put us on this. If word of that letter gets out, every wacko in town's going to come out of the woodwork, saying he's the killer, writing us letters, calling us up, maybe—a few of them—even killing someone. We got to get this guy sooner rather than later, but we don't want to run ourselves ragged before we're even started. . . . Call McIver and Bloomfield—they're hanging on till they hear from me—and tell them to check out the Arizona: was Giles there, when did he come in, when did he leave, who did he talk to, like that. Tell them unless they find that he wasn't, not to bother me about it till tomorrow. Tell them they find out he wasn't, to get me on the car radio. I'm taking Giles home, then I'll head home. . . . Not till noon tomorrow, all right?"

Redfield put his hands on Neuman's and gave them a quick squeeze. "Thanks, Jake."

"Yeah."

"You keep a secret, Giles?" Neuman said.

Giles turned from the car window—he had had his face in the breeze, clearing his head even further—and smiled smally. "Me?"

"A professional secret," Neuman said. "I hear it on Channel Three or read it in the papers in a way that makes me think it came from you, I'll have your ass in a sling."

Giles's smile broadened. "I appreciate what you've done for me, lieutenant. Yes, I can keep a secret."

"Chris Kaiser's killer wrote a letter saying she wasn't going to be his last victim," Neuman said. "He sent it to the *Express*, hoping that since they offered the guy they call the Samaritan Killer a chance to tell his story, they might be more interested in his story, since it has some sex in it, along with the violence. They would've—the *Express*, I mean; printed it, that is—but I nixed that. I don't hold out much hope of its staying a secret for long, though. They'll find a way to get it into print. They'll find some other cop who knows about it—plenty do, by now, from the guys who're giving the typeface a going-over (it was a typewritten letter), all the way up to the brass—and they'll make him their source. Or maybe they'll go to court saying they got a right to print the letter since it's their property since it was sent to them. I suppose they do. I suppose they ought to, even. But I don't want them to do it just yet. . . .

"The guy—I'm sure it's a guy, although I shouldn't close my mind to the possibility it's a girl pretending to be a guy, but I don't think so—the guy says in the letter he's fed up with women like Chris Kaiser getting ahead in the world on account of what I guess you'd call their sex appeal. Reading between the lines, I guess what he means is the whole point about Women's Lib was supposed to be that men weren't supposed to treat women as, you know, just sex objects, and then there's a woman like Chris Kaiser who's in these ads on the subways, the billboards, all over town, looking like . . . well, like a sex object, when what she's supposed to be is a journalist. Like you, like a hundred other guys and quite a few women who seem to be able to do their job without . . . well, getting undressed for it."

Giles laughed. "I'm afraid I agree with this individual, lieutenant. As much as I'm shocked by Chris's death, I can't rid myself of the feeling that she was a blot on the escutcheon of the profession. . . . Does that return me to the ranks of suspect?"

Neuman honked at a cabby who cut him off. "Well, I'm not sure I know what an escutcheon is, and as far as returning you to the ranks of suspect, I can suspect you all I want; it doesn't look like you were in the right place at the right time, unless you hired someone to do your dirty work, in which case just tell me so I can book you and stop all this talking, I've talked enough for one day, and been talked to more than enough. . . . Reason I'm telling you all this—about the letter, I mean—is you've been in the television news business for a long time. I spent most of today talking to other people in the television news business: your producer, the other people on your show—none of them thinks you killed her, by the way, if that's any consolation to you—"

"It is," Giles said softly.

"—and the thing that struck me was how . . . ephemeral it all is."

Giles laughed louder. "You're *sure* you don't know what an escutcheon is, lieutenant?"

"Yeah, well," Neuman said, "it's like a shield, isn't it? I guess I do remember a few things from my college days, even if it was four thousand years ago. . . . As I was saying, it struck me how ephemeral it all is, how you can be on top one minute and out on the street the next, what with the ratings being as important as they are, and all, and it occurred to me that it isn't just somebody from the *in*side, somebody like you, who got bumped from the top spot by Chris Kaiser, who'd be glad she's dead—not that you're glad she's dead; I'm just talking hypothetically here, to use another big word—but that somebody from the *out*side, from another news show on another channel, might be just as glad. And I was wondering, given what you know about the television news business and what I told you about the letter, if you have any ideas about who such a person might be."

Giles thought for a while before speaking. "I can't think of anyone, lieutenant. That surprises me, because my business is not only ephemeral, it's cutthroat. The producers, the anchors, the executives of all the other news shows on all the other channels in New York will be *glad*, in some sense, that Chris is dead, because she represented a competition they were unable to meet. At the same time, they know that Chris, herself, didn't matter. She was simply the embodiment of an idea—the idea of a producer, a news director, an advertising executive, a media consultant—of someone, or several people perhaps, in the front office as to what a nighttime news anchor should be. At one time, I embodied a similar idea, put together by different individuals under different circumstances. If I had died—naturally or violently—I would have been easily replaced by some other embodiment of that idea, who surely existed somewhere. The same is true of Chris: she'll be replaced—not by me, not by someone from one of the other channels, for they're embodiments, whether male or female, of different ideas—but by someone who for all practical purposes might as well be her. And before you ask who is that person and might *she*—it would have to be a woman—have killed Chris, the answer is, No one and no. Chris's replacement doesn't exist yet; she's being created somewhere in the front offices of Channel 3—at this very moment, I wouldn't at all doubt—so she can't very well have murdered Chris in order to advance her cause, because she wouldn't've known *who* she was going to be. . . . I'm very tired, lieutenant. I'm not sure if I'm making myself clear."

"Clear enough," Neuman said, and thought, Talk, talk, talk. All that talking—and listening—to find out that if he wanted a suspect in the murder of Chris Kaiser he had better look elsewhere than at the other television channels in New York. "This is your building, isn't it? On the corner?"

Giles flinched a little as he recognized his apartment house. "It is, yes."

"Like I said, I had one of my men—Sergeant Bloomfield—call your wife to say you were okay and on the way home. I guess she'll be waiting up, I don't know. I'm going to hold on to your gun for a while, not 'cause I think you killed Chris Kaiser with it, but because I'd feel bad if I gave it back to you and you blew your head off with it. . . . Good night, Giles. Or I guess it's morning by now."

Giles opened the door latch but didn't swing the door open. "I owe you a great deal, lieutenant."

"You don't owe me shit," Neuman said. "Your debt is to the people who care about you—if there're any of them left. My old man—ah, fuck it. You ought to get upstairs."

"Was an alcoholic? Is that what you started to say?"

Neuman closed his eyes and pressed on them with the tips of his fingers, making fireworks of green and black. "What difference does it make?"

Giles pushed the door open but didn't get out. "I naturally over-heard your discussion with Sergeant Redfield. I can understand his distress."

"Oh, yeah?"

Giles touched Neuman's arm. "Didn't you know?"

Neuman opened his eyes and looked from Giles's hand to his face, which was wrenched with concern. "Know what?"

Giles waved his hand, as if to dispel what he was about to say. "I don't know this for a certainty, but I believe he and Chris are—were—friends."

"You believe it? Why?" Neuman said.

Giles thought for a moment. "About a year ago, Sergeant Redfield was a guest on a panel show on Channel Three—"

"I know about it," Neuman said.

Giles nodded. "I wasn't on the panel—Chris was the moderator—

but I watched it at home. Some time after that—maybe a few months, maybe only a few weeks; I have nothing to measure it against—I saw them together."

"Them?"

"Chris and Sergeant Redfield. I recognized him from the panel show and from his photographs in the newspapers—you two are an often-photographed couple."

"Yeah. Saw them where?"

"The Control Room—a bar just down the block from Channel Three. It's a hangout for people from the station."

"And they were hanging out?" Neuman said.

"The only word I can think of to describe their posture," Giles said, "is intimate."

Neuman shifted out of park into drive, keeping his foot on the brake. "'Night, Giles."

"Good night, lieutenant."

Driving over the Triborough, heading for Ultima Queens, the Bedroom Borough, his birthplace and, he never doubted, his resting place too, for it was also the Borough of Cemeteries, Neuman thought, *Why the fuck didn't he just say so?*

SEVENTEEN

"I asked you not to come here anymore," Susannah Keyes said.

"You let me in."

"I let you in because if I hadn't you'd've done something absurd. Scaled the garden wall or something. Something macho."

"You always liked it a little rough."

"Liked," Susannah said. "Would you please go now? I really don't want to see you."

"I read your book."

She laughed. "You would. You love to punish yourself."

"I guess you'll get your wish now—being a guest on the Johnny Carson show."

"It's not a wish, it's a fantasy. And, yes, I've been invited."

"And a shot at your other wish. Or is it a fantasy, too? Fucking Carson."

Susannah smiled. "He's an attractive man."

"It's too bad the women who read that book aren't going to know it was written by a nymphomaniac. *Womanlove*. Shit. It's high-class pornography, that's all—intended to get men hot and to get you hot at the thought of getting them hot."

"Why, thank you. High class. My."

"You got anything to drink?"

"Not for you. I want you to leave. If you don't leave, I'll call the police."

He sat in her Eames chair and folded his hands behind his head. "And yell rape? That's actually your style, isn't it? Call the cops, yell rape, a couple of good-looking young cops show up, you describe in detail everything I did to you—even if I didn't—pretty soon the three of you are climbing the walls and, pretty soon after that, each other."

"And you'd just watch?" Susannah said.

He lifted his chin toward the stack of manuscript pages on her desk. "What're you writing now?"

"A novel. Yes, you're in it, you'll be sorry to hear."

"What is it you always say, a writer can only write about what he knows?"

"Or she. You don't come off all that badly, actually—or you won't if you leave right now. I had a mind to turn you—your character— into a murderer, a gynecidal maniac."

"Gynecidal? Is that the word?"

"It would've complicated the plot unnecessarily. And besides, for all your posturing, you're really a pussycat. And a masochist. You wouldn't kill the women who cause you so much pleasant pain."

He smiled. "I'd like to read it."

Susannah snorted. "Nobody reads my work in progress. Not my agent, not my editor, nobody."

He laughed. "You're really a dumb cunt, you know that?"

She arched her neck.

"That's exactly what I wanted to know. And I didn't even have to ask you."

She frowned. "Wanted to know it, why?"

He drew a pistol from inside his jacket and pointed it at her face. "Because when I take it, it'll cease to exist."

She blinked uncontrollably. "Put that away."

"And since nobody else has read it—not your agent, not your editor, nobody—nobody'll be able to put two and two together and say I'm one of the characters."

"*Please* put it away."

From inside his jacket he took a silencer and screwed it into the barrel.

"I'll scream."

"This is New York. People scream all the time. It's a local custom."

"*Please.*"

He got up from the chair and came to her and with the silencer brushed her rich black hair away from her face.

She shivered. "Please."

"You put your finger on it. Gynecidal maniac, hunh? I like that."

"Martha has a copy," she said, or tried to. She moved her lips, but nothing came out. Her tongue was limp and helpless and her throat was dry. She forced a swallow and tried to say it again, *Martha has a copy*, but before she could he had fired a bullet into her brain.

EIGHTEEN

Linda Walsh closed her eyes and tried to see in her mind's eye the younger of the two men who had come into the Green Tree as she and Ray were leaving.

She opened her eyes and looked at the photograph on the front page of the *News*, which a customer had left on the bar—in lieu of a tip, the cheap bastard.

It was the same man.

She read the caption, which she'd read half a dozen times already:

TOP COPS HUNT NEWSWOMAN'S KILLER. Detective Sgt. Robert Redfield (l.) and Lt. Jacob Neuman (back to camera) talk to reporters outside studios of Channel 3, where they began investigation into shooting death of news personality Chris Kaiser. Story: p. 3.

And the story, which she'd read twice:

Police Commissioner Daniel Clarity has assigned two of the department's crackerjack homicide detectives to spearhead the investigation into Saturday's murder of TV anchorwoman Chris Kaiser, THE NEWS learned today.

Detective Lt. Jacob Neuman, 60, and Detective Sgt. Robert Redfield, 39, were ordered to head the investigation following a direct appeal to Mayor Berger by Thomas K. Minchenberg, president of Channel 3, whose Midnight News with Chris Kaiser was the highest-rated local news show in the nation.

Informed sources told THE NEWS that Minchenberg presented the mayor with information indicating that Miss Kaiser was not murdered by an intruder, as had originally been believed, but by what the sources called "a cold-blooded killer who intends to kill again."

The information, the sources said, was contained in a letter written by the alleged killer and sent to an unidentified newspaper. According to the sources, the police have asked the newspaper not to publish the letter.

Attempts to reach Mayor Berger, Commissioner Clarity and Minchenberg for comment on the report were unavailing as none of them would return telephone calls to their homes and offices.

100

Other police officials, however, confirmed the assignment of Detectives Redfield and Neuman—known to their colleagues as Redford and Newman after the popular actors who have been paired in such films as "Butch Cassidy and the Sundance Kid" and "The Sting"—to head the investigation into Miss Kaiser's death.

The two detectives, who have an arrest record unsurpassed by any other homicide detectives in the city, had previously been assigned to the much-publicized killing of a young hoodlum by an unidentified man whom the media have dubbed the Samaritan Killer.

And so on, with background material on investigations Redfield and Newman had brought to successful conclusions.

Redfield. The name on the ticket envelope in Ray's jacket pocket, with an address on East 72nd Street. Linda had already looked in the phone book to see if a Robert Redfield lived on East 72nd Street. No number was listed, which made sense; he was a cop—with enemies.

One of whom might be the man who was staying in her apartment—Linda had persuaded Ray to move his things (one light duffel-bag) from the YMCA on 63rd Street into her place—the man who had told her his name was Ray Howell, but who had bought a plane ticket under the name Paul Howell, the man about whom she knew almost nothing except that he liked Annie Dillard and baseball, the man she could, if she let herself, fall in love with.

Linda started at the sound of a key in the door. The digital clock on the refrigerator said it was four thirty in the morning. How could she fall in love with a man who came home at four thirty in the morning and wouldn't, she knew, tell her where he had been? She folded up the newspaper and thrust it deep down in the garbage pail, then went to the kitchen door with what she hoped was a smile on her face. "Hi."

"Hi," Ray said. "When did you get home?"

True, she often worked until closing time and didn't get home until three thirty or four herself. Maybe there was nothing to be suspicious about. Maybe he had gotten a job in a bar and didn't want to tell her lest she feel some professional jealousy.

Stop kidding yourself, Linda. This guy could be dangerous.

101

"I left a little early. Lou owed me some time. I hoped you might be here."

"I went to see a friend. I told you I'd be late."

"I know. It's just . . ."

Ray came to her and put his hands on her shoulders. "Linda . . ."

She twisted out of his hands. She hated being held that way. It reminded her of the way her father had held her—before slapping her in the face or hurling her against the wall. "Don't say it. I know what you're going to say. I'm sorry. I can't help it, that's all. I can't help it if I like you. I can't help it if I want you around."

Ray put his hands in the pockets of his jeans and scuffed at the floor. "Maybe I should go."

Let him, Linda. Let him go. "No. I won't let you. Even if it's only going to be for a while, I want that while." She went to him and pulled his hands from his pockets and placed them on her breasts. She reached up and grasped his hair and pulled his mouth down to hers.

You're crazy, Linda.

So? The worst that can happen is he'll kill me. Then I won't have to miss him.

*   *   *

While she slept, Ré remembered.

He walked for a week, heading west, toward home. He traveled by night and slept by day, living off the land.

On the evening of the eighth day he was awakened by someone poking at his belly with a bayonet—a young Vietnamese in tatterdemalion: the remnants of an ARVN uniform, a pair of GI-issue shorts, a headband woven of elephant grass, a pair of Adidas running shoes. Ré had nothing to lose, and grabbed the man's rifle barrel and tried to wrest it from his grip. Someone behind him clipped him behind the ear with something solid.

It was pitch black when he woke, but he heard the crackling of a fire and smelled the smoke and the scent of cooking flesh. He thought perhaps his captors had blinded him, but he felt no pain. When he touched his eyes he discovered that he was blindfolded.

Someone crouched next to him and touched his shoulder gently.

He smelled like an American. "We'll take the blindfold off when we're sure who you are, bro. Meanwhile, eat this."

The meal was the flesh of a wild hog, some kind of fried fruit, water sweeter than any he had ever tasted. He asked for more of everything, and it was given to him.

The American lighted a cigarette and put in it Ré's lips. The smoke made him dizzy but then relaxed him.

"You're a deserter," the American said in an accent that was slightly southern—white southern.

Ré hadn't thought of it that way, but he guessed that it was so. Although it hadn't been a question, he nodded.

"We've got good intelligence," the American said. "Better, in some ways, than any of the armies fighting this dog-assed war. It's how we survive. Our intelligence says there're no American units operating within a hundred klicks of here, so you must've come a long way."

"My unit was operating around Firebase Enid," Ré said. "The Fourth of the Two-oh—"

The American put his fingers over Ré's lips. "Rule Number One is, your past is your own. We don't need to know anything about you to take you in. All we need to know is that you want in."

Ré felt for his shoulder flash, but it had been ripped from his blouse. His name tag was gone, too, and the ID tags on the chain around his neck.

There was a smile in the American's voice. "The guys who brought you in buried all your ID. Since they don't speak English, even they don't know who you are, what outfit you were in. . . . Yeah, you're probably thinking most ARVN speak a little English, but they weren't ARVN. One's a VC, one's NVA—or they were. They're with us now."

"VC? NVA? And you? Who's 'us'?"

"We've tried to avoid having a name. Having a name leads to having ranks and having ranks leads to dissension. But some of the guys call us the People. We're Americans, ARVN, NVA, and VC. Deserters, our former leaders would call us—and do—but we like to think of ourselves as people who saw the light, who saw that killing and being killed was a way of life with no future in it." The American laughed. "There were eight of us originally: three GIs, an ARVN scout, and four NVA regulars. We all dove for the same bomb crater during an artillery barrage that some dumb fuck walked right on top of us instead of a hundred meters up the ridge like we told him to. We sat there for a whole night, eyeball to eyeball, our rifles in each other's faces, safeties off, fingers on the triggers. Around dawn, somebody laughed. I forget who it was, but pretty soon we were all laughing— laughing at being alive. We dropped our guns and danced around like maniacs, laughing and screaming. When we finally calmed down, I made a suggestion—that instead of going back to our units, and maybe later that day blowing each other away, why not join up, pool our resources, our skills, and sit the war out? We knew a damn sight more than any officers, any generals, any politicians, any presidents. I'd never thought about anything like that until I suggested it. From the looks on everyone's face—our scout put my idea into Vietnamese—they'd never thought about it either. But from their second looks it was damn clear it was an idea they thought a lot of, once they'd heard it. To make a long story short, we joined up. That was eighteen months ago now, and since then we've grown to twenty-four. You'll make twenty-five."

Ré touched his blindfold. "Can I take this off now?"

Someone behind him untied the blindfold. It took a moment for his eyes to adjust to the firelight, but when they had he saw that he was at the center of a circle of energy more powerful than any he had ever felt. There were Americans in black pajamas, Vietnamese in fatigues, others in T-shirts bearing gaudy American slogans, others in loincloths, still more Americans in gym shorts and running shoes, looking as though they were about to get up a game of touch football, others in full combat gear—except that their uniforms bore no insignia.

Ré gave a shy wave. "My name's—"

"Your name's whatever you want it to be," the American said. He was slight and blond and wore blue jeans and combat boots, no shirt. "So think it over for a while before you tell us who you are. It's a chance we don't get that often—to be whoever we want. My name, my real name, is a name I hated ever since I was a kid. It was my father's name too—still is, I guess—and he hated it too, so I guess

104

you can tell what he must've thought of me, giving me the same name. Anyway, I call myself Huck now—like Huck Finn. He was always my favorite book character when I was a kid, and as soon as I thought of it I couldn't think of a better person to be."

Ré thought for a moment, staring into the fire, feeling the eyes of all the others on him. "I met a Vietnamese woman once who had a baby boy she wouldn't name because she was sure he was going to die."

"That's up to you, bro," Huck said. "You want to have no name, that's up to you. We've got one fellow—he's out guarding the perimeter right now—who's been with us six months and hasn't thought of a name yet. He wants it to be just the right name, and the right name hasn't come to him yet."

Ré looked up from the fire into Huck's eyes. "I want a name. I want a name because I don't feel I'm going to die. I think a name'll keep me from dying." He extended his hand to Huck. "Pleased to meet you, Huck. I'm Tom."

Huck hesitated for a moment, but then a glint came into his eyes that said he had hoped without knowing it that that was the name Ré would choose.

NINETEEN

Susannah Keyes's body was found on Tuesday afternoon, by two uniformed cops who were the last links in a chain of concern that had been growing since that morning.

A driver for a private limousine service had arrived at Susannah's apartment at six o'clock to drive her, ironically, to the studios of Channel 3, where she was to have been a guest on *Good Morning,*

New York, a news and entertainment program. Getting no answer to his continuous rings on her front doorbell, the driver called his dispatcher, who called the *Good Morning, New York* talent department, which had booked the limousine. The talent department called the show's producer, who, when he had scraped up a substitute guest—a junior high school gym teacher who had recently had a sex change operation and was suing the Board of Education to retain her job—called the publicity department at Willow Press, Susannah Keyes's publisher. The publicity department called Susannah's editor, who called Susannah's agent, who, suspecting cold feet rather than foul play, called Susannah's apartment and, getting the answering machine, left a stern message saying that having written a controversial book Susannah had to be prepared to cope with the controversy. It wasn't until the agent returned from lunch, found that Susannah had not returned her call, made another call, and got the answering machine that she decided the matter required something other than telephonic handling. She took a cab downtown, rang Susannah's doorbell fruitlessly, cajoled a neighbor into letting her into the building, rang and knocked at Susannah's apartment door, and then, disturbed at the unpleasant stench coming from the apartment, called the police.

Meanwhile, in their afternoon mail deliveries, every newspaper in town got a typewritten letter, postmarked Monday morning at a post office near Susannah's apartment, announcing her death and stating that it was the second in the series that had begun with Chris Kaiser's. The letter recapitulated the sentiments expressed in the letter delivered to but not published by the *Express*, urged the newspapers' editors to ignore the police's effort to suppress these communications, and ended by saying there would be still more deaths—"until the cunt-bitches are wiped out."

The afternoon papers kept the presses running to get extra editions onto the street in time for the evening rush hour. The morning papers planned extended press runs. Television crews, rankled by not having received copies of the letter—which looked to have been typed individually, rather than photocopied—and barred from the block Susannah Keyes had lived on, settled for filming the newsrooms and

106

pressrooms of the newspapers, focusing on reporters brandishing an edition of one paper or another fresh from the presses.

The *Express* had something no one else had—a mention of the fact that in the wastebasket by the mailboxes in Susannah Keyes's apartment house—the basket was emptied once a week, on Fridays—the police found a letter addressed to Susannah and containing a piece of paper bearing the words "Your next." The source was Jake Neuman, who with that trifle repaid the *Express* for not having printed the text of the original letter.

"I could kick myself around the fucking block," Neuman said. "If I'd let them print the letter, and if she'd read it, she might've put it together—understood that this was a warning."

"There was no way you could've known, Jake," McIver said. "Besides, it looks like a hoax, don't you think? The grammar, I mean. The guy who wrote the letters isn't an illiterate."

"Maybe he wants us to think he is," Redfield said. "But that doesn't make sense, does it, since, as Tim says, the letters don't have any grammatical mistakes."

"A department shrink's looking at the letters now," Neuman said, "trying to put together a profile of the guy. I could save him the trouble—the guy's a wacko."

"He must've known these broads, don't you think, Jake?" McIver said. "I mean, how else do you account for the clean entries and exits? They must've let him in—or he had keys—and he locked the doors when he left—with the keys he had or keys he took. Bloomfield's talking to what's-her-name, Keyes's agent, putting together a list of male friends, associates, whatever—something to match with the list of Kaiser's friends."

Neuman nodded, but he didn't see the point. "You think we're looking for a woman here? What's-her-name—the agent—tells me Kaiser's book is about, you know, being a lesbian. Maybe it's female friends, associates, whatever, we should be looking for."

"The only thing, Jake," Redfield said, "is there's nothing in the book that would make a woman angry enough to kill her. It's men it comes down hard on."

"You've read it, have you?" Neuman said.

107

Redfield shook his head. "Read about it. There was a long piece in the Sunday *Times*. It's pretty strong stuff. She was calling for a kind of Amazon society: women living together, raising children bred by artificial insemination, doing without male relationships of any kind. On that list of male friends, associates, whatever, there might be a guy maybe once had something a little different in mind when it came to having a relationship with her, with Susannah Keyes."

"Yeah, well," Neuman said, "in that case, Tim, why don't you go over and help Bloomfield with that list. Not that I don't trust him, but he doesn't always ask the next question after the question he just asked. Lean on what's-her-name—the agent—make sure she tells you every name she can think of even if she doesn't think she can think of it right off. . . ."

"Which reminds me, Bobby," Neuman said when McIver had climbed the steps to Susannah Keyes's building, in whose superintendent's apartment they had set up a primitive command post, "you forgot to tell me that you didn't just meet Chris Kaiser, that you knew her."

Redfield picked a leaf from the privet hedge alongside the sidewalk in front of the building, where they had come to get some air. "Giles?"

"What difference does it make? What difference does it make if a little bird told me? You're the one who's supposed to tell me things like that."

Redfield folded the leaf in half between his fingers, then in quarters. "It was six months ago, Jake. I met her on that show, like I told you. She looked right through me, like I told you, so I was as surprised as anybody when she called me up about a week later, asking me to have a drink. We went to a bar near where she worked, had a couple of drinks—she had to work that night, so she had Perrier—and talked mostly about the weather—and about how it would be impossible for us to have a relationship, what with her hours and mine."

"Is that what people talk about these days?" Neuman said. "Sounds kind of pessimistic."

"I think it was her way of leading me on without having to come across," Redfield said. "I've known a lot of women like her: career women. They tell you how interesting you are, how attractive, how surprisingly sensitive you are given that you're a cop—cops're supposed to be tough as nails—then they tell you what long hours they work, how they haven't had a vacation in years, how much responsibility they have. It's like they're flirting with you with one hand and drawing the line with the other."

"Flirting with *you*, you mean," Neuman said. "So you never saw her again?"

Redfield shook his head. "Only on the tube."

"How'd she get your number?" Neuman said. "You said she called you, and you're not listed."

Redfield cocked his head. "What is this, Jake? You trying to punch holes in my story? I'm leveling with you, for Christ's sake."

"Didn't say you weren't. I just like to know things like that."

Redfield shrugged. "I never asked her. I assumed she got it from the producer who put together the panel show. His name was Bryan or O'Brien or something like that. He had my home number."

"And after the drink did you take her home or what? Don't look at me like that. I'm not trying to punch holes in anything; you're my partner, for Christ's sake, not a suspect. I'm just wondering, since you might've been to her place, if you saw anything, saw anyone, noticed anything that might be of interest to us."

"I already told you, Jake—she had to work that night."

"So you did, Bob. So you did. . . . Okay, well, that's enough chitchat. Let's go upstairs and see what kind of list of friends, associates, whatever, what's-her-name—the agent—'s come up with."

The agent—her name was Zoe Zell—came up with two hundred names over that day and the next and kept calling to add more. Seventy-five of them, then eighty, then eighty-five, were also on the list of friends, associates, whatever, of Chris Kaiser.

Fifty of them lived outside New York. Eight were out of town on business or pleasure when Chris Kaiser was killed, six (four of the eight plus two others) when Susannah Keyes was. Of the twenty-five who were therefore in town when both murders were committed, thirteen had witnesses who could account for their whereabouts at the times of both murders, four had alibis that disqualified them as Chris Kaiser's killer, three as Susannah Keyes's. Of the five remaining friends, associates, whatever, of the two women, one was a seventy-five-year-old woman who had been crippled by polio since childhood, one was the rector of St. Bartholomew's Church, one was blind.

That left Zoe Zell herself, who had not only been Susannah Keyes's agent but had known Chris Kaiser, as she put it, "casually—which was about the only way anybody got to know her," and Thomas Minchenberg, who had not only been, as president of Channel 3, Chris Kaiser's boss, but had known Susannah Keyes, as he put it, "more intimately than I ought to have, since I was still married at the time—and she hadn't yet decided that men were anathema."

Neither Zoe Zell nor Thomas Minchenberg had witnesses who could corroborate their contentions that they were asleep and watching television, respectively, when Chris Kaiser was killed; that they were both asleep, alone, when Susannah Keyes was. Minchenberg did remember that he had been watching *To Have and Have Not* on Channel 9 and that he had been quietly glad when the projector broke down about one forty-five in the morning. A call to Channel 9 confirmed the breakdown, although the log showed that it came at one twenty-eight.

Neither Zoe Zell nor Thomas Minchenberg had a license for a .38-caliber Smith & Wesson semiautomatic equipped with a silencer, which, Forensics had determined, was the gun used to kill both Chris Kaiser and Susannah Keyes.

Neither Zoe Zell nor Thomas Minchenberg owned Olivetti portable manual typewriters—especially with worn-out lower-case *e*'s and *r*'s—which, Forensics had determined, was the machine used to write the letters and the note to Susannah Keyes.

More importantly, neither had a motive to kill his or her bread and butter.

When Neuman reminded Zoe Zell of that—they were sitting in her office on Friday afternoon, looking out over most of the world east of Third Avenue—she said, "Especially since it looks like I'm out one novel."

"Novel?" Neuman said.

"Suze's novel," Zoe Zell said. She picked up a copy of the inventory list the police had made at Susannah Keyes's apartment and flicked a fingernail at it. "It's *not* on here. It's not *on* here."

"This is a novel she was writing?" Neuman said.

110

"She was nearly finished. She may have been entirely finished. It was going to be the most important book in a long time. It was going to knock the New York literary world on its collective ear."

"How so?" Neuman said.

Zoe Zell slumped a little. "I haven't read it—not a word of it. That's the way Suze was. Other writers show me their work chapter by chapter. They want me to sell it based on a few chapters and an outline. They want input—from me, from an editor. Not Suze. She didn't want any input until a book was finished, and then she'd listen to only absolutely the strongest, most reasoned arguments as to why she should take something out or put something in or do something differently. Her feeling was that it was *her* book—not mine, not her editor's, not her publisher's—and that if I was going to represent it, her editor was going to edit it, her publisher was going to publish it, it had to be on *her* terms."

"Makes sense," Neuman said. "I guess. I mean, doesn't it?"

"Things get lost, lieutenant," Zoe Zell said. "The annals of literature are full of stories of writers whose work has been lost, strayed, or stolen. Fires. Whole opuses have been destroyed in fires. Well-meaning cleaning women have thrown away chapters. Single pages. Why, there's a famous case of a novelist whose infant son destroyed the last page of a novel his father was working on. He knew how the book ended, of course, but he couldn't exactly recall the words he used. The second effort, he felt, fell short both in its poetry and its philosophy. Ideas are flimsy things, lieutenant. Why, Suze herself once told me she had an idea for a novel while she was in the shower. By the time she got out and dried herself off enough to go to her desk and get a pad and pencil, she'd forgotten it and never remembered it."

Neuman thought a long time about what his next question should be. All he could think to say was, "So?"

"The novel's *gone*, lieutenant," Zoe Zell said.

"And you think the killer took it?"

"*I* certainly didn't. *You* certainly didn't. None of your *men* took it. . . . Did they?"

Neuman shook his head. "And what you're saying is there's no copy?"

"*None* . . . unless. . ."

"Yeah?"

"Well," Zoe Zell said, "Suze mentioned to me once, a couple of months ago, that a friend of hers, a woman named Martha Wine, was upset about the direction the novel was taking. Martha . . . well, Martha was Suze's guru, in effect. Martha inspired Suze to write *Womanlove* and also encouraged Suze to give up the men in her own life. They were lovers, lieutenant, to answer the question in your eyes. Then, after the manuscript had been sold, Martha up and left Suze and moved to California—Sausalito, near San Francisco. She told Suze that since she was about to become a sort of guru herself—for other women who read the book when it was published, that is—she no longer needed Martha; she needed to develop her philosophy and her life-style on her own. Suze was shattered and, predictably or not, started taking up with men again. A lot of this—I know this from what Suze told me—was in the novel. I gathered, when Suze told me Martha was upset about the novel's direction, that maybe Suze was wavering in her feeling that women could do entirely without men. I don't know; as I said, I haven't read a word of the book, and I don't know that Martha had either. She may have just responded to what Suze told her."

Neuman thought for a long time again. "Let me get this straight. Do you think this Martha Wine—she was on your list, as I recall, of out-of-town friends—do you think she took the novel?"

Zoe Zell shook her head. "Suze may have sent her a copy of the novel—the whole thing or a few chapters."

Neuman thought for a still longer time, during which he began to feel excited for the first time since these investigations had begun. "This is an autobiographical novel, right? It's about Susannah Keyes and people she knew. Since there's a good chance she knew her killer, there's a chance—maybe not a good one, but a chance—that he's in the book. Not in so many words, I mean, but in a way that if we put our minds to it we could recognize him. Yes?"

Zoe Zell nodded.

Neuman stood up. "Well, thanks for your time, Miss Zell. You sure have an impressive memory. All those names just off the cuff, and Sergeant Redfield told me before I came over that you called him with still a couple more. He's checking right now on their alibis. Be sure to keep calling, and we'll call you if there's anything we need to know."

"Does that mean I'm no longer a suspect?" Zoe Zell said.

Neuman smiled. "Well, I don't know that you were ever exactly a suspect in the strictest sense of the word. We would've liked it a lot better if you could've accounted for your whereabouts when the murders were committed, but, well, if you were in bed you were in bed."

Zoe Zell smiled. "It's the fact that I was alone that bothers you, isn't it, lieutenant?"

Neuman shuffled. "Well . . ."

"You're wondering why, since I was Suze's friend and agent, and since I obviously agree with the *con*cept if not the letter of Suze's work, why I wasn't in bed with a woman, aren't you?"

"Well, I—you know . . ."

"Suffice it to say, lieutenant, that I'm considerably farther down the road of misandry—that's abhorrence of men; males—than Suze was, than even Martha is. I'm fed up with women, too. I spend my time alone; I sustain myself and I please myself."

"Yeah, well, if it works, if it gets you through the night."

Zoe Zell laughed. "But what I really wanted to ask you, since it seems I *am* no longer a suspect, is if you have any interest in writing a book."

"A book?"

"A book about your career in general and about these two murders—and more if the killer keeps his promise—in particular. Do you think there'll be more murders?"

"Not if I can help it."

She smiled. "And of course you can't—not really, not unless you get a lot luckier than you've been so far. Isn't that right?"

"Maybe. Maybe not."

"That's good, though," Zoe Zell said, "because three murders would make a better book than two. Don't look so shocked, lieutenant. I'm a businesswoman. I know what's commercial. And I know that publishers're going to be a lot more interested in a memoir by a homicide detective who tracked down the killer of three women than in one by one who tracked down the killer of two."

"I work with a partner," Neuman said.

"Oh, I know. Redford and Newman. I think it's wonderful."

"And with dozens—hundreds—of other people who never get the credit they should for cracking a case, but who it couldn't've been cracked without them. When this case is cracked—and it will be, because guys like this, guys who write letters to newspapers, notes to their next victims, want to get caught—"

"This is wonderful, lieutenant. I hope this would all be in the book."

"—when this case is cracked, it'll be one of those hundreds of people who's responsible for cracking it. I'll make the arrest, most likely, along with Sergeant Redfield, and we'll get the glory, but it won't be us who should write a book about it; it should be some cop on the beat who notices somebody hanging around night after night at a place no one ever hung out before, some clerk in—"

"I get your point," Zoe Zell said. "But I do wish you'd think it over. We're not talking peanuts here; we're talking six figures."

"Six figures? You mean like one hundred thousand dollars?"

"One hundred Gs, lieutenant. Isn't that what you call them? Possibly two hundred Gs—depending on whether a paperback deal could be made in advance."

"And you get—what?—ten percent?" Neuman said.

"Fifteen. But then, I don't charge my clients for long-distance phone calls, for postage—"

"So if this novel doesn't turn up," Neuman said, "you stand to be out—what?—fifteen thousand minimum, since from what I understand, Susannah Keyes writes books that're—what did you call it?—commercial, and publishers'll probably be a lot more interested in a novel by a woman who was murdered by a psycho than in one who was just, you know, alive and kicking. And what you're really worried about is that if the novel does turn up—if this Martha Wine did get sent a copy, or if Susannah Keyes hid it where we didn't find it or put it in a safe deposit box for safekeeping—that it's not really yours to make a percentage off, since your contract with your client probably isn't a multi-book package but for one book at a time, with either of you having the right to nix the business arrangement on the next book.

"Don't look so surprised, Miss Zell, I had occasion to learn a little about the book business a couple of years ago when I handled a case of a murdered author. Murdered by his agent, as it turned out—you must remember the case—'cause he was having a thing on the side with the agent's wife—the author, that is. The other thing I learned about the book business is that the author, even though he was dead, had his ante upped—as a result of being dead, that is. He was more fortunate than Susannah Keyes; he had *two* books ready to be published. Fortunate's the wrong word: the agent hadn't been able to sell them, which was why there were two of them. Soon as the guy was dead, bingo, the agent sold them—not for six figures but for a lot more than the guy was getting when he was alive, and a lot more than the agent was getting, although he only charged ten percent, 'cause I guess he charged his clients for long-distance calls, postage, whatnot"—*talk, talk, talk*—"but then you know all this, Miss Zell. You're in the same racket. You must've read all about it in *Publishers Weekly*.

"Well, I'll be going now, and no thanks, I don't think I'm interested in writing a book, and maybe you're not a suspect anymore and maybe you are, so don't go taking any trips without telling me or Sergeant Redfield where you're going. So long."

Descending in the elevator, Neuman thought, *Six figures? Maybe I should write a book. But who would read it? It'd just be full of talk. Talk, talk, talk.*

TWENTY

"You busy, lieutenant?" Steve Federici said.

Neuman looked at his feet, which were up on his desk. "I guess not, Steve. I mean, when I'm busy I tend to be standing up, running around, or at least sitting so I could write something down if somebody told me something important, or could reach the phone if it rang. Don't I? I don't know. What's up?"

Federici pulled a chair over to Neuman's desk, put one foot on it, and rested his elbow on his thigh. "Is the sarge around?"

Neuman looked around the squad room. "Don't see him, Steve. So I guess he's not around. Doesn't surprise me, really. I got him doing shitwork. Checking alibis of some people who might've killed Chris Kaiser or Susannah Keyes. Or then again, they might not've. I don't know."

Federici frowned. "You okay, lieutenant?"

Neuman felt his throat, his chin, his cheeks. He looked at the backs of his hands, the palms. "I guess I'm okay. I thought before I might be getting a cold, but I don't think I am. Or maybe I am, and I just don't know it yet. I don't know. How're things with you?"

Federici took his foot down from the chair and looked around the squad room, as if for help.

Neuman laughed. "Okay, Steve. I'll level with you. I didn't level with you, but now I'll level with you. The fact is, I'm fed up. I'm fed up with people killing people and then running away and hiding so we can't find them. I'm fed up with looking for people who've killed people and then run off and hid so we can't find them. I'm fed up with asking people who knew the people who were killed who might've killed them. I'm fed up with asking the people the people who knew the people who were killed said might've killed them if they killed them. I'm fed up with the people who might've killed them saying they couldn't've killed them because they were playing poker or at a party or at a ball game or home with their family when the people who were killed were killed. How come I'm not playing poker, or at a party, or a ball game? I can't remember the last time I went to a ball game.

"No, I can remember. It was when the Mets won the series. Nineteen sixty-fucking-nine. I was TPF then. We were called in for crowd control. *Crowd* control. You couldn't've controlled that crowd with submachine guns—with *tanks*. They tore up the whole fucking infield. They stole home plate and the pitcher's rubber. The bases. I got to confess something; I took a little bit of infield grass myself. I didn't tear it up or anything; somebody else did, then dropped it. I took it

116

home and put it in the den for a while. I don't know why. I don't even like the Mets. The Giants; I was always a Giant fan, even when they moved to San Fran. Which reminds me, I'm expecting a call from San Fran. If I go out to the head and you hear the phone ringing and it's from San Fran, don't take a message or anything, just come and get me, okay? I've been trying for three hours to get through and the line was busy—busy, busy, busy. I finally got through a few minutes ago and all I got was an answering machine. I left a message and . . . Aw, what the fuck do you care, Steve? What were we talking about? The Mets. I don't even like the Mets. You like the Mets, Steve?"

"The Yankees."

"The Yankees. I might've known. They always got all those Italians—DiMaggio, Rizzuto, Berra . . . You know what I'm most fed up with, Steve? Talking. I'm tired of talking. I'm thinking of checking into a monastery somewhere when this case is wrapped up, sometime around the year two thousand, and taking a vow of silence. Not for too long—just a couple of years. Five years, maybe. How you doing? You got any leads on what's-his-name—the Samaritan Killer? How you getting along with McGovern, the lazy fuck?"

Federici put his foot back up on the chair. "That's what I wanted to talk to you about. McGovern—a lot of the guys, but McGovern especially—McGovern thinks this guy did the right thing: popping the punk, I mean. He's just letting the case slide, going through the motions. Like the Nassau County thing. He didn't even want to go out there. He as much as told me *not* to go out there—that it was a waste of time. I went on my own, lieutenant, and it wasn't a waste of time. It's connected. This guy's on a roll."

"You're getting a little ahead of me, Steve," Neuman said. "I've been so tied up I haven't read the papers, haven't heard much about what's going on around the house. What Nassau County thing?"

"A guy named Joe Smith got popped in Mineola late Sunday night, early Monday morning," Federici said. "A twenty-two-caliber pistol, in the chest. It was the same gun—and get this: Smith was in the same outfit as Stearns. Oh, right; you don't know about that. Okay, let me tell you. The Detroit cops I-D'd Cariello's drug dealer. Detroit, Cariello called him, but his name was Clarence Stearns. Remember Cariello told us he had a tattoo—a dragon on his shoulder and down

117

his back? One of Cariello's men, Pursinger—they call him Pursesnatcher—was in 'Nam and said it looked like a tattoo that might've been done in 'Nam. Well, it was done in 'Nam. Or at least he was *in* 'Nam—Stearns, I mean. Cariello'd sent his prints to the Pentagon, and sure enough he turned up in their files. Enlisted in February 'sixty-eight, trained at Fort Leonard Wood, went to 'Nam in June 'sixty-eight, re-upped in May 'sixty-nine, served another six months in 'Nam, then got stateside duty at Fort Meade, honorable discharge December 'sixty-nine. Went in a private, came out a private, a couple of marksmanship medals but nothing important. No bad marks, either; he was just a soldier. His first arrest was in November 'seventy-one, selling weapons to some black militants in Detroit. Army ordnance. Stolen. The Detroit cops think it came by way of 'Nam; they think Stearns was connected with the black market when he was over there, stayed connected when he got out. They think that was his source of drugs, too. He beat the weapons rap on a technicality—a Miranda thing—but he was nailed again three months later, on narcotics charges this time, and did two years in a federal pen in Michigan. His next arrest—

"Shit, you don't need to know all this. All you need to know is that Clarence Stearns was popped with a twenty-two-caliber pistol on Friday night, and on Sunday night or Monday morning, Joe Smith, who was in the same outfit as Stearns, was popped with the same gun, which was also the gun that killed Carlos Pabon, who sure as shit picked the wrong guy to fuck with."

Federici changed the foot he had up on the chair. "Reason I know about Smith at all—he ran an auto body shop, stripped hot cars on the side, was popped in his office, it looked like robbery, didn't rate a line in the New York papers—reason I know about him at all is a Nassau homicide dick—Graves is his name; good name, hunh, for a homicide dick?—Graves read in the paper about the connection between Stearns's killing and the thing on the subway and about Stearns's tattoo. Smith had the same tattoo. Graves called us—good thing McGovern was out to lunch; I got the call—told me about the tattoo. As soon as I got off with him I called the Pentagon, and they ran Joe Smith through the computer and came up with about three hundred Joe Smiths, but only one who answered the description of the DOA in Mineola, and he was in the same outfit as Stearns. I got a car and went looking for McGovern—he's a hard guy to find when he wants to be, which is most of the time—and told him what I'd found out, and he said, So? And I said, So let's take a ride out to Mineola. He said, What for? I said, 'Cause the guy's on a roll is why. He said, Roll? You call popping a punk, a pusher, and a hot-car stripper a roll? I call it a public service. I said— Well, never mind what I said. What I did was I went out to Mineola on my own time, like I told you, and looked things over and saw the ME's photographs of Smith's body, and it was the same tattoo, all right."

Federici changed feet again. "Turns out Graves knew Smith when they were kids. They grew up together. Smith was in trouble a lot and joined the Army at the suggestion of a judge out there that maybe it was a way to stay out of it. Graves lost touch with him after that, but he heard about him from time to time, heard that he came back from 'Nam with a lot of cash in his pocket, that he was hooked up with some local undesirables, that before he got into stripping hot cars he was into small-time narcotics pushing, loan sharking, pimping for some semi-high-class call girls, like that."

Federici stood with both feet on the floor, gripping the back of the chair in both hands. "I told McGovern all this. He said, See? I said, The thing of it is, the way he's going, the guy's going to kill someone else. He said, He keeps up the way he's been going, we should give him a medal. I said, What do you want to do next? He said, Wait. I don't know, lieutenant. I mean, he outranks me; I've got to do what he says even if I think he's wrong. But I can't do nothing, even if that's what he says to do. It doesn't feel right. You got any ideas? Reason I wanted to talk to the sarge was, he was in 'Nam, maybe he heard of Stearns or Smith or both. Maybe he has an idea why someone would want to kill them, and who. I know there were thousands of guys in 'Nam, I know it's a long shot, but I got to try something. I can't just wait."

Federici, Neuman thought, would go far in this business. He'd been on the force only six years, had his gold shield for only two, and he could already talk, talk, talk with the best of them. "You must have a contact in the Pentagon by now—right?—what with calling down there so much," Neuman said.

Federici looked down at the floor and mumbled something.

"Hey, look, I'm not asking you to tell me the guy's name," Neuman said. "A source is a source. I just had an idea of a favor you could ask him."

Federici spoke more clearly but didn't look up. "It's not a guy, it's a girl, and McGovern's been giving me a hard time 'cause I spent about an hour with her on the phone the other day, but it turns out she's from Bay Ridge too, and we know some of the same people, and, well . . ."

Neuman smiled. "So ask—what did you say her name was?"

"Toni," Federici said. "Antoinette. Major Antoinette da Silva, Public Information."

"A major, yet," Neuman said. "Well, well. So ask the major if she can put together a list of everybody who was in the same outfit as Stearns and Smith, with addresses as up to date as they've got, which'll probably be their addresses when they were discharged, which'll probably be their parents' addresses, most likely, which won't do you a hell of a lot of good. But start calling anyway. Maybe you'll get lucky, you'll find a guy who's still living at home, or in the same town anyway, the parents'll give you his number, you'll find somebody who knew Stearns and Smith or both of them, knows if there's anyone from those days with a reason to kill them, and to kill anybody else he might know of. You might ask, too, if he knows of anybody else who's been killed with a twenty-two-caliber bullet lately—anybody from that outfit, I mean, 'cause for all we know Stearns and Smith were not the first ones on this guy's list. It's shitwork, I know, but it's got to be done, and I don't see any other way to do it, 'cause McGovern's right, in one sense; there's not much you can do but wait—wait till the guy screws up, which is sometimes the only thing you can hope for, although this guy doesn't strike me as the screw-up type—but that doesn't mean you have to sit on your ass while you're waiting; you can stir things up, ask questions, and maybe something'll turn up that's just what you want to know. Which reminds me: did Carlos's pals ever turn up?"

"Zilch, lieutenant," Federici said. "I figure they're holed up, maybe even skipped town, until this thing cools off, maybe longer. One way or another, they show up, someone's going to come looking for them, either us or the Samaritan Killer."

"Yeah, well," Neuman said, "the reason I ask is if they do show up and the killer has any reason to think they can I-D him, like you say, he's going to be looking for them, so maybe the thing to do is put out the word that they're back—it doesn't matter if they aren't—put out the word in the papers, I don't remember that we ever I-D'd them to the press, then put a man on their apartments—that's right, we've got men on them anyway, don't we, in case they show—so tell the men on their apartments to keep an eye open for somebody who looks like the killer and starts hanging around the neighborhood. Which also reminds me, we never told the press about the book the guy was reading, did we? What's-its-name, Pilgrimage to Something Creek?"

"Pilgrim at Tinker Creek."

"Yeah, well. That's the kind of thing, somebody reads it, it might ring a bell. Who knows, maybe somebody saw his next-door neighbor reading it on the elevator—or carrying it in his pocket, anyway, 'cause people don't generally read in elevators, they just look at the numbers over the door, or maybe you call that reading—his next-door neighbor who's been coming home late a lot lately, or early, depending on how you look at it, acting funny, keeping to himself."

Federici's face beamed, then quickly clouded over. "McGovern'll say it's a waste of time. I'd have to clear it with him first."

Neuman waved a dismissive hand. "I'm not talking about doing something formal, calling a news conference or whatever. Just call up a few reporters—guys you owe a favor, guys you'd like to have owe you one. Don't let them use your name. Just tell them you're a source close to the investigation or some such. McGovern's so dumb he won't think it's you, he'll think it's somebody downtown, somebody in McGillion's office."

The cloud passed. "Thanks, lieutenant. Thanks for listening."

"Anytime, Steve." *You're a hell of a talker.*

Federici turned away, then about-faced and gripped the chair again. "There's one other thing, lieutenant."

"Yeah?"

"Well, I don't know how to ask this, exactly. . . ."

"Do I think a major would date a detective two?" Neuman said.

Federici blushed. "It turns out Toni's coming up to see her folks next month, and, well . . . she's got this terrific voice. I mean, I don't know what she looks like, of course, but she *sounds* great."

Neuman looked at the ceiling. "Seems to me if you were a—you know, a civilian, she wouldn't think twice about dating you. I mean, she wouldn't think any more about it than she would think about it in the first place. Now, the Department is a sort of paramilitary organization, although I don't know if anybody ever actually comes out and says that. But we've got ranks—no majors, but we've got ranks, although a major is the equivalent of, I guess, a DCI, so we sort of have majors, except we don't call them that. But we've got ranks.

"Now, a detective two is somewhere in between. You outrank a uniformed patrolman, a uniformed sergeant, but not a uniformed lieutenant, a captain, and so on. And you don't outrank a detective sergeant, like our own Bobby Redfield, who got his picture in the paper the other day and what did I get, my back to the camera. And you certainly don't outrank a DCI, which would be the equivalent, like I said, of a major, and I don't think a DCI would date a detective two, if it was possible, if you know what I mean. But the Department's only a *para*military force, which means that it's not really a military force at all, just sort of. So it has nothing to do with the Army or the Air Force or the Marines or the Navy. I mean, we don't have to salute them, and they don't have to salute us. So what it comes down to, I'd say, is that her being a major and your being a detective two has nothing to do with anything."

Neuman stopped abruptly, although he could have gone on for quite a while longer, because his phone started ringing. "So, *mazel tov*, Steve, as they say in France."

"Thanks, lieutenant," Federici said. "Thanks a lot."

"Miss Wine, thank you for calling back. My name is Neuman, Jacob Neuman, lieutenant, New York City Police Department, Homicide Division. I'm investigating the murder of Susannah Keyes, who I understand was a friend of yours. I want to express my condolences at the death of your friend and assure you we're doing everything we can to bring the perpetrator to justice.

122

"The reason I'm calling is Miss Keyes's literary agent, Zoe Zell, mentioned that Miss Keyes had discussed with you a novel she was working on at the time of her death. The novel seems to be missing from her apartment. We don't know if the killer took it or if it's just lost or misplaced. Miss Zell wondered, since you'd discussed the novel with Miss Keyes, if you'd happened to read it, either the original or a copy. The reason we're interested is, since Miss Zell said the novel was an autobiographical novel, we hoped there might be some clue in it as to the identity of Miss Keyes's killer, since we have reason to believe that she was killed by someone she knew. I don't propose to go into why we think that, but our reasons are good ones, I can assure you.

"So I'm calling, Miss Wine, to ask if you, in fact, have read Miss Keyes's novel, either the original or a copy."

"Yes."

"I see. And, uh, was it the original or a copy?"

"A copy. An unproofread carbon copy."

"I see. Unproofread. Meaning, if she made a mistake on the original, she didn't correct it on the copy, even though she corrected it on the original, presumably."

"Yes."

"I see. And, uh, do you still have the copy?"

"Yes."

"I see. And, uh, am I right in thinking it's a copy of the entire novel?"

"Yes. Susannah sent me a chapter at a time. The last chapter arrived in the mail the day I learned about her murder."

"Terrible. I mean, it must've been a terrible shock."

"Yes."

"Yes, well . . . can you send me the copy, Miss Wine? As I said, we're hoping that there might be some clue in it as to the identity of Miss Keyes's killer—"

"There is."

"There is?"

"Yes. Beau killed her."

"Bo? B-o or B-e-a-u?"

"The latter."

"The latter. Right. And, uh, do you know who Beau is, Miss Wine? I mean, I assume that's the name of a character in the book and not somebody's real-life name."

"Yes."

"And do you know what Beau's real-life name is?"

"No."

"I see. Well, I surely would like to read that book, Miss Wine. Is there—?"

"I'm flying to New York tonight, lieutenant. I couldn't bring myself to attend Susannah's funeral, but I want very much to visit her grave. I'll bring the copy of the manuscript with me. I'll be staying at the Shoreham, on Fifty-fifth Street. Why don't you come by tomorrow about eleven, say?"

"The Shoreham? Eleven? Sure."

"Goodbye, lieutenant."

"Uh, right—goodbye."

Neuman hung up and shut his eyes to keep his head from spinning. Now there was a woman after his own heart. No gab, no chatter, no reminiscence, no divergence, no digression, no tangents. Just plain, simple yeses and nos, just plain simple facts. Not talk, talk, talk. Just talk, period.

TWENTY - ONE

"Where're you going?" Linda said.

"Out."

"What're you going to do? 'Nothing,'" she sing-songed.

He stopped with his hand on the doorknob. "How about a movie later? You're off tonight, right?"

Linda punched the arm of the couch. "I *told* you. I have to work. Lou's mother died. You weren't even listening to me, were you? You never listen to anything I say. What were you thinking about? Or who? Were you thinking about Leila?"

His eyes narrowed and he came away from the door.

"I looked in your wallet while you were sleeping this morning," Linda said. "I found her picture. 'To André, with all my love, Leila.' Who's Leila? Who's André? And who's Paul Howell—Paul Howell who has an ID card saying he works for the International Red Cross, but whose picture on the card is a picture of you? And who're you? Are you André? Are you Paul Howell? Are you Ray Howell? Who the fuck are you?"

He went into the bedroom and came out in a moment carrying his duffel bag and his copy of *Pilgrim at Tinker Creek*.

"That's right," Linda said. "Run for it."

He stopped in front of her. "I'm sorry."

"Sure."

"Goodbye."

She wanted to embrace him, to pull him down onto the couch, to undress him, to feel him inside her. She sat on her hands.

"And who's Redfield? And Stearns? And—who was the other one—Smith?"

He dropped his bag and gripped her shoulders. "Forget those names. Forget me. Forget everything."

Linda looked into his eyes and said evenly, "Let . . . me . . . go."

He released her, picked up his bag, and headed for the door.

She laughed. "Aren't you going to kill me too? The way you killed Chris Kaiser and the other one, the writer? Or aren't I glamorous enough? I could get some new clothes, do my hair differently. I could look real good if I put my mind to it. I'd do it for you. Even if you'd kill me. Please don't go."

But he was gone, and for a moment it was as though he'd never been. Then the pain welled up and filled every inch of her.

Should he take Redfield now? He didn't want to. He wanted to wait. He was enjoying making Redfield sweat. And he knew he was sweating. He was so careful, always checking his back, varying what Ré had come to know were his regular routes. But not so careful that he ever picked Ré out of a crowd. He expected a disguise, expected him to move furtively. He never expected Ré to stride right past him, as he had done several times in recent days. To be open, uncamouflaged, unguarded, Ré knew, is often the best disguise. He had learned that in the jungle.

*   *   *

The Americans were gone. It was an Asian war now, as it always ought to have been. And, as would have happened much sooner had it been, the North seized the advantage.

All around them the land emptied of people. Whole villages were abandoned in a trice. Tilled fields were left unplanted, tools lay where they had been dropped, animals that could not be carried were left to starve.

Rumor had it that the northern soldiers were murdering men, enslaving women, eating children. The truth was that they simply marched southward, toward Saigon, unopposed by the South Vietnamese army, which for all practical purposes had ceased to exist.

Some of the band wanted to join the river of refugees flowing toward the sea. Others wanted to go by way of Cambodia, which had already fallen to the Khmer Rouge. Still others wanted to stay where they were. They had lived like savages, but not savagely, for five years; they had forgotten civilization, as it had forgotten them; this was the only life they knew.

Huck was among the last group. "There's nothing for me back in the States. I was already an outcast when I left. Why should I expect things to be different for me now? Besides, even if you got on one of those boats, even if you made it to the carriers that're supposed to be picking people up, what makes you think they'd just take you on board, no questions asked? They'd throw you in the brig, man, which was the place you ran away from in the first place."

"I was framed," Ré said. "Maybe by now the truth's been told."

Huck shook his head. "I love you, Tom, but sometimes you're about as dumb as they come. A lot bigger lies than the lie that was told about you—whatever that lie was, and I don't want to know what it was—a lot bigger lies than that lie are written down in the history books. A lot more important people than you have been framed and'll never be unframed. It's the way of the world, man: one man lies and another swears to it and another tells another and another writes it down in a book. One of the reasons this bunch has stayed together as long as it has, with as few problems as it's had, is that we never tried to convince each other that what we said about ourselves was the truth, that what everyone else said was a lie. I mean, for all I know, you fragged a colonel, raped a nun, lined up a bunch of women and children and emptied a clip at them. It doesn't matter. I only know you to be who you've been since you walked in here—or were carried, actually. And I know you to be honest, hard-working, loyal, with a lot of common sense and a pretty good sense of humor. What more could I ask? Whatever you did in the past hasn't made you a fuck-up, a liar, a cheat. But nobody back home's going to feel that way. To them, what you did—what somebody else said you did—is what you are. There's no way you can ever be anything else to them. No way."

"I have to go back," Ré said. "There's a girl—she's a woman now. I can't have her believing a lie. I have to tell her the truth."

Huck swelled up to protest but checked himself. He put a hand on Ré's shoulder. "Then go now, Tom—today. It's best."

Ré hugged Huck and they held each other wordlessly for a long time. Then Ré gathered up his things and with only a wave to the others—they answered his wave with waves of their own, with V signs, with clenched fists—he stepped into the jungle and was gone.

He walked for a week, heading west, the way he had set out five years before. He came to a river and swam it. The land was the same, but he felt it was another country. He wished he had a map, to count up the number of countries he had to walk through to get to the country that had been his.

One evening, he smelled cooking, heard babies crying, children shouting, dogs barking—the sounds of peace. He crept close and saw that what accounted for the peace was a high barbed-wire fence. Thousands, maybe tens of thousands, of Asians were jammed inside it. From a flagpole by a gate flew a flag—not of a nation but of those without nations, homes, hope—the flag of the International Red Cross.

A young Caucasian was hunkered down by the gate, his face drawn, his eyes red with sleeplessness, dust covering his hair and bush clothes.

Ré walked up to him and crouched down to look him in the eye. "You're in charge here?"

The man nodded.

"These people running from the Communists?"

The man nodded.

"There's been a lot of killing?"

The man nodded.

"Anything I can do?"

The man smiled. "I'm glad you're volunteering, because I was going to draft you. The first thing you can do is get rid of that rifle. I can't have any guns here. The next thing is, what languages do you speak?"

"Vietnamese, a little Khmer, a little more Montagnard. And Spanish."

The man laughed. "You're the official camp interpreter." He extended his hand. "I'm Paul Howell. I'm a Canadian, in case you're worried I might turn you in."

Ré shook his hand. "I wasn't worried. I'm . . . André Keller. People call me Ré."

Three weeks after Ré arrived at the camp, Paul Howell stepped on a mine and was blown to pieces. He and Ré had been out walking and he was in the middle of a recitation of his life story: born in Toronto of a Presbyterian father and a Jewish mother; educated in public schools; attended McGill University for one year, then decided he was getting an education that was "too Canadian, not worldly enough," and transferred to Columbia University in New York; studied history, played shortstop on the baseball team, drank at the Gold Rail when not in training, sang alto in the glee club, worked part time at the Law School library, dated a few Barnard girls, a few nurses from St. Luke's; decided, when the antiwar movement reached its peak, that the place to be in any controversy was not on either side but in the middle, where the greatest tragedies occurred; joined the Red Cross as an administrative assistant, became a field officer in a remarkably short time, worked in Appalachia, Bangladesh, Lebanon, and, finally, Cambodia. Just before he died, he said that should he die, only his employer would know it; his parents, both only children, had died in an airplane crash, and he was their only child. He had become a wanderer and had few friends, none of them close.

In the days that followed, Ré wondered: Was he offering me an identity, seeing as how he seemed to know, though he never asked, that mine was useless?

There wasn't much time to wonder, for Ré took over the administration of the camp and was busy from before dawn until after midnight, trying to hold things together for these many thousands of people whose worlds had become undone.

He did, in the words of a senior Red Cross official who visited the camp after it had been in existence three months, "a masterful job." He was, in the words of the same official, who paid another visit after three more months, "a magician." He could, the same official said six months later when the camp had been closed, new homelands having been found for all its occupants, "write his own ticket," go anywhere he wanted for the organization.

Ré chose to go to its headquarters in Geneva, for he wanted to be on neutral soil, to prepare for his eventual return to the United States without risking a case of the psychic bends.

TWENTY - TWO

Martha Wine sat very still, as she often did since hearing of Susannah's murder. She was afraid to move too quickly—even as innocuous a gesture as reaching for the teacup on the table beside her easy chair—lest the careful ordering of her emotions that she

129

had accomplished go off balance and her feelings come tumbling down.

She hadn't known she was still in love with Susannah or how much she loved her. She might never have known had Susannah not been killed, for she had been determined never to see her again, to resist Susannah's entreaties that they get together when Susannah came west to promote her book.

But she had to move, for there was a second knock on the door of her hotel room, and if she didn't get up to answer it, who would?

She got up slowly, holding her head just so, and started for the door, then realized that she couldn't answer it as she was dressed, for she wore only panties and the oversized man's work shirt that served as her pajamas. Susannah had loved to see her dressed like that and would peel the panties off and make love to her without removing the shirt. She couldn't entertain a police officer like that. Newman? Was that his name?

But she had nothing else to wear. A careless stewardess had poured red wine onto the lap of the linen pants she wore on the plane, and some serious dry cleaning would be necessary to save them. She had packed only one skirt, putting it in the same shoulder bag in which she carried Susannah's manuscript—Martha Wine hated waiting for luggage and traveled only with what she could carry—and it had gotten hopelessly wrinkled. She had gotten up at eight and called the valet service to have it pressed, but it wasn't picked up until nearly nine thirty and wouldn't be ready until eleven, the hour the police officer was to come and interview her. Or Newcombe?

But it wasn't eleven already, was it? Carefully, she looked down at her left wrist and read the time on her watch: ten twenty. Then it wouldn't be the police officer, would it? Perhaps it was the bellhop with her skirt, prematurely pressed, as Susannah had been prematurely murdered.

But who wasn't—prematurely murdered, that is? One could die prematurely, as well as maturely, and even postmaturely; but one could be murdered only prematurely; murder was never in the cards, never scheduled.

130

Or was it? Didn't some people expect to be murdered? Even *ask* to be murdered? Criminals—mafiosi—it went with their territory. And cops, too; they were targets. She would have to talk about it with the police officer. Newsome?

Whatever his name was, he wouldn't want to talk about that; he'd want to talk about Beau. On the plane, Martha had reread the second half of Susannah's novel, the half in which Beau figured strongly. She was less certain that Beau—or the man on whom Beau was based—was Susannah's murderer and was unable to recapture the feeling that had made her originally certain. Perhaps it was that she had hated Beau so on the first reading, hated any man with whom Susannah could claim to have fallen in love; perhaps it was that, on rereading, she found Beau less credible, less interesting.

Beau was neither short nor tall, neither dark nor fair, neither garrulous nor taciturn. He had no past—or didn't talk of it to Grace, the protagonist—and Grace didn't inquire. She was interested only in the present, and since Beau was present, he was interesting. It was more or less as simple as that. He was a tool, in more ways than one, and Grace was using him to get revenge on Judith—Martha herself—for leaving Grace—and in particular for leaving her without the wherewithal to have another affair with another woman; for Grace's prowess was with men. With women, she could not be a seductress; she could only be seduced.

Another knock.

Move it, Martha. The policeman is here.

I can't. I have to work this out before he gets here.

It's not him. It's someone else. It's too early.

Right.

Martha pulled down the tails of her shirt and held the collar closed about her neck and put her mouth close to the door. "Who is it?"

"Room service," a man said.

Room service? She hadn't ordered room service. Or had she? She had a pot of tea, so she must have. But that had been hours ago, shortly after getting up. "I—"

Of course. The room service bellhop was back to collect the pot and dirty cup and saucer. "Uh, just a minute."

She went to the table and picked up the teapot and the cup and saucer and carried them to the door. She stood for a moment, then took them back to the table. This was room *service*; she didn't have to carry dirty dishes around.

Should she let him see her like this? Why not? She hadn't seen the face of the room-service bellhop when he delivered the tea; she had called through the door to leave the tray on the floor. But he had just been getting on the elevator when she opened the door and she had seen that he was young and tall and powerful. He would enjoy seeing her in her shirt and panties, with her long blond hair in attractive disarray. It would make his day. Perhaps he would make hers. Not now—the policeman was coming—but later, when he got off work. She had no plans; she was only going to see Susannah's grave. The bitch.

Martha Wine smiled at her reflection in the mirror over the dresser. She understood now why she had come to New York—not to mourn over Susannah's grave but to dance on it, to celebrate her—Martha's—ultimate triumph.

Or was it Beau who had triumphed? Martha had had Susannah and left her. Beau had had her and killed her. More dramatic, more pointed—more final. It was like Beau.

In the novel, Beau warned Grace—Susannah—that he could, if he cared to, kill her with his bare hands. "I've been trained to," he says.

"In the Army?" Grace says. "In Vietnam?"

"Whatever," Beau says.

The closest thing in the novel to a revelation about Beau's past. But nothing more said, for Grace wants to know only about his present. Once, when he says, "In my work, you learn to mistrust everyone, because everyone thinks you mistrust them and behaves falsely, covers up," Grace interrupts:

"Don't tell me what you do. I want to know only what you do to me."

Another knock.

"Coming," Martha Wine called, and went to the door—after first unbuttoning another button of her shirt—and unlocked it.

The bullet traveled only a few feet before striking her forehead. Yet

132

such is the miracle of the human brain that in those few milliseconds Martha had time to wonder:

Beau?

TWENTY - THREE

It was funny, Neuman thought, how you could know what someone was talking about even when you didn't know what they were talking about.

Like the day Kennedy was shot. Jack Kennedy. Neuman had had the day off and had gone to Gertz with Maria to do some shopping. Maria had the stamina to shop until they threw her out the door at closing time, but Neuman got weary after an hour, so he had gone to the snack bar in the basement to drink a cup of what they called coffee and read the sports pages of the *News*, which he hadn't read at breakfast, purposely.

Two men—men like himself, working stiffs who now and then had a Friday off and paid for it by going shopping with their wives—were standing in the hall outside the snack bar, drinking coffee from containers and talking.

"I can't believe it," one of them said. He wore a plaid hunting shirt over a gray T-shirt.

"Fuck you mean you can't believe it?" the other one said. He wore a yellow nylon windbreaker and a Mets hat. "You can't believe that in nineteen sixty-three there're a lot of psychos on the loose?"

That was all he said, yet Neuman knew that something had happened to President Kennedy. He couldn't have said how and he couldn't say now, but he knew. Maybe it was something about the way the men were standing—a little stiffly, perhaps, holding their coffee containers far from their mouths, as if they might toss them away if someone came up to them and said this wasn't really a time to be drinking coffee. Or maybe it wasn't. Neuman couldn't say.

Nor could he say how he knew that the bellhop at the Shoreham had found Martha Wine dead in her room, but he knew. Maybe it was the bellhop's bleached face and the way he held his chin tipped up just a little, as if to keep something from spilling out of his mouth—words, sobs, vomit. Or maybe it wasn't. Neuman couldn't say.

"Ohmigod," was all the bellhop said when he finally spoke. He said it only once, yet Neuman knew what he was talking about even though he didn't know what he was talking about.

Neuman had arrived at the Shoreham at a few minutes before eleven and sat in the lobby and watched the metal arrow over the elevator door swing from left to right as the elevator went up and from right to left as it descended. He would wait for one more round trip before going up to six-oh-six.

The bellhop came down the stairs—not pell-mell, but with a careful haste. He was built like a halfback and Neuman wondered for a moment if he always used the stairs, to stay in shape. Then he saw that bleached face and that tipped-up chin and heard that "Ohmigod."

The elevator was on four and going up and Neuman took the stairs—two at a time for the first flight, then one at a time. He was altogether winded by three; by four he thought he would die; by five he was sure he was dead and he didn't remember making it to six, but he did.

Six-oh-six was right by the stairway. The door was wide open and on the hallway carpet, draped over a hanger and encased in plastic, lay a woman's beige skirt. He put it together, breathless or not: the bellhop was delivering the skirt, cleaned or pressed, from valet service; he found the door to six-oh-six ajar or wide open; he looked in; he dropped the skirt; he ran down the stairs.

Wheezing through his nose, Neuman looked in six-oh-six and saw what the bellhop had seen: a woman. On her back. Dressed in a blue shirt and yellow panties. Dead.

Neuman took a quick look around and saw what the bellhop had not seen—that nowhere in the room, not in the dresser drawers or the drawers of the endtables or the writing table, not in the closet, not under the bed, not in Martha Wine's one piece of luggage, was there a manuscript of a novel.

"Klinger's on the phone, Jake," Tim McIver said. "He wants an update."

"Tell him to go fuck himself," Neuman said.

"Jake."

"All right. Tell him I'll call him when I'm sure the guy's not still in the hotel."

"We've been through every room, loo," Bloomfield said. "The basement. The roof. It's clean."

"It's clean of someone hiding under a bed, you mean," Neuman said. "Or in a closet or behind a standpipe on the roof. But it's not clean till we've talked to every guest, every bellhop, every maid, every cook, every busboy, everyone."

Redfield moved close to Neuman. "I've got everyone who was on duty in the lobby in the manager's office, Jake. You want to talk to them now?"

Talk? Neuman thought. No, I don't want to talk to them. I want the one who shot her to confess. Or I want someone to finger the one who shot her. But I don't want to talk. But he said, "Yeah," and followed after Redfield.

Redfield stopped with his hand on the doorknob of the manager's office. "You all right, Jake?"

"Still out of breath, but, yeah, I guess."

"Tough break, Jake. The bellhop must've missed the guy by seconds. You missed him by minutes."

"Yeah, well. I'd be more surprised if he'd walked right into my arms than if I just missed him. . . . The thing of it is, Bob, who knew she was here?"

Redfield shrugged. "Friends on the coast, maybe. Friends here. Friends of Susannah Keyes's. We'll have to go down the list again—what's-her-name's list. We'll have to talk to them all again."

Talk, Neuman thought.

The bellhop's name, fittingly, was Porter. He was sobbing hysterically. Neuman asked him a few questions, but all he got was wails, so he turned to the manager, whose name was Ness.

"We run a very quiet hotel here, lieutenant," Ness said before Neuman could ask him anything. "Nothing like this has ever happened here."

"What the fuck do I care?" Neuman said. "I don't want to hear a song and dance, I just want answers to the questions I ask you. Short answers. How many rooms in this place?"

"Thirty rooms. It's a small hotel."

"You see what I mean?" Neuman said. "That's what I consider a long answer, and I asked for short answers. Thirty rooms would've been a short answer. That's the kind of answer I want. . . . And how many guests in those thirty rooms?"

"Forty-three. Not . . ."

"Not what? You were going to say something else. Not what?"

"Not including Miss Wine," Ness said.

"Cute," Neuman said. "Very cute. . . . And of the forty-three guests, not including Miss Wine, how many have been guests here before?"

"Twelve are permanent residents. Of the remaining thirty-one, fourteen have stayed here at least once before."

"And you can vouch for them?"

"Vouch?"

"Is any one of them a killer?"

"No. Emphatically not."

"Emphatically? That's pretty good. Emphatically. How about the others, the ones who're here for the first time? Any of them strike you as the murdering kind?"

"No."

"But not emphatically?"

"Yes! Well . . . I would be speculating."

"Speculate. It's a free country."

"There is one guest," Ness said, "who strikes me as, well, suspicious. His name is Krystal—with a K. He arrived yesterday afternoon with no luggage, no reservation, no idea how long he would stay. He paid for two nights in advance—with cash—and as far as I am aware he hasn't left his room since he checked in, which would have been approximately one P.M. He hasn't ordered dinner or breakfast from room service, he hasn't had any food delivered, as some

136

guests do. There are some excellent Japanese restaurants down the block, lieutenant, and—"

"Okay," Neuman said. "This answer's getting a little longer than I'm interested in. My men spot-checked all the rooms. Presumably Mr. Krystal with a K was in his and not dead of a heart attack or lying in the shower with a bump on his head from slipping and falling, right? Bobby?"

Redfield paged through a list. "Krystal, four-oh-four. He was in, Jake. Want me to get him?"

Neuman nodded.

Redfield left.

Porter moaned.

"What's the matter, Porter?" Neuman said. "You didn't kill her, did you?"

"Really, lieutenant," Ness said.

"Shut the fuck up, Ness," Neuman said. "So, Porter, who'd you see around the lobby this morning?"

Porter shook his head.

"Come on, Porter. What'm I, a fucking jerk?"

"There was quite a lot of traffic through the lobby this morning, lieutenant," Ness said. "It's unusual for us to have a full house at this time of year, but twenty of our guests—they're occupying twelve rooms—are attending a convention at the Hilton, down the street, and there was a problem there with overbooking. We accommodated some of the overage."

"Overage?"

"Yes."

"Overage. So what Porter's trying to tell me isn't that he didn't see anyone in the lobby this morning, he saw a lot of people?"

"Yes."

"And didn't notice anyone unusual."

"I can't speak for him, but—"

"Speak for him. He's having trouble speaking at all."

"I didn't see anyone unusual, lieutenant," Porter said.

"Oh, you can talk now," Neuman said.

"Yes."

"You got control of yourself."

"Yes."

"You figure you better start talking or people'll start thinking you didn't just find Martha Wine's body, you murdered her."

"Lieutenant, really."

"Ness? Fuck you. . . . Did you kill her, Porter? You didn't answer me before."

"No."

Redfield put his head in the door. "Krystal."

"Bring him in. No, never mind. I'll come out. You take over here."

"Mr. Krystal?" Neuman said.

"Yes?"

"Krystal with a K?"

"That's right."

"Where were you this morning between ten and eleven?"

"In my room."

"Four-oh-four?"

"Yes."

"And you'd been in your room since one o'clock yesterday afternoon?"

"That's right."

"You didn't go out for dinner, didn't go out for breakfast, didn't order anything from room service?"

"No."

"You don't get hungry, Mr. Krystal?"

"I was having too much fun."

"Fun. Uh hunh. Doing what? Never mind, I can guess. Where're you from, Mr. Krystal."

"Des Moines, Iowa."

"Des Moines. Iowa. You here on business?"

"No. Pleasure."

"Yeah, I can see that. You married?"

"Yes."

"Kids?"

"Seven."

"Jesus. Your wife know you're here?"

138

"She thinks I'm in Omaha on business. I lease farm equipment."

"Omaha. Farm equipment. Well, don't worry; I won't tell her."

"Thank you."

"Thank *you*," Neuman said. "Oh, Mr. Krystal—there is one thing: the manager said you checked in without any luggage."

"Yes. The trip to Omaha was to be just a day trip. I couldn't take luggage or my wife would've gotten suspicious."

"Right. Well, won't she be suspicious that you've been gone this long?"

"Oh, no. I called yesterday evening—yesterday afternoon Central time—and said I'd been delayed. It's happened before; she's understanding."

"I can see that. Well, since you didn't bring any luggage and since you haven't left your room since you got here, does that mean you stole the dress from another guest?"

"The woman in four-oh-two. She's a perfect twelve, just as I am. It makes it all the more exciting, lieutenant."

"I can imagine. Look, Krystal, since she hasn't reported the dress stolen she probably doesn't know it's gone. Go back upstairs, take the dress off, put your clothes on, hang the dress on the knob of four-oh-two, come back down, go out the door—I'll clear you with the cop on the door—go back to wherever it was—"

"Des Moines."

"Des Moines. You have fifteen minutes. If you're not out by then, I'll bust you from here to Des Moines with a little Duluth thrown in."

"Thank you," Krystal said.

"You're welcome," Neuman said. "What about the shoes? They stolen, too?"

"Oh, no. They're mine. The shoes and the lingerie and the jewelry are all mine. I carry them in pockets I had specially sewn into the lining of my topcoat. There's one for the wig, too."

"Uh hunh. What do you call that color?"

"It's called Distinguished Blue. Do you like it?"

"On you, it looks good."

"Martha Wine took TWA flight sixteen from San Francisco to JFK," Redfield said. "She landed at ten fifteen, fifteen minutes early.

Tail winds. She must've taken a cab because she was here at quarter to eleven. She left a wakeup call for eight, called the desk a little after, asking for valet service to press a skirt, called room service a little after that and ordered a pot of tea. The valet service didn't pick up the skirt until nine thirty and told her she couldn't get it back before noon— the extra guests Ness mentioned. She said she had to have it before eleven, that she had an appointment—with you, Jake—and didn't have anything else to wear. She had a pair of slacks, but they have a stain on them—wine, it looks like, from the flight, maybe. Porter brought the tea up. A guy named Ramirez picked up the skirt and would've brought it back, too—he handled stuff like that—but she'd made her point about needing the skirt before eleven, so Porter brought it up, found the door open, and so on. That's what I've got."

Neuman snapped his fingers. "So Ramirez did it, when he picked up the skirt."

"There was a maid cleaning across the hall," Redfield said. "Svetlana Gorayavich. She saw Ramirez knock, saw Wine answer, saw her give him the skirt, saw Wine close the door, saw Ramirez get in the elevator."

Neuman snapped his fingers. "Ah, well."

"Like Ness said," McIver began, "there're thirty rooms, forty-three guests—not including Wine—"

"Not including Krystal, either," Neuman said. "You can include Krystal out."

McIver laughed. "Twenty-nine rooms—or twenty-eight, I guess, not including Wine—twenty-eight rooms, forty-*two* guests, including Krystal out—"

"Tim?" Neuman said.

"Yeah?" McIver said.

"I can count."

"Of the forty-two, twenty—the ones Ness said were from the convention at the Hilton—twenty were out of the hotel by ten o'clock. Another twelve were out before nine. Six went out before ten and were back before ten. Another four were still in their rooms at ten. Two of them left after ten but were back before eleven. Two of them never left their rooms before we sealed the place up—"

"How the fuck do we know all this?" Neuman said. "This is a hotel, for Christ's sake. People come and go all the time."

"It's Ness, Jake," McIver said. "The guy's paranoid."

"Not paranoid enough," Neuman said.

McIver went on: "The bullet was a thirty-eight—a Smith. The ME says she died between ten and twelve. We know she didn't die after eleven, so she died between ten and eleven. Nobody on the floor, nobody in the rooms above and below heard a shot, so he must've used a silencer. Forensics is still working on that, and on whether it's the same gun that killed Kaiser and Keyes."

"It's got to be the same guy," Neuman said. "Doesn't it?"

"It doesn't fit, Jake," Redfield said. "The newspapers haven't heard from the guy. Wine wasn't a public figure in the way Kaiser and Keyes were. She wasn't a nobody, but she wasn't a somebody in the same way they were—their pictures in the papers, being on TV, like that. It doesn't fit."

"If the gun fits, then it fits," Neuman said. "So far, since it's a thirty-eight Smith, I'd say the chances of its fitting are pretty fair, maybe even above average. Look at it this way: the guy kills Kaiser, he kills Keyes, he takes the manuscript of the novel from Keyes's apartment because he knows, or figures, that he's in it—that there's a character based on him and that if someone read the novel carefully they'd finger him. He also knows that Keyes made a copy of the novel and sent it to Wine. How he knows that, I don't know, but what's-her-name, the agent, knew—or suspected—so maybe the killer knew, or suspected, too. How he knows Wine is coming to New York and bringing the copy of the novel with her I don't know, but it wouldn't've been the hardest thing in the world to find out. Maybe he knew Wine; maybe he called her up and said, 'Hi, how you doing?' and she said, 'Okay, considering my ex-girlfriend got bumped off—and by the way, I'm coming to New York to visit her grave and bringing the cops a copy of her novel because there's a guy in it—Beau—who's the killer.' I mean, it might've been that simple. We don't know anything about her. Maybe she had a big mouth. Maybe she called *him* up. . . .

"Okay. So. He finds out where she's staying. That would've been simple too. But what isn't simple, what he can't plan in advance—and this is why he doesn't send letters to the newspapers, Bob—is when is he going to pop her. A hotel's not like an apartment building.

141

For one thing, there're paranoids like Ness working in them. For another, you can't just come and go without people noticing you. In an apartment house, you can come and go without people noticing you, but in a hotel, you come—they want to know if you're staying there or visiting or what; you go—they want to make sure you're not skipping out on your bill. So he has to wait for the right time, which may mean he was hanging around since last night, which is why, Tim, you should send a guy up and down the block—there're mostly offices on this street, and a few apartment buildings, but maybe somebody was working late—and see if anybody saw anybody hanging around.

"On the other hand, night, or early morning, probably wouldn't've been the best time, seeing as how there would've been more chance of being noticed coming in and going out. There's a fire exit in the back of the main floor, but the front door's the only way in unless he pried the fire door off its hinges, which he didn't do, unless he put it back when he left, which he also didn't 'cause there's about a hundred years of dirt on those bolts.

"So morning's the best time, probably after nine when people're up and around, going to breakfast, buying newspapers, heading out to conventions at the Hilton and whatever else people do who stay in hotels like this. He comes in, he mingles, he looks ordinary, he's not wearing his gun outside his pants, he gets a chance and he goes up the stairs, probably, I can't see him taking the elevator, unless he took it to another floor, then walked up or down, but I can't see it. He goes up the stairs, knocks on her door, maybe even says who he is—maybe she's even *expecting* him, 'cause we've got to figure she knew him; otherwise how would he know she was coming to New York with the manuscript? I mean, nobody knew that."

"There's something I have to say, Jake," Redfield said.

"Speak. I'm not the only one around here who's allowed to talk."
Talk, talk, talk.

"*We* knew she was coming to New York," Redfield said.

"So we did."

"I can't help thinking, Jake—it's just a hunch; I don't have any good reason to think it—but I can't help thinking that maybe this guy is someone we know."

"Someone we know?"

"A cop."

"A cop?"

"Let me tell you why I think it," Redfield said. "Remember the guy on the subway, the Samaritan Killer? We both thought he might be a cop because of the way Briggs the graffiti king said he held his gun, because of the way he handled the situation. We don't know how this guy holds his gun, obviously, but we do know that the guy who killed Kaiser and Keyes seemed to have a very easy time getting into their apartments. We've been thinking he had an easy time because they knew him, but maybe that's not it. Maybe he had an easy time because, when he knocked on their doors or rang their bells and they asked who it was, he said he was a cop and showed his badge.

"You're looking at me funny, Jake. I said I didn't have a good reason for thinking it. But I just thought I better talk it out. You know how you always say if you talk about something enough maybe something'll come out."

Neuman nodded. There were times when he thought every criminal must be a cop. Who knew better the ways of criminals—and, better still, the ways of cops? But not this time. This time he had no reason to think the killer was a cop—except that, as Redfield had begun by saying, a number of cops had known that Martha Wine was coming to New York with a copy of Susannah Keyes's novel. "I don't know, Bob. I mean, it's not an idea I'd reject out of hand. On the other hand, I'm not about to spend any time at this point going through the roster and trying to figure who's a psycho and who's not. I still like the idea that the killer knew Kaiser and Keyes and maybe Wine, too, which is why I'd like to get my hands on that novel. Why the hell didn't I have somebody meet Wine at the airport? Why the hell didn't I put a man on her just in case?"

"You couldn't've known, Jake," Redfield said.

"No way, Jake," McIver said.

"Umm," Neuman said.

Bloomfield knocked on the door of the manager's office and said Forensics had determined the bullet had been fired from a gun with a silencer, the same gun that killed Chris Kaiser and Susannah Keyes.

"So what else is new?" Neuman said.

Bloomfield also said Deputy Chief Inspector Lou Klinger had called again asking for an update.

"So what else is new?" Neuman said.

Bloomfield also said that there was a crowd of reporters outside the hotel demanding that Neuman give them a briefing.

"So what else is new?" Neuman said.

Bloomfield also said that a large number of spectators had gathered across the street behind police barricades and that there had been complaints from a jeweler and a hairdresser whose entrances were blocked.

"Why the fuck're you telling me this?" Neuman said. "Find some uniformed brass and tell him to get them the fuck out of there."

"I just thought you'd like to know, loo," Bloomfield said.

"The only thing I'd *like* to know," Neuman said, "is who the fuck is killing these women."

But Jake Neuman would have liked to know, would have been very interested to know, that in the crowd of spectators blocking the entrances to the jeweler's and the hairdresser's, watching, listening, making mental notes, was another killer he had briefly looked for:

Ré.

TWENTY - FOUR

Ré walked down the block when the police dispersed the crowd, then jaywalked to the other side and made his way back to the hotel just as the detectives came out to face the reporters. He stood close to a television cameraman and made himself look as if he belonged.

The plump cop in bold, jarring checks and plaids—the one Ré had seen in the Green Tree—did the talking. The Irish cop and the Jewish cop stood behind him, Redfield at his side. Redfield kept his eyes down most of the time, except once when he looked up to answer a question addressed to him, except once when he panned the crowd with his eyes, panning right over Ré's face.

Ré smiled. And remembered.

He had walked down one side of the main street of his hometown, passing face after face he knew and that knew him not. He had coffee at the coffee shop and was served by a waitress who had served him hundreds, thousands, of times before—not coffee, but cherry Cokes and Devil Dogs. He went into the five-and-ten and bought a pack of cigarettes—he had stopped smoking, of necessity, in the jungle, but had started again in Geneva—from his Aunt Ruth. Leaving, he held the door for his father's partner in a construction business, who thanked him. He drove his rented car out to where his home had been—it had been razed and replaced by one of a dozen identical homes in a subdivision called Maplewood, even though there were no maples for miles. He knocked at the door and inquired about himself of a young woman—little more than a teenager—with a two-year-old twin on each hip.

"There's no André Keller here—oh. You mean the deserter?"

"I haven't seen him in years," Ré said. "I met him in basic training. He went to 'Nam and I went to Europe. I don't know about his deserting."

"Well, he did," the woman said. "My husband knows all about it. You should talk to him, only he took his rig to Barstow. Won't be back till Tuesday."

"I won't be here that long," Ré said. "What happened to his family?"

"'Bout what you'd expect would happen when they heard their son raped a woman and killed an officer who tried to stop him. They died of shame, that's what they did. The old man just keeled over on the steps, he heard the news. The mother took a while longer—about a year—before she cashed in her chips."

Tears welled in Ré's eyes, and he turned away and looked out over the parched lawn. "He had a fiancée too, I remember. What happened to her?"

"She's dead too."

Ré whirled so suddenly that the woman drew back and the twins put fingers to their mouths. "Dead?"

The woman's eyes narrowed. "Say, how'd you know this was where he lived? This ain't the house he lived in, the name of the street's been changed. How'd you find this place?"

"Died where?" Ré said evenly. "Died when? Died how?"

The woman took another step back and began to close the door with her foot. "You're him, ain't you? You son-of-a-bitch."

Ré turned and went down the walk and got in his car and drove away in a spray of dust and gravel. A police car passed him on the main road, going at speed, but it was answering some other alarm. He drove to Leila's house and knocked at the door. Leila answered.

No. It wasn't Leila. It was her sister, Diane, who had been in diapers the last time he had seen her and was now the age that Leila had been when he met her.

"Is your mother home?" Ré said.

Diane shook her head. "She went shopping. Are you here to fix the pickup?"

Why not? Once upon a time, car engines had been his forte. "Yeah."

"Daddy was cussing you 'cause you said you couldn't come till tomorrow."

Ré smiled. "That's why I came today. I don't like your daddy cussing me."

She watched while he worked—it was a simple matter; the idle motor, which didn't work anyway, had rusted off and become lodged under the accelerator cable, jamming it—and after they had talked about the weather for a while, he said, "I used to live around here, then moved away and now I'm back. When I was in high school there was a girl who looked a lot like you. Her name was Leila Stone. She any relation?"

Diane mumbled, "She was my sister."

"Was?"

"She's dead."

146

"I'm sorry to hear that. How'd it happen?"

"I'm not supposed to talk about it."

"I can understand that," Ré said. He stood up, shut the hood, and brushed off his hands. "That takes care of it."

"I don't have any money to give you. Momma won't be back for another hour."

"I wouldn't take any money from you. But I would like to wash my hands and have a glass of water."

In the kitchen, Diane stepped close to him as he dried his hands. "She was murdered."

Ré fought to keep from crying out. "Uh hunh."

"She had this boyfriend? Who was in the Army? In Vietnam? He killed somebody? Another soldier? He ran away? Leila—my sister— she said everyone was liars? That he wouldn't kill anybody, least of all another soldier? She ran away, too? To L.A.? She didn't have any money? She started going with guys? You know, touching them and stuff for money? She was a heroin addict. She got killed by this guy she was supposed to give the money to she made from going with guys? He gave her this overdose? With a needle? I'm not supposed to know any of this. I stayed up nights, listening to people talking. See that little hole up there? It comes out in the bathroom upstairs. I used to lie in the bathtub and listen to people talk. Where're you going? You didn't drink your water."

Back in Geneva, back at his desk, Ré resolved that not enough people had died—not yet. When they had, then he could be at peace.

TWENTY - FIVE

The phone rang and rang even after Neuman answered it. He yanked out the modular plug at the back of the base, and still it rang.

Without opening her eyes, Maria said, "It's the doorbell, Jacob."

And so it was, although it was two o'clock in the morning. Neuman hadn't gotten home until one, had had a beer and some cold meat loaf Maria had left in the refrigerator, and had gotten into bed at one thirty, without taking a shower, although he needed one badly. He had set the alarm for five thirty so he could take one before heading back to Manhattan at six, with only a hard-boiled egg and some warmed-over coffee for breakfast.

He put on his plaid bathrobe over his checked pajamas, stepped into his striped slippers, and went downstairs. He stopped at the bottom landing, wondered if he should go back for his gun, decided the hell with it, and padded across the living room to the front door. He put his face to the glass and jumped back, for Steve Federici had his face to the glass on the other side. His nose was flattened by it and he looked demented.

Neuman got his breath back, tightened the belt of his robe, and opened the door. "What the fuck, Steve?"

Federici held his hands up, helplessly. "I'm sorry, lieutenant. I didn't want to use the phone. I mean, it could be tapped or something."

"Tapped?"

"I don't know. I just don't know."

They stood there for a long moment until it occurred to Neuman that Federici expected to be asked in. "You want to come in?"

"I got to talk to you, lieutenant. Yeah, I'd like to come in."

"Come on in, then," Neuman said, and stood aside to let Federici pass. He looked up and down the street, but the only cars parked there were his and his neighbors'. "You walk, or what?"

"I didn't want to drive my car. I thought I might be followed."

148

"Followed?"

"I took the subway to Union Turnpike, then got a cab to a couple of blocks away and walked from there. It's funny; it turns out I know this neighborhood. A girl I used to date in college lived around the corner."

Neuman wondered if he should ask her name. It would be a neighborly thing to do. But he didn't want to know her name. He didn't want to know anything at all that would keep him from getting back into bed as soon as possible. "You want some coffee?"

Federici rubbed his hands together. "Geez, I'd love some, if it's not too much trouble."

"It's no trouble," Neuman lied, for though he could boil water he could never dole out the right amount of grounds. His coffee was as thin as water or as thick as mud. And he would have to make some, for Maria would have left only a cup's worth for him to drink in the morning, and to make it in the morning, with sleep confounding his already faulty judgment, would be out of the question.

He gasped on pushing open the swinging door to find someone in the kitchen.

Maria. Making coffee. "¡Qué barbaridad!"

"Sí," Neuman said, kissing her on the cheek. "Thanks, babe."

"I'll leave it here, Jacob. You'll hear the buzzer when it's ready. I don't want your friend to see me in my nightgown."

"It's one of my men, babe. Thanks again. I'll be up soon."

She smiled, for she knew he wouldn't be up at all.

Neuman left the swinging door open so he could hear the coffeepot buzzer and went into the living room. Federici, who had been sitting in Neuman's favorite chair, stood up.

"Sit down, Steve," Neuman said.

Federici looked at where he'd been sitting. "Here?"

"Why not?" Neuman sat in Maria's chair, shifted to slide a knitting needle out from under him, crossed his legs, and opened his eyes wide. "So?"

"I'm really sorry about the time, lieutenant. I didn't realize it was so late."

"It's late," Neuman said. "Or early—depending on what direction you're going, I guess."

Federici studied his palms. "I'll give it to you as quick as I can."

Neuman remembered Major Antoinette da Silva of the Pentagon Public Information Office and hoped she wasn't the reason for Federici's visit. If she was, she would also be the reason for Federici's demise, for Neuman would march upstairs, get his service revolver, march back down, and put a bullet through Federici's brain.

"Last Sunday night, early Monday morning, like I told you, a guy named Joe Smith got popped in Mineola with a twenty-two-caliber pistol. Like I told you, it was the same gun used to pop Carlos Pabon on the subway Friday night and, a few hours earlier, Clarence Stearns up in Harlem. Like I told you, Stearns and Smith were in the same outfit in Vietnam. Stearns, you know this from Cariello, was a small-time dealer; Smith, like I told you, ran an auto body shop, stripped hot cars on the side. I heard about Smith from a Nassau County Homicide dick named Graves, who knew Smith when they were kids.

"Graves called me tonight—I mean *last* night; I'm really sorry about the time. It's just that I didn't believe it at first, and by the time I made myself believe it, well, it was a lot later than I thought—or a lot earlier. . . . Anyway, like I just said, Graves called me last night and said how come I wasn't working on the subway shooting anymore. I thought, Oh, shit, that fucking McGovern has got me moved off the investigation, and to top it off he hasn't even told me, and I said, What do you mean, not working on it? Last I heard I was working on it. He said, That's funny, 'cause a homicide dick named Redfield called me yesterday and wanted to know everything I knew about a DOA named Joe Smith. Said it was connected to a case he'd just been assigned to, a guy getting killed on the Broadway local, another guy, a small-time drug dealer, getting killed up in Harlem. . . .

"Now maybe I should've done something right then, lieutenant—called you, called McGovern, called Klinger, called Redfield, even—and said, What the fuck is going on? You take a guy off a case, put me on it, then put the guy back on it without even telling me. I mean, I know I'm not running the case, but I'm *work*ing on it and I got a right to know who I'm working with. But I didn't. I didn't call anybody because something else had come up just before Graves called me and it was making me crazy and I had to get it sorted out and the call from Graves was tied into it. . . .

"Like I told you, I made this contact at the Pentagon." Federici blushed. "Say, lieutenant, I got to thank you for your advice. You were right. Toni's got no problems about dating a detective two, and when she comes up to see her folks next month we're going to go out for a little dinner at this place I know in Bay Ridge, Eighteen and Seventy-second. . . .

"Anyway, like I said, I made this contact at the Pentagon, and like you suggested, I asked her if she could put together a list of everybody who was in the same outfit as Stearns and Smith, with addresses as up to date as she had. It didn't take that long. She's got this computer— she asks it a question and it answers, just like that, not like the computer we've got, you ask it a question, it takes a nap or blows a fuse. She made up the list, Toni, she put it in the mail—Express Mail, you know, mail it by five, delivery's guaranteed by three o'clock the next business day, two pounds for nine thirty-five. I figured, what the hell, nobody's going to complain if I put in a chit for nine thirty-five, even if she could've mailed it first class and it probably would've got here by Friday or Saturday. . . .

"So I got the list on Thursday. A hell of a long list. I don't know how many names on it—a couple of hundred, anyway. I didn't get a chance to do anything with it 'cause the other thing that's been going on is, like you suggested, I talked to a guy I know on the *Times*, a guy I owe a favor, he helped me to get some tickets to the Millrose Games last winter, and told him about the Samaritan Killer carrying a copy of *Pilgrim at Tinker Creek*. It was in Thursday's paper. I've been getting calls up the wazoo. Everybody on the East Coast who knows somebody he doesn't like who's read the book has called me up to say, Look no further for the Samaritan Killer, I have got your man. I haven't even checked them out. If they smell over the phone, I figure they're going to smell in person. But it's kept me tied to the desk. You were right, by the way, about McGovern. He never figured I leaked the item to the *Times*; he figured it was somebody in McGillion's office. He's been on the phone for hours every day, trying to find out who. He put that much effort into finding the shooter, we'd've nailed him by now easy. . . .

"Anyway, the point is, I didn't get a chance to look at the list real close until this afternoon. McGovern took off to check out a supposed lead on Stearns's killing—some junkie who did business with him, thought he knew someone who wanted to kill him. Christ, from what Cariello said, everyone in Harlem wanted to kill him. Anyway, McGovern was out of the office and I had a chance to look at the list. I didn't know where to start, there were so many names. I thought, for the hell of it, that I'd start with Stearns and Smith. I mean, I knew they were dead, but I thought I'd see what addresses the list had for them. If they were recent addresses, then I'd be ahead of the game, I figured, when it came to getting in touch with the other guys on the list. So I turned through the pages looking for the *s*'s. I landed in the *r*'s. I was just about to turn over to the *s*'s when a name just jumped out of the page at me. You know how that'll happen, lieutenant? You're looking in the phone book or something and all of a sudden a name'll pop out at you—not a name you were looking for, but a name you know. It happened to me once with my own name. I was looking—"

"Redfield," Neuman said.

"Yeah," Federici said.

"Holy shit."

"Yeah."

Neuman heaved himself around to reach for the phone, then changed his mind and sat back facing Federici. "And it was just after you noticed Redfield's name that Graves called you?"

"About an hour. Like I said, I was going crazy trying to figure it out. I mean, Redfield saw the picture Cariello had of Stearns, didn't he?"

"Yeah," Neuman said.

"And he heard Cariello tell about Stearns's tattoo, didn't he?"

"Yeah."

"So even if Stearns has changed since 'Nam, even if we didn't have an ID on him at that point, nothing but that he called himself Detroit, you'd think Redfield would've I-D'd him, wouldn't you?"

"Yeah."

"But he didn't."

"No."

"And the thing about Smith, like I told you, is it didn't get a line in the local papers—just *Newsday*, and not more than a line there. Like

152

I said, he got popped in his office. It looked like a holdup. And because of McGovern not thinking there was anything to it, we didn't give anything on it to the local papers, not even when we made the connection that the guy who popped Smith also popped Pabon and Stearns. So if Redfield knew about Smith getting popped, then he had to know 'cause he found out on his own. I mean, I didn't tell him and McGovern didn't tell him. Jesus Christ, lieutenant, you don't think Redfield popped Smith, do you?"

"No. Try not to go off half cocked on this, Steve. Smith, Pabon, and Stearns were all killed with the same gun. We have a description of the guy who killed Pabon, and it's not a description of Redfield. Where's the list?"

"What list?"

"The list of the guys who were in the same outfit in Vietnam—Redfield's outfit."

"At the precinct. I'm sorry, I guess I should've brought it with me, but—"

"Let's go," Neuman said, and was on his feet heading for the stairs. On the way, he realized that the coffeepot buzzer was buzzing, and had been for quite a while. He went in and shut it off and found that Maria had made a lunch: three ham and swiss cheese sandwiches on rye bread with mustard, four sour pickles, three hard-boiled eggs, a packet of salt, and a packet of pepper. The sandwiches were wrapped in wax paper, the pickles and eggs in clear plastic sandwich bags. They stood beside a brown paper bag on which Maria had placed a blue thermos bottle. Propped against the bottle was a note:

Dear Jacob,

Put the sandwiches, pickles, eggs, salt, and pepper in the paper bag.
Fill the thermos with coffee from the pot.
Take the paper bag and the thermos with you.
Don't drink from the thermos while you are driving

Love,
Maria

When he had dressed, Neuman saw that Maria was awake and watching him.

"Did you unplug the coffeepot?" Maria said.

153

"I didn't, but I will."

"Be careful."

"I will." He bent over to kiss her mouth. "I love you, babe. I don't know what I'd do without you."

"Without me, you would do nothing. You would starve. You wouldn't wash, you wouldn't shave. You would live as you dress. Look at those clothes. That is the jacket to another suit."

"The jacket to this suit's too tight. It doesn't look so bad. They're both plaids."

Maria rolled over. "*¡Que barato!*"

TWENTY - SIX

L inda Walsh read for the hundredth time the item she had clipped from the *Times*:

Homicide detectives have identified the paperback book carried by the man who shot and killed a 19-year-old Hispanic youth last Friday night on an IRT subway train.

According to a source close to the investigation into the murder of Carlos Pabon, the killer, a tall, slim Caucasian in his mid to late 30s, was reading a copy of "Pilgrim at Tinker Creek" by Annie Dillard. The book, which won several awards and was a best-seller in the mid-1970s, was identified by a passenger who had read it and recognized the cover, the source said.

No other progress was reported in the search for the killer, who eyewitnesses said shot Pabon to prevent him from assaulting a nurse.

The item ended with a phone number the police had asked anyone with information about the case to call. All calls would be kept confidential.

As she had hundreds of times in the three days since she had first read the item, Linda sat down at her kitchen table, pulled the phone to her, lifted the receiver, and dialed the number. This time, unlike the other times, she did not hang up immediately after she finished dialing. She let the number ring.

It rang five times, which she thought was two times too many. She nearly hung up, sure that the police didn't really care, sure that they would laugh at her when she told them what she knew.

Just as the sixth ring began, the phone was answered. "Patrolman Mazilli."

"Sergeant Redfield, please," Linda said in a whisper.

"Hello," the patrolman said, nearly shouting by way of encouraging her to speak up.

"Sergeant . . . Redfield . . . please."

"Who's calling?"

"I don't want to tell you my name. I have to talk to Sergeant Redfield. It's about the man in the subway."

"You have information regarding the perpetrator of the subway shooting?" the patrolman said.

"Yes."

"And what is the nature of the information?"

"I want to talk to Sergeant Redfield."

"The sergeant isn't available at this point in time. If you would care to inform me as to the nature of your information, I can assure you that your call will be kept confidential."

Linda hung up.

An hour later, after drinking a glass of wine, although it was not yet nine o'clock in the morning, she called again.

The phone rang once. "Hello?"

"Sergeant Redfield, please."

"Just a moment. . . . Sarge! She called back."

Another voice said, "Redfield."

"Sergeant Redfield?"

"Yes."

"I, uh . . ."

"What's your name, ma'am? Don't worry. I won't ever make it public. It's just that it'll be easier to talk if I know your name."

"Linda."

"Linda what?"

"Are you the Sergeant Redfield whose picture was in the newspaper the other day?"

"Yes."

"And did you have lunch last Saturday—not yesterday, but a week ago—at the Green Tree restaurant?"

"Yes."

Linda didn't speak for a long time.

"Linda?"

"I'm afraid."

"I can understand that. Where are you?"

"Home."

"Is he with you?"

"He? Oh. No. He—" She remembered that if you talked long enough, the police could trace the number you were calling from. She had talked long enough already. Hadn't she? "I'll meet you somewhere. I'll come to where you are. To your police station."

"No," Redfield said. "He might be watching you. He might follow you. Let me come to where you are. I don't wear a uniform. He won't know I'm a police officer."

"He knows you!" Linda shouted.

"I know," Redfield said softly. "Let's meet somewhere, Linda. Do you know the Terminal Diner, at Forty-fourth and Tenth? It's a good place to meet—out of the way, but busy. I'll meet you there in twenty minutes. Take a cab. I'll pay you back. You know what I look like, right? From the newspaper?"

"Yes."

"Twenty minutes, Linda. And, Linda?"

"Yes?"

"Don't be afraid."

"All right."

TWENTY - SEVEN

The sun had risen red as blood, but it was turning out to be a beautiful morning.

So much, Neuman thought, for that weather watcher's rhyme.

He and Federici had arrived at the precinct at three fifteen and had gone over the list swiftly once, in the hope some name would ring a bell. None did, and they went over it more slowly, looking for a pattern that they doubted they would recognize. They found none.

"Okay," Neuman had said. "Call her."

"Who?"

"The major. Toni. Your lady friend at the Pentagon."

"Jesus, lieutenant, I don't know her home number. Only her work number."

"Call it. It's the Pentagon, for Christ's sake. They got to be open twenty-four hours a day. I mean, what if somebody started a war?"

Federici called the Pentagon and, after much cajoling, got the duty officer to call Major Antoinette da Silva at home. She called back, listened to Federici's appeal, and said she would be at her office by six. She doubted whether she would have anything for them before noon.

And what would it be when she had it? Neuman wondered. All they had been able to ask was whether anything "unusual" had happened involving that outfit during the more than six years Robert Redfield was one of its members. He wouldn't be surprised if she called at noon the next day, or never.

The phone rang at nine fifteen. Federici started to answer it, then stepped back. "You better get it, lieutenant. If it's Toni, and if she's got something . . ."

"If," Neuman said, and picked up the receiver. "Neuman."

"Hi, lieutenant. This is Major Toni da Silva. Army PIO?"

She sounded like fresh flowers, and Neuman tried not to sound like what he was—an exhausted cynic. "Hello, major."

157

"Lieutenant, Detective Federici said you were interested to know if anything 'unusual' has ever been reported regarding the Fourth of the Two-oh-sixth."

"That's right."

"I told Ste—Detective Federici there's no specific button marked 'unusual' on this big old computer I'm sitting in front of, that he'd have to be more specific. He said he couldn't be, that you guys weren't exactly sure what you were looking for. I said did he mean 'unusual' in terms of battlefield performance, as in an unusually high number of medals—Bronze Stars, Purple Hearts, and so on—or, on the other side, an unusually high number of courts-martial, dishonorable discharges, whatever. He said probably the second. I hit the appropriate buttons and didn't come up with much. That outfit wasn't particularly razzle-dazzle, wasn't especially lackluster. It was ordinary, real ordinary—except for one incident. I don't know if it's what you're looking for, but I thought I'd save time if I tried it out on you."

"Please do," Neuman said.

"This was back in 'seventy-one. A captain, Ronald Phelps, age thirty-six, of Shreveport, Louisiana, was shot and killed by a private first class, André Keller, age twenty, of Atascadero, California."

As she spoke, Neuman paged through the computer printout, putting checks alongside the names of Phelps and Keller.

"This stuff's real shorthand, so all I can make out is that Phelps apparently caught Keller in the act of assaulting a female Vietnamese civilian, tried to stop him, and Keller shot him. Keller escaped before he could be apprehended and has never been heard from since. According to the file."

"Meaning what?" Neuman said. "Meaning the files aren't always accurate?"

"It's accurate as far as it goes," Major Toni da Silva said. "The crime was committed, reported, and never prosecuted because of the absence of a perpetrator. The file reflects that. What the file doesn't reflect is the report concerning Keller's whereabouts. I only found that by cross-checking under Keller's name. I got a blip."

"A blip," Neuman said.

"A flashing light indicating that there had been some recent inquiries regarding the individual in question. Keller, that is. If there had been solid information regarding Keller's whereabouts—if his body had been found, if there had been positive identification from a reliable informant, if he'd turned himself in—obviously that would have been entered in the file. The blip means that there'd been only a report, an unverifiable sighting."

"But there was a report?" Neuman said.

"There was a report," Major Toni da Silva said. "About a year ago, August fifteen last, to be exact, the Atascadero Sheriff's Office contacted us and said a man believed to be André Keller was seen in the area asking questions of some local residents. A woman resident—her name isn't on the report—called the sheriff and said a man came to her house and said he was a *friend* of Keller's, hadn't seen him since they were in the service together, wondered what had happened to him. Her house is apparently built on the site of the house where Keller and his family lived. Something about the way the man behaved—the report doesn't say what—made her think he was Keller. She didn't call the sheriff until two days after the man's visit. The report doesn't say why. . . .

"Now, concerning the other names, lieutenant, that Ste—that Detective Federici said you were specifically interested in: Stearns, Clarence; Smith, Joseph; and Redfield, Robert. Interestingly, all three had blips."

"All three," Neuman said.

"All three. They were routine inquiries as to most recent address. We get lots of queries like that, guys wanting to look up their old service buddies. There's no indication—there never is—as to whom the inquiries were from."

Whom? Neuman thought. She not only talks and talks, she talks well. "Major, this is all very helpful, and I can't tell you how much I appreciate what you've done—and Steve too. Detective Federici, that is. I know it's Sunday, I know it's your day off, I know you dragged yourself out of bed to come in and do this, but there's one more thing I'd like to ask. Your computer is terrific, and, like I said, this is all very helpful, but the computer can't talk—I've read about some that're supposed to be able to and maybe someday yours will—but until then what we really need is to talk to somebody about these people: Stearns, Smith, Captain Phelps. For reasons I can't go into at

159

the moment, we are unable to talk to Mr. Redfield, although I know that Steve has probably mentioned to you that he is a colleague of ours. And since Stearns and Smith and Captain Phelps are dead as well, it goes without saying that we can't talk to them.

"What I'd like to ask, therefore—and you've been over this list a couple of times; maybe you could go over it once more very quickly—is there anybody on the list you *know*, anybody you've maybe happened to serve with somewhere, who would remember those days in Vietnam, whom we could call up and talk to for a while just to flesh out these very interesting facts that the computer's coughed up? I know it's Sunday, I know it's your—"

"Way ahead of you, lieutenant," Major Toni da Silva said. "The first time through the list one name popped out at me. Mickey Chavez. Miguel Chavez, that is. Mickey runs a counseling center for Vietnam vets up your way. Newark. He was my top sergeant when I was in basic. Fort Ord. A confirmed lifer, or so everybody thought. Then one day he just up and quit—resigned his commission, forfeited a full pension, the works. It seems he was having terrible headaches, nightmares; a car'd backfire and he'd dive under a table. He read something in the paper about other vets—Vietnam vets, that is—who were having the same kind of problem. Post-traumatic stress disorder is the fancy name for it. Delayed shell shock is what it is. Mickey decided—he never told *me* this, understand; I was just a grunt; but about a year ago I read something about him in an article about Vietnam vets in *Time*. No, *Newsweek*. No, maybe it was *Time*. . . .

"Anyway, a magazine . . . He decided, according to the magazine, that training people to fight in the next war, wherever that's going to be, wasn't what he should be doing with his energy; he should be helping people who were suffering the way he was from fighting the *last* war. So he quit, worked for an outfit in California—Venice, I think, near L.A.—that sort of pioneered the whole counseling effort, then came back East, where he was from, and set up an office in Newark, where there're a lot of vets, mostly blacks and Hispanics. Mickey Chavez was in that outfit in 'Nam, lieutenant, and he'd be a good man to talk to. You got a pencil? I'll give you his number."

"Actually, why don't you give his number to Steve, major?" Neuman said. "He'll want to have a word with you anyway, and you can give him the number while you're at it. In the meantime, let me just say again what a help you've been and how thankful I am and if you're ever in New York, which I understand you're going to be because Steve tells me your folks live up here, if you're ever in New York I would be honored if you would stop by and say hello, I'll even show you our computer, which if you kick it hard enough and kind of tilt it to one side can sometimes add two and two and come up with the right answer, not always, but sometimes. And if you can't stop by, which I would fully understand because we're located in a neighborhood that isn't exactly the kind where you can walk down the street and be absolutely certain somebody isn't going to whack you over the head and grab your wallet, then maybe you would just call up and say hello and we could meet somewhere for a beer, or whatever your pleasure is, and thanks again, major."

"Call me Toni, lieutenant. Please."

"Toni? Okay, I will. And, Toni?"

"Yes?"

"Call me Jake. Please."

"Jake? Okay. Jake it is. . . . Jake?"

"Yeah?"

"I probably really shouldn't ask this. I mean, I know it isn't fair and Steve's probably right there and everything, but, well . . . is he as cute as he sounds?"

"Yeah, I guess he is. I mean, I don't know if that's the word I'd use. I mean, it's not a word I use much, but, well, yeah, I guess he is."

"Good," Major Toni da Silva said. "Oh, good."

Miguel Chavez was as terse as could be, so terse that Neuman kicked himself for taking the time to drive to Newark when it all could've been said on the phone in a few minutes. Why didn't people just tell you you weren't going to have to drag it out of them?

"There were five of us," Miguel Chavez said. "Buddies. Joe Smith, Clarence Stearns, Bobby Redfield, Ré Keller—André, but we called him Ré—and me. It was us against the world, us against the gooks, us against Phelps. Phelps was a ballbreaker. In Nha Trang, once, on a weekend pass, we got these"—he pulled down the neck of his T-shirt and showed Neuman a bit of an elaborate tattoo—"Ré's idea, although it wasn't really Ré's trip. But he wanted to get at Phelps. He knew Phelps would hate them. Phelps chewed us out. Ré talked back. Not about the tattoo, about the operation we were on. We were overextended, we shouldn't've been as far out as we were without support. Phelps threw Ré in the brig, along with three Vietnamese civilians— an old woman, a young one, the young one's baby. I had late guard duty. I brought them some food. Phelps hadn't been going to feed them. Phelps relieved me. I thought he was going to throw me in after them for bringing the food, but he said he was going to take the duty.

"It didn't make sense. He never took a duty, no matter how whipped we were. Phelps tried to rape the young woman. Ré grabbed his pistol and shot him. That was Ré's story. I believed it. I thought everybody did. But Bobby—Redfield—and Smith, they were afraid, afraid that word would get out that Phelps had chewed us out for the tattoos, that he'd been on our case generally, that we'd all be charged with fragging him. They told the MPs Ré did the raping, that Phelps tried to stop him, that Ré shot him. Ré was gone by then, into the jungle. He freed the Viets, too, and they took off. We tried to find them but never could. So Ré's back? Well, I'm not surprised."

"Not surprised that he survived in the jungle for however many years without weapons, supplies?" Neuman said.

"I helped him get away," Chavez said. "I got him his gun, ammo, grenades, canteens. I knew he'd make it. There were rumors—stories, I guess you'd call them, stories guys'd tell late at night—that there was another army out there, an army of deserters from all sides: MACV, ARVN, NVA, VC, that they got together out of a need to survive and stayed together. I figured Ré'd end up with an outfit like that, and that he'd make it. I guess I was right."

"He's not after you, then," Neuman said. "You helped him, so he's not after you. Smith, Stearns . . . and Redfield are the ones he was after."

"Can you blame him, lieutenant?" Chavez said.

"I'm not in the blaming business," Neuman said. "I'm just trying to keep score."

TWENTY - EIGHT

"Linda?"

"Hello, Sergeant Redfield."

"Call me Bobby, Linda. This is real informal."

"You said you'd be inside, in a booth. Is something wrong?"

"I have a car here. I thought it'd be safer—not that there's anything to worry about, but safer nonetheless—to take a little drive rather than sit around in a public place. If you want coffee or something, I'll get it and you can have it in the car. Breakfast, even. On me."

"No, thanks," Linda said. "I'm . . . I'm not hungry."

"It's the blue Chrysler over there, Linda. I thought we'd take the tunnel, go up the Palisades. It's real pretty this time of year."

"Okay."

They didn't speak until they were through the tunnel, heading north. Traffic was light, industry had the day off, the air was crisp and clean. Linda couldn't remember the last time she had been in a car, the last time she'd been out of the city.

"Well, Linda," Redfield said, "why don't you just tell me everything. Start from the beginning, try not to leave anything out. You will, of course, but I won't interrupt you. When you're finished, we'll go back over it and I'll ask about the things I think you probably left out."

"I don't know where to start," Linda said.

"Start at the beginning."

"It was last Friday—God, only last Friday. He came into the Gold Rail, a bar on Broadway, up by Columbia. I tend bar there. Nights. He ordered a beer, a Bud. He had a bruise on his hand. I went to get a clean towel from the kitchen. When I got back, he was gone. He'd been watching the television. Chris Kaiser? The one who was murdered? Her show was on, and he was staring at the set. Then he was gone. . . .

"I went out for a walk the next morning, and there he was, walking

163

down the street, reading a newspaper. It had a headline about the killing on the subway the night before. The Samaritan Killer? He wouldn't let me read it. He threw it in a trash can. I—I liked him. I wanted to get to know him. I said let's have lunch, at the Green Tree. It was a nice lunch. We didn't talk much, but . . . we liked each other. I knew we'd . . . go to bed afterwards, and . . . we did. You came in just as we were leaving the restaurant—you and your partner. I didn't know who you were—I didn't see your picture in the paper until a couple of days later—but I knew he knew you, that he didn't want you to see him. He went to the pay phone and stood with his back to you until you went past him. You went into the men's room, then he came out to where I was waiting. . . .

"He said his name was Ray Howell. He had cards—a driver's license, an ID card—saying his name was Paul Howell. He had a plane ticket, made out to Paul Howell, from Detroit to New York. I looked in his stuff. He stayed with me for a couple of days. He'd been staying at the Y, but I asked him to stay with me and he did. But he was out all the time—out late at night, out early in the morning. He was out when those women were killed—Chris Kaiser and the other one, the writer. Keyes. Susannah Keyes. And the third one—Martha, was it? Martha Wine. He killed her too. I'm sure of it. He killed all of them.

"Who're Smith and Stearns? And why did he have your name? He had your names written down on the back of his airline ticket. Smith, Stearns, and you—with your addresses. Why? Who is he? What is he doing? He killed the kid on the subway too. He was reading that book—*Pilgrim at Tinker Creek*. It's my favorite book, and he was reading it. The bastard."

The traffic thickened as they neared the George Washington Bridge and didn't thin out until they had passed the interchange and were on the tree-lined Palisades Parkway.

"Okay, Linda," Redfield said. "Let me ask you a few questions. You say he called himself Ray. Did he ever spell it? Was it R-a-y Ray or something else?"

Linda shook her head. "I don't—no. He never spelled it."

"Did he ever mention the name André?"

"No. Yes. André. To André. There was a picture. A picture of a girl. To André, with all my love."

"Did he say who Paul Howell was?"

"Well, no, he never said who he was, but he said he'd had a friend—he never said his name—who went to Columbia in the sixties, drank at the Gold Rail. That was why he came in there. He said he wanted to see the places his friend'd talked about. I think that was Paul Howell. He works for the International Red Cross."

"Cambodia," Redfield murmured. "So that's how . . ."

"What?" Linda said.

Redfield shook his head. "You say he was out when Chris Kaiser was killed, Linda. She was killed sometime after midnight Friday—early Saturday morning. But he left the bar while her show was on the air and you didn't see him again until almost noon on Saturday. Isn't that right?"

"Yes. I just meant . . . I wasn't with him then."

"And you say he was also out when Susannah Keyes was killed. She was killed early Monday morning. He was staying at your place by that time?"

"Yes, and he was out. Since Sunday night."

"And you say he was out when the third woman, Martha Wine, was killed? She was killed Saturday morning, between ten and eleven."

"He . . . he wasn't out. He was gone. He left me that morning. He . . . he left me."

"Why?"

"I told him I knew—knew about the women he killed."

"And what did he say?"

"He didn't say anything. He just left. I asked him who you were—what you were to him. And Stearns and Smith. I asked him what you were to him."

"And what did he say?"

"'Forget those names. Forget me. Forget everything.'"

So suddenly that not until it was over did Linda piece together the links in the maneuver, Redfield turned sharply left, drove across the grassy median, turned left again, and was headed south, back the way they had come.

"Where . . . what is it?" Linda said.

"We're going back to New York, Linda," Redfield said. "To your apartment."

"No. I can't. He might . . . come back."

"Why should he come back, Linda?" There was contempt in Redfield's voice. "He left you, he told you to forget everything, to forget him. Why should he come back?"

"Then . . . then why're we going to my place?"

With controlled patience, Redfield said, "The man you went to bed with, Linda, the man you fell in love with, is a killer. He killed Clarence Stearns, he killed Joe Smith, and he wants to kill me."

"Why?"

"Why? Why is it that when women're told something, they always want to know why? They're told what, but they want to know why. Isn't *what* enough? Isn't it enough to know that he's a killer and that he wants to kill me?"

"I . . . I . . . ."

"He's been following me," Redfield said. "He probably followed me today, to the diner. He probably doesn't have a car. He didn't say anything about a car, did he? You haven't seen him with a car, have you?"

"No."

"So I've lost him, for the time being. But he'll be back, he'll pick me up again. And when he does, I'm going to lead him to your apartment. Don't ask why, Linda. Don't ask why. He'll follow me to your apartment, and when he does, I'll have him where I want him."

"But why don't you . . . ?"

Redfield looked away from the road and smiled. "Why don't I what, Linda? Why don't I what?"

"You're a policeman. Why don't you just . . . arrest him?"

Redfield looked at his watch. He switched on the car radio and turned to a station that was broadcasting news. The news was the news of a slow Sunday: The City Council president warned of a subway fare increase; Ninth Avenue was the scene of a food festival; there had been a smoky fire in a Bronx social club; Con Ed workers continued their two-week-old strike. The last item, filler for the final seconds of the newscast, said that the city's newspapers had received new com-

166

munications from the killer of Chris Kaiser, Susannah Keyes, and
Martha Wine; the killer promised to kill again.

Redfield switched the radio off and didn't speak again, except to ask
Linda her address.

Linda wanted to know why she had to be in her apartment. If Redfield was setting a trap, wasn't it enough that he be there? And why
her apartment? But she was afraid to ask.

TWENTY - NINE

Patrolman Mazilli found it difficult to think with Lieutenant Jacob
Neuman's face only inches from his.

"Why, Mazilli," Neuman said, "would you tell Redfield about the
call on the special number and not tell Detective McGovern or Detective Federici, who're the detectives handling the job the special
number was set up for?"

"L-like I s-said, sir, the woman asked for Sergeant Redfield."

"Who is *not* handling this job."

"But he w-was, sir. The two of you . . . I mean, originally . . ."

"Originally, Mazilli, is over. Now is now, and now Sergeant Redfield is not handling this job, Detectives McGovern and Federici are
handling it, and they are to be notified of all calls on the special
number, if possible while the calls are still in progress, which is why
you've got that fucking buzzer on your desk which if you pressed it
would ring upstairs and somebody from the squad, if not Detectives
McGovern or Federici then someone who's working on the same job
they're working on—working now, not originally—would come down
and find out what the fuck was going on. Play the tape."

Mazilli swayed from side to side. "I can't, sir."

Neuman followed Mazilli with his eyes. "So not only did you not press the fucking buzzer but you forgot to tape the fucking call. You know, Mazilli, you got a pretty nice job here. You sit around and read the newspapers and when the phone rings you answer it, and even if it doesn't ring you still collect a paycheck and you don't have to worry much on an assignment like this about getting shot or wearing a hole in your shoes. What did she sound like, the woman who called and asked for Redfield, since you forgot to tape the call?"

"I didn't forget, sir," Mazilli said, changing from swaying to rocking. "The tape was erased."

Neuman stepped back, lest Mazilli rock right into him. "Erased? You mean, like Watergate?"

"Sergeant Redfield erased it, sir. I tried to tell him that's what he was doing, but he just waved me away."

Neuman nodded slowly. "So what did she sound like, Patrolman Mazilli?"

Mazilli was about to say she sounded like a woman, but McGovern came in just then and said, "Redfield's not at his place, loo. I called and got no answer so I sent a white-top around, they rang and got no answer, they got the super to let them in and there's no one around," and while McGovern was saying it Mazilli realized he would have to do better than that. And when Neuman nodded to McGovern and looked back at him for his answer, Mazilli said, "She was more young than old, lieutenant. Not a teenager, but not in her forties, either. I'd say twenty-five to thirty-five. No real accent—not black or Hispanic or Irish or Italian. But a New Yorker, definitely a New Yorker. . . ."

Mazilli paused, wondered whether he should go on, decided he should. "She asked for Sergeant Redfield right off, sir. I answered the phone, I said my name, and she said, 'Sergeant Redfield, please,' in like a whisper almost. I heard what she said, but I wanted to be sure, so I said, 'Please speak up, ma'am,' and she said—she said it louder—'Sergeant . . . Redfield . . . please,' kind of pausing between words. I said, 'Who should I say is calling, please, ma'am?' and she said, 'I can't tell you my name, I want to talk to Sergeant Redfield about the Samaritan Killer—' "

"Did she call him that, Mazilli?" Neuman said. "Did she call him the Samaritan Killer?"

"Uh, no, sir, I guess she didn't. She just said she had to talk to Sergeant Redfield about the killing in the subway. I asked her what was the nature of the information she had concerning the perpetrator of the subway shooting and she said, 'I have to talk to Sergeant Redfield,' or, 'I can only talk to Sergeant Redfield.' or, 'Only Sergeant Redfield will understand,' or something of that nature, sir."

"They're very different, aren't they, Mazilli?" Neuman said. "Which was it?"

"I believe she said, 'I have to talk to Sergeant Redfield.'"

"And you said?"

"I said, 'The sergeant isn't available at this point in time. If you would care to inform me as to the nature of your information I can assure you that your call will be kept confidential.' It's s.o.p., sir, to reassure the callers that their calls'll be kept confidential."

"And she said?"

"She hung up, lieutenant."

"And you then called Sergeant Redfield at home."

"Yes, sir."

"And told him that someone with information about the subway killing was trying to reach him."

"Yes, sir. I told him it was a woman, sir."

"And he said?"

"He said he'd be right in. He said he'd handle things, not to call Detective McGovern or Detective Federici. Or you, lieutenant."

Neuman nodded. "Then what?"

"He came in, sir. Sergeant Redfield. About fifteen minutes after I called him. He hadn't shaved or anything, he went down the hall to shave, he told me to yell if the phone rang, he was back in about five minutes, he sat around, had some coffee, looked through the papers. An hour after the first call—the first call was at seven fifty-two, the second call at eight forty-eight—an hour, almost, after the first call, the phone rang again. He was by the window, looking out at the street. I said, 'Do you want to get it, Sergeant?' He said, 'You get it, I'll take it if it's for me.' I answered the phone, I said, 'Hello?' the

169

woman said, 'Sergeant Redfield, please,' I said, 'Sarge, she called back.' He came to the phone, pointed to the door meaning I should go wait out in the hall. I pointed to the tape recorder, meaning he should tape the call; he nodded and hit the rewind button. I waved my hands, meaning, No, he shouldn't do that, that it would rewind to the head, that he'd record over the first call. He just ignored me, hit the record button, pointed to the door, meaning I should wait out in the hall. And I did."

"Then what?" Neuman said.

"He talked for—I don't know—a minute, two minutes. I could hear him through the door, but I couldn't hear what he was saying, except I could hear he didn't say much. I heard him hang up and I started to go through the door; then I decided I'd better wait till he came and got me. I waited, I don't know, two minutes, three minutes. Finally, he came out, he had his coat on—he'd taken his coat off when he went to shave; that leather coat of his, lieutenant—he had his coat on. All he said was, 'I'll be in touch, Mazilli,' and he went out to the street and got in his car and drove off.

"I went back inside. He didn't tell me to listen to the tape, but he didn't tell me not to either, and, well, I had to log the call, it's my job, so I rewound the tape to the head and hit the play button and all there was was dead air, sir. Either he hadn't taped the call at all or he'd taped it and then erased it. . . . That's it, sir. When Detective McGovern came in I mentioned the call and, well, I guess he called you, sir."

Mazilli waited for Neuman to say that at this time tomorrow he would be walking a beat in the South Bronx. But all Neuman said was, "Okay, Mazilli. That's all. You didn't do it by the book, but you did what you thought was right. Thanks."

"Yes, sir," Mazilli said, and slipped out the door.

When he had gone, and when Federici, McIver, and Bloomfield had joined Neuman and McGovern, Neuman said, "André Keller shot Clarence Stearns and Joe Smith and he's hunting for Redfield. He also shot Carlos Pabon, but that doesn't count, he was just doing a good deed; I guess you *could* call him a Samaritan Killer. Redfield knows Keller's hunting him. If the woman really knows Keller, then Redfield wanted to see her to find out where Keller is, where he's staying, whatever. Keller's from out of town, he might be staying at a hotel, at a Y, but I doubt he's staying under his own name, I think he must've left his own name in 'Nam, so I'm not going to waste time checking hotels.

"I think if we find Redfield, we'll find Keller, which is something we want to do since he's killed a lot of people, low-lifes or not, and meanwhile I'm supposed to be finding the guy who killed three women, and so is Redfield, for that matter, and what the fuck is he doing trying to handle this thing on his own? Put out an all-points for Redfield, Tim, and update the all-points on the Samaritan Killer; tell them his name is André Keller, though I doubt if he's using it. Matt, I'm running this case now, I don't care what Klinger says, and he won't say anything for a while 'cause he doesn't know about it and if he calls just say I'm busy, which I'm not exactly, I should be finding the guy who killed three women, and I'm not finding him, all I'm finding is garbage—"

Neuman stopped his hand halfway to his head, which he'd been intending to rub, for it itched, for he hadn't taken that shower he needed so badly. He stood that way for a long moment, then said, "Garbage."

McIver, his hand on the door, ready to go out and deliver the all-points to Communications, turned back. "Garbage."

"Yeah," Neuman said.

"The hotel garbage," McIver said. "The guy who popped Martha Wine wouldn't want to be seen walking out with the manuscript in his hand; he might've dumped it in the garbage."

"Yeah," Neuman said. To Bloomfield, he said, "It's a weekend, they might not've had a pickup. Call what's-his-name—the manager. What the fuck was his name?"

"Ness," Bloomfield said. "Like Eliot Ness. Loo?"

"Call Ness and tell him and tell him not to let that fucking garbage go anywhere. Get six men—no, get ten men. Get ten men and go through that fucking garbage with a fine comb, find that manuscript. You don't find it, go through the garbage that's still in the rooms, Wine's room and every other room. What're you guys standing there for? Get moving."

"Loo?" Bloomfield said.

171

"Get . . . moving."

"Loo, there's something you should know."

"There're a lot of things I should know, Bloomfield, like what the fuck is going on. This better be good."

"It's about the garbage, loo," Bloomfield said. "Bobby said he'd go through it."

"Bobby?"

"Sergeant Redfield."

"Go through it?"

"He said he'd get some men and go through the garbage, looking for the manuscript."

"Did he?"

"I don't know, loo. I mean, I know he said it, I don't know if he did it; I was interviewing hotel guests."

"What the fuck was I doing?" Neuman said.

"I think it was when you were talking to what's-his-name, loo— Krystal. The guy in the dress?"

Talking, Neuman thought. Talk, talk, talking. "He never said a fucking thing to me about it. I don't think he did it. Why didn't he do it? It was a good idea. He couldn't have . . . could he?"

"I don't know, loo," Bloomfield said. "Like I said, I know he said he was going to do it, I don't know if—"

"I don't mean the garbage," Neuman said.

"Oh," Bloomfield said.

"He said he thought the killer was a cop," McIver said.

"I know," Bloomfield said.

"That doesn't mean *he* did it, Jake."

"That," Neuman said, "I don't know."

THIRTY

Ré drank coffee at the luncheonette catty-corner from Redfield's apartment building. He had been a regular customer there since the day he arrived in New York. He told the counterman he was watching for a man who owed him money. The counterman, who had a brother-in-law who was a welsher, commiserated and let Ré sit without ordering when business was light.

Ré had been there in the morning, when Redfield left—in a hurry, in his car. He had taken a bus uptown to the precinct and had seen Redfield's car parked outside. It wasn't, as Neuman had told Major Antoinette da Silva, a neighborhood to hang around in, and Ré had taken another bus back downtown, just riding until he felt like walking, walking until he felt like sitting, riding a bus uptown and going to the luncheonette.

"Ha, ha," the counterman said. "There was a patrol car across the street before. I told myself maybe they're looking for your friend, maybe you're not the only guy he stiffed. They went inside, stayed about ten minutes, came out, drove off."

"It's a big building," Ré said.

Ten minutes later, Redfield drove into the building's garage. Five minutes later, he came out the lobby door and walked west on Seventy-second Street.

Ré left a dollar on the counter.

"Hey," the counterman said, "you don't need to leave a tip like that, a guy like you a guy owes money. What're you doing?"

Ré waved, and said softly, "I won't be back."

"Hey," the counterman said. "You coming back? I'll see you later."

Redfield walked on the north side of Seventy-second, Ré on the south, until Park Avenue, where Redfield crossed over to the south side. Ré bent over a car door, as if unlocking it, and when Redfield continued west followed after him, staying behind him on the same side of the street.

At Fifth Avenue, Redfield went into the park, walking on the sidewalk along the Transverse Road, which was full of Sunday cyclists, joggers, walkers, skaters.

Ré followed, thinking, He knows I'm here. He wants me to follow. He doesn't want to take me, or be taken, but he wants me to follow.

At Central Park West, Redfield walked north, staying on the east side, the sunny side. He walked to Eighty-sixth Street, then crossed and walked west, walking on the south side of Eighty-sixth.

Ré followed on the north side.

At Columbus Avenue, a police car was double-parked; its occupants were writing a ticket on a taxi driver. Redfield slowed down to let a pack of Cub Scouts headed home from the park shield him from the policemen.

At Broadway, Redfield descended into the subway, taking the stairway on the southeast corner.

Ré hesitated, started down the stairs on the northeast corner, then went back up, crossed the street, and took the same stairs Redfield had.

Redfield had gone through the turnstile and was leaning against a pillar on the northbound platform. He had his back to the turnstile, but he was standing where he could be seen.

Ré bought a token, went through the turnstile, and stood against the wall twenty yards from Redfield.

It was ten minutes before a train came.

Redfield got on at the front of the car, Ré at the rear. Redfield stood. Ré sat where he could see Redfield through the scrim of passengers but could not himself be seen.

Redfield got off at One Hundred Tenth Street. Ré followed, walking behind three nuns.

Redfield started north on Broadway, then turned suddenly. If he had looked, he would've seen Ré face to face, but he didn't; he went into a deli.

Ré retreated to the corner and stood behind a newsstand next to the subway stairs.

Redfield came out in five minutes carrying a brown paper bag. He walked north on Broadway—passing the Gold Rail—and turned east on One Hundred Eleventh Street.

174

Ré glanced in the window as he passed the Gold Rail, but he knew he wouldn't see Linda or she him. She worked at night.

Redfield walked down One Hundred Eleventh to a building near the end of the block and went inside.

It was Linda's building.

Ré stopped, stood still for a moment, then walked back to Broadway and back down to the Gold Rail. He went in and ordered a beer—a Bud.

THIRTY - ONE

One of Bloomfield's ten men, a cop named Tough—he was known as Extra Tough and had been called E.T. long before the popular motion picture gave the initials an irrevocable other meaning—found the manuscript at the bottom of a gigantic bag of trash on the fourth floor of the Shoreham Hotel. It was soaked with coffee and stank of the remains of somebody's breakfast.

Neuman placed it in the middle of his desk and poked at it with a letter opener. "Now who the fuck is going to read this?"

"Lieutenant?" Federici said.

"Yeah?"

"I know you're down on him, but Mike Mazilli, he's not a bad cop, and he knows how to speed-read."

"Speed-read?"

"Speed-read. You know, that thing where you move your finger down the page and you can read a book in about twenty minutes."

"Twenty minutes," Neuman said.

"Well, maybe not twenty minutes, lieutenant. Maybe an hour. But fast. I've seen him go through the sports pages in about three minutes—on a Monday, with all the Sunday scores."

"Go get him," Neuman said. "Put somebody else on that phone."

When Mazilli had been gotten, Neuman said, "Get your chin up off the floor, Mike. You look like you think I'm going to tell you you're going to be walking a beat in Staten Island. I'm not going to tell you that, I want you to do something for us. This manuscript here— it's a little wet and smelly, but from what Detective Federici says you won't take very long to read it—this manuscript is an uncorrected carbon copy, meaning that if the author made a typo on the original she didn't bother to make the correction on the copy too, it was just for safekeeping; it's an uncorrected carbon copy of a novel that was written by a woman who was murdered, and we have reason to believe that the murderer may be in the book, not in so many words or anything, but as, you know, a character. We have reason to believe especially that the murderer may be a character named Beau, so don't spend a lot of time going over parts of the book that Beau isn't in, just the ones he is in, and as soon as you come across anything that gives a hint as to who Beau is in real life—that's Beau B-e-a-u, not B-o—give a holler. You can take this down the hall to Detective Randolph's desk, he won't be needing it, he's on vacation, the lucky son-of-a-bitch. Any questions, Mike?"

"No, sir," Mazilli said. "Thank you, sir."

"Yeah, well," Neuman said. When Mazilli had gone, carrying the manuscript carefully before him, Neuman said, "Now what?"

Federici handed him a slip of paper. "You wanted to see the note the killer sent to the papers, lieutenant. Here's the one he sent to the *Times*. I got it from the guy I owed a favor, he paid me back. The thing of it is, as you'll see, he didn't send a separate letter to each paper, he just made carbon copies. And all it says, as you'll see—"

"Let me look at it, will you, Steve?" Neuman said. "I won't see anything if you don't let me look at it."

"Sorry, lieutenant," Federici said.

Neuman read the note:

Martha Wine was number three. There will be more.

"He's in a hurry," Neuman said.

"That's what I thought," Federici said. "I mean, such a short note, and making carbons. He's in a hurry."

"Somebody's getting close to him," Neuman said.

"That's what I thought," Federici said.

"I wonder if it's us," Neuman said.

The buzzer rang.

"It's Tough," Federici said.

"What's tough?" Neuman said.

"Tough, the cop who found the manuscript in the garbage. I put him on the phone in place of Mazilli. There must be a call."

Neuman went to the phone that had an extension for the special number, picked up the receiver, and listened.

"This is Patrolman Tough speaking," Neuman heard. "How may I be of assistance to you?"

"I want to talk to a detective," a man said.

"What is the nature of your communication?" Tough said.

Why, Neuman wondered, did all cops talk that way on the phone? They didn't talk like that on the street. On the street, Tough would've said, What do you want?

"I want to speak to Neuman," the man said. "Lieutenant Jacob Neuman."

"Are you calling with information regarding the perpetrator of the shooting incident on the southbound Broadway local at approximately—"

"This is Neuman," Neuman said. "I've got it, Tough."

"Yes, sir."

There was a pause during which Neuman knew Tough was wondering whether to tell Neuman that the tape was rolling. He silently pleaded with him not to. He didn't.

"Hello," Neuman said. "This is Lieutenant Neuman. . . . What do you want?"

"You're looking for the man who killed those three women?"

"That's correct," Neuman said. "However, the number you called is not the number we gave out for information regarding those crimes. The number you called is a number set up in an attempt to establish the identity of the perpetrator of—" He was doing it too; it must be something about the telephone; it discouraged ordinary conversation. "Why'd you call this number?"

177

The man snorted softly. "What difference does it make? I wanted to talk to you. I'm talking to you."

"The only difference it makes," Neuman said, "is maybe you called this number because you happen to know it by heart because you happen to be the guy who killed not only the punk on the subway but Clarence Stearns and Joe Smith too, and who's looking for Bobby Redfield."

There was a long pause, after which Neuman said, "Ré?"

Another pause. Then Ré said, "Give me another number to call—a number you don't have tapped. And don't put a trace on the number I'm calling from."

"Why should I do that, Ré?"

"I know who killed those women."

"Yeah, well. I know you killed three men and're looking to kill a fourth."

"I don't want Redfield," Ré said. "You can have him."

"Oh? And why would I want him? I want him safe, is all—safe from you."

Another pause. Then Ré said, "I'm calling from a phone booth in a bar on Broadway. I'll give you the name when I'm hanging up. Don't bother to send a patrol car. I won't be here when they get here. You can get here in five minutes from where you are."

"How do you know where I am, Ré?"

"I'll call the number in eight minutes—the number of the booth. Then we'll talk."

"Why can't we talk now, Ré?"

"The Gold Rail. On Broadway."

Ré hung up.

"Shit," Neuman said.

McIver put his head in the door. "We traced the general area, loo. Somewhere on—"

"Broadway," Neuman said. "One-Ten and Broadway. The Gold Rail. I'm going alone. I want backup. I want backup for the backup. But I want everybody—*everybody*—to be real, real quiet. No sirens, no heavy brakes, none of this SWAT shit. I want to be sneaky."

THIRTY - TWO

The phone rang three minutes after Neuman arrived at the Gold Rail, eight minutes after Ré hung up.

"Right on time," Neuman said.

"Redfield's on One Hundred Eleventh Street," Ré said. "The building with the awning, almost at the corner of Amsterdam. In the apartment of a woman named Linda Walsh. Apartment Four-B—"

"B as in balls, Ré?" Neuman said. "I must say you got a lot of balls. That was clever, real clever, getting me off that phone. Another two minutes, we'd've had white-tops driving up the side of this booth. You must be close by, though, hunh? You in another booth, or're you calling from an apartment?"

"Redfield killed those women," Ré said.

"And I'm the king of Siam, Ré," Neuman said. "Or what's it called nowadays? Thailand?"

"You cops," Ré said. "You're so loyal to your partners that you can't see the dirt on their faces."

"The only dirty face I want to see, Ré, is yours. So why don't you do me a favor and just come back to this bar, your hands out in the open, and we'll do our talking face to face instead of on the phone? I can't talk on the phone. I get headaches, I start losing my train of thought. Where're you calling from anyway, Ré? Another bar? I think I hear a ball game in the background, or is that just the ball game they got on the tube here?"

Three minutes nearly had passed. If the operator came on asking for more money, Neuman would at least know that Ré was in a pay phone. Big deal, Neuman thought.

"Last Saturday morning," Ré said, "Redfield left his apartment at twelve thirty and took a cab—"

"*Your three minutes are up,*" an operator's recorded voice said. "*Please deposit five cents for an additional three minutes.*"

179

Neuman heard a coin fall.

"Maybe I should call you, Ré," Neuman said, "so you don't use up all your change."

"—he took a cab to Sussex Towers on Central Park West. . . . Does that address mean anything to you, Neuman?"

"Yeah."

"Chris Kaiser's address," Ré said. "He got there at about twenty to one—"

"How do you know all this, Ré?" Neuman said. "What've you been doing, following him?"

"That's the point, Neuman," Ré said. "I've been following him. If you know about me, if you know about Stearns and Smith, about Redfield, about 'Nam, then you know I've been following him. That's the point."

That was indeed, Neuman was afraid, the point.

McIver came in the bar, trying not to look like a cop, but looking like nothing but. Neuman waved at him and when he came to the booth wrote a note on his pad and handed it to McIver:

Pay phone. Maybe a bar. No uniforms. Just clothes. Don't take him. Just watch.

McIver left.

"You there, Neuman?" Ré said.

"Uh, yeah. You were saying? About Bobby going to Chris Kaiser's apartment?"

"He had a key to the lobby door. The doorman left the door for a few minutes. Redfield let himself in then, took the elevator to the top floor—"

"How do you know that, Ré? Were you in there with him?"

"I could see the elevator panel from the front door."

"Right."

"Chris Kaiser came home a little after one, in a taxi. The doorman was back by then. He let her in, she took the elevator up to the top floor. Redfield came down about five minutes later—not out the front door, out a side door on Seventieth Street. He walked up to Seventy-second and got a cab. . . . You want to hear more?"

"Yeah, Ré, I'd like to hear more."

180

"You want another dead woman on your hands?" Ré said.

"Meaning what?"

"Meaning Linda Walsh."

"Oh, yeah. Linda Walsh. What was that address again?"

"Okay, Neuman, I'll give you more. Sunday night, Monday morning. West Twelfth Street. Redfield, on foot this time, he parked his car over by the river, rings the bell of a woman named Susannah Keyes. No, I wasn't with him, Neuman, I saw him push the bell, I went up on the steps after he went inside and looked at the bell he'd pushed and read the name. Susannah Keyes. He was there a long time—three hours—"

"Don't you ever sleep, Ré?" Neuman said.

"When he left he walked to Sixth Avenue and mailed some letters—it looked like more than one—in a box on the corner. Then he took a cab over to the river and got his car."

The receiver was hot in Neuman's hands. The earpiece hurt his ear. "And what about Saturday morning, at the Shoreham Hotel?"

"Good," Ré said. "You're catching on. Redfield—"

"Wait," Neuman said. "Let me try. . . . I had a meet set up with a woman at the Shoreham at eleven. I figured I'd go alone, no sense dragging a lot of people downtown. I told Bobby—Redfield—to come in at noon, by which time I figured the meet'd be over, we could discuss what I'd found out. . . . Redfield went to the Shoreham ahead of me, right?"

"About ten-fifteen," Ré said. "He took a cab down from his apartment to the Plaza Hotel, then walked to the Shoreham."

"He go in the front door?" Neuman said.

"Yeah."

"How long was he in there?"

"Ten minutes, at most."

"He come out the front door?"

"Yeah, and walked over to Fifty-first and Lexington, took the subway uptown. To the stationhouse, I figured, or maybe his apartment. I didn't follow him. I went back to the Shoreham."

"And saw me go in," Neuman said. "A little before eleven."

"And then saw a lot of reinforcements."

"Including Bobby—Redfield—who was at his desk when I called in the homicide."

"I wouldn't know," Ré said.

"Who's Linda Walsh, Ré?" Neuman said. And why hadn't he given McIver her address? Did he still not get the point?

"A woman I know. She thinks . . ."

"Thinks what, Ré?"

"That I killed those women."

"Why is that?"

"I've been out a lot. Out when they were killed."

"Out following Bobby?"

"Yeah."

For want of anything to say, Neuman said, "What's with this phone? They haven't asked for more money in a while."

"I put in a quarter."

"Right . . . Ré?"

"Yeah?"

"What did you find out, when you went to California last year?"

"You know a lot, don't you?"

"I know a little. I don't know as much as I should."

"I found out my folks had died of shame, that my girl had run away—out of shame. She got into stuff she couldn't handle, wasn't made to handle. It . . . it killed her."

"Ré?"

"Yeah?"

"I have to go talk to my men for a minute. Just a minute. I want to get some of them over to Linda's place—"

"Go quietly. He's expecting me. He's waiting to kill me."

"Yeah, I know, Ré. I get the point. . . . Will you still be here when I get back—still be on this phone, I mean?"

"No."

"No, I can't say I blame you. Do me a favor, though, will you? Call me tomorrow morning, say, at the number you called before. If I'm not there, someone'll find me. I want to talk to you some more."

"I'll be gone by tomorrow."

"Call me long distance, then. Collect."

"Good luck, lieutenant. You have that address?"

"I got it," Neuman said, "And I got the point."

McIver came running up to Neuman outside the bar. "Zip, loo. We checked every pay phone we could find between here and One Twenty. Bars, restaurants, on the street. There must be a million phones in this area. We didn't even start on the schools—Barnard, Columbia. They probably have about a million apiece."

"Forget it," Neuman said. "We're going to One Hundred Eleventh Street, a building with an awning almost at Amsterdam. Apartment Four-B as in . . . boy. We're going very quiet, very sneaky."

Federici came running up. "Mazilli called on the radio, lieutenant. He found stuff about Beau. He's like a private detective. And get this, loo—he's got a tattoo. A big tattoo all over his shoulder and back—like Stearns, like Smith, like Chavez, like Keller, like . . ."

Neuman nodded.

"Jesus, lieutenant."

"Yeah," Neuman said.

"There must be an explanation, Jake," McIver said.

"Yeah. The explanation to why all these years we've been partners I've never seen Bobby with his shirt off. I guess he thought it was something to hide. I guess he was right."

THIRTY - THREE

7:27, 7:28, 7:29.

Linda watched the digital clock tick off the minutes.

7:30.

"This doesn't seem very—I don't know—official," Linda said.

At the window, Redfield grunted.

183

"I mean, where's your partner? Aren't you the famous team, Redford and Newman?"

Redfield moved to the other window, which looked out on Amsterdam Avenue.

"I mean, I don't get this at all. You said it yourself—he said he was leaving, he left, he's not coming back. Why should he come back?"

Redfield laughed. "You *don't* get this at all, do you, Linda?"

"I *said* I didn't get it. . . . Can I turn a light on?"

Redfield pressed himself against the wall to see farther down the street.

7:36, 7:37.

"If this is how cops spend their time, it's no wonder this city's such a hellhole. For all you know, he could be out killing some other woman right now."

7:39, 7:40.

"Can I turn on the radio?"

Redfield glanced over his shoulder at her. "Fix me something to eat, will you? Some soup or something. Don't turn the kitchen light on."

Linda laughed. With a swagger in her voice, she said, "'Fix me somethin' ta eat, will ya? Some soup or somethin'.' . . . You've got to be kidding. This is the nineteen eighties, Jack. You want some soup, you can fucking well fix it yourself."

Redfield came to her, drew a pistol from his shoulder holster, and placed the end of the barrel against her lips. "Now, cunt."

Linda amazed herself by pushing the gun barrel away and spitting dryly. Then she got up with exaggerated fussiness. "Oh, fuck, I'll make some eggs. I'll make an omelet. You like westerns? I make a good western."

Redfield caught up with her and shoved her aside and went into the kitchen ahead of her. He opened drawers until he found the utensils. He grabbed handfuls of knives, handfuls of forks, and dumped them in the garbage can. He took the paring knife, butcher knife, and bread knife down from the magnetized board on the wall and dumped them in the garbage can. With his pistol still pointed at her, he opened the door to the service elevator, lifted the garbage can out into the hallway, closed the door, double-locked and latched it. He opened cabinets until he found the canned food, took down a can of minestrone soup, put it in the electric can opener, pressed the switch, removed the top from the opener, and sailed the lid out the partly open kitchen window. "Soup."

Linda laughed.

Redfield hit her in the mouth with the back of his free hand, sending her sprawling backward over the table. She fell onto a chair, rolled, broke her final fall with her hands, came up sitting under the table, and stayed there. "You crazy fuck."

The phone rang.

"Answer it," Redfield said.

"Answer it yourself, motherfucker."

Redfield dragged the table away, grabbed her under an arm, and lifted her to her feet. He thrust her against the wall on which the wall phone hung. Her momentum knocked the receiver from the hook. It hit the floor, bounced up on the coiled cord, fell, and hit the floor again.

Linda screamed. Something struck her behind the ear. It hurt at first, then turned into a sweet sensation. Her head grew lighter and lighter and lifted her feet up off the ground. She flew higher and higher, then fell slowly, slowly, slowly to the floor, which was soft and billowed under her as she landed.

THIRTY - FOUR

"Shit," Neuman said.

"What, Jake?" McIver said.

"Somebody answered—dropped the phone, like; it bounced on something a couple of times. A woman screamed. There was a sound like somebody sapped somebody. Then the phone got hung up."

"You going to call back?"

"I guess." Neuman dialed the number again, listened, hung up. "Busy. Off the hook, probably."

"I can call Verification, lieutenant," Federici said. "They can tell whether it's busy or off the hook."

"It's off the hook," Neuman said. "You can call, but it's off the hook. He's not going to talk to us. He's been on this end of deals like this. He knows how we can wear you down."

They were in the Green Tree Restaurant, which they had commandeered to use as an operations center. The owner, dismayed at first as he watched his customers herded out the door, some of them having been routed in the middle of their entrées, was mollified when told it might be a long night, that there would be a lot of cops to be fed and provided with coffee, that the city would foot the bill.

Neuman, who had done the mollifying, hoped the city would.

Federici, having called Verification, reported that the phone was off the hook.

"Now what?" Neuman said.

"We need more men if we're going to do this right, Jake," McIver said.

"We ask for more men, we tell them why, we'll get Special Services, we'll get the hostage negotiators, they'll take this away from us," Neuman said.

"Maybe it's best, Jake," McIver said. "You're too close to it."

"Tim's right, loo," Bloomfield said. "You're too close to it."

"You're fucking right I'm close to it. He's my partner."

"Not anymore, Jake," McIver said.

McGovern hung up another phone. "I got the super, loo. Name's Ruiz. Doesn't live in that building, lives across the street. He's coming over with keys and to give us the layout."

"Lieutenant?" Federici said.

"Yeah?"

"I'd like to go up, lieutenant. I mean, I volunteer."

"Thanks, Steve, but I'll go up."

"Jake," McIver said.

"He's my partner, Tim. You say he's not my partner anymore, but I

186

say he's still my partner and I say he's in trouble and who the fuck else should go but me."

"I say we don't go up at all," McIver said. "I say we wait him out. A day, two days. He's got to sleep."

"There's a woman up there, for Christ's sake, Tim," Neuman said. "An innocent woman. I can starve him out, wait him out, wear him down, but I can't do that to her."

McGovern brought a slight Hispanic man to the table. "This is Ruiz, loo. The super."

"Have a seat, Mr. Ruiz," Neuman said, "and thanks for coming out on a Sunday night on such short notice like this. You have keys, I guess. You want to show me what's what?"

Ruiz explained the keys: one for the downstairs door, two for the front door of the apartment, two for the rear door, which opened onto the service elevator.

"The front and rear doors—they have chains on them?" Neuman said.

Chains and latches, Ruiz said.

Neuman tossed the keys and caught them. "So these won't do me a hell of a lot of good, will they? Oh, well, I guess I didn't really expect to just walk in like it was my own place or anything. Here's a napkin, Mr. Ruiz, and here's a pen. Could you draw me a map of the layout of the apartment? It doesn't have to be beautiful, just a rough map."

Ruiz drew a rectangle—"This is the living room"—and on its right a narrower rectangle—"This is the bedroom"—and on its left a square—"This is the kitchen and dining room." He made marks for the doors and windows.

"That's real simple, isn't it?" Neuman said. "There's a bathroom, too, I guess. You must've left it out."

Ruiz smote his forehead and drew a small square in one corner of the bedroom.

"Good," Neuman said. "Your basic apartment. One way in, one way out. Two in this case, but it's really the same thing because I guess somebody has to come and get you in the service elevator, right? You can't run it yourself."

Ruiz said that was right.

"And there's no fire escape," Neuman said. "Just the fire stairs, right?"

Ruiz said that was right.

Neuman stood up, tucked in his shirt, smoothed his hair, felt his whiskers. "I'm going up."

"For Christ's sake, Jake," McIver said. "We haven't evacuated the building yet. You can't just go up there, not with hundreds of civilians in their apartments. They'll throw the book at you, Jake. Honest to God."

Neuman tossed the keys and caught them. "Tim, you've been on things like this before. You know as well as I do that going by the book means making a lot of noise. White-tops all over the place, snipers behind the fenders, cops in flak jackets running into the building, breaking down doors, stomping up and down the hallways hollering on bullhorns, women screaming, kids crying, guys yelling that their home is their castle, you can't make me leave if I don't want to, where's your warrant? pigs, Nazis, fascists, the whole bit. Then you got to get the people out of the building, some of them down the same hallways this apartment's on, you got to get them in wagons or buses, you got to take them someplace till the thing's over, feed them, give them coffee, donuts, sandwiches. Meanwhile, everybody else in every other building on the block is hanging out the windows trying to see what's going on, standing out on the sidewalks kibitzing, drinking beer from bags, generally having a good time being in the fucking way. . . .

"The way it is now, hardly anybody knows we're here. The people in the building don't know, the people on the block don't know, even Bobby's not sure—unless he made Bloomfield when I sent him across the street to have a look."

"He didn't make me, loo," Bloomfield said. "I'm sure of it."

"So even Bobby's not sure," Neuman said. "And that's the way I'd like to keep it, 'cause the more noise that gets made, the more people who're around, the shorter everybody's fuse gets. The snipers want to snipe, the guys with the gas want to throw the gas, the guy inside starts thinking, Well, if I'm going to go I might as well take a few people with me. I don't want that. The way it is now, I can go up there, tell him, Look, so far the only evidence I've got against you is the word of someone I may never see again, although I'm going to have to send somebody around to your apartment and see if you've got a typewriter like the typewriter used to type the notes, to see if you've got a thirty-eight Smith with a silencer, to see if maybe you've got the original of Susannah Keyes's manuscript stuck in a drawer somewhere—"

"It's done, Jake," McIver said.

"What's done?"

"I called Klinger when you were back in the head. I told him what's going on, told him we needed a warrant to search Bobby's apartment. I know I shouldn't've done it without telling you, but I felt you were too close to it. I still do. Klinger said he'd take care of it, that he'd be over right after he got off the phone with the judge."

"With more troops?" Neuman said.

"With more troops."

Neuman tossed the keys and caught them. "In that case, I'm going up." He started for the door.

"Jake?" McIver called.

Neuman stopped but didn't turn around. "You're going to tell me Klinger said you should take over. You're going to tell me he said you should arrest me if I didn't follow your orders, take my gun away, my badge, my cuffs. You're going to tell me if I don't give you these keys you're going to have to take them at gunpoint. You're—"

"All I'm going to tell you, Jake," McIver said, "is good luck."

Neuman started up again. "Thanks. When Klinger gets here, try to keep him from making too much noise."

THIRTY - FIVE

Before letting himself in the front door—why, he knew not—Neuman read all the names on the buzzers: Follett, White, Muldoon, Cosby, Imperiali, Singleton, Kammerstein, Neuberger, Olmedo, Flam, Reed, Esposito, Worsley, Webb, Freund, Jeffries, Neal, Whitesides, Hubble, Walsh, Arnold, Morgan, Greenburger, Neuman.

He wondered if Neuman was any relation. He wondered if Worsley was Gump, who used to play goalie for the Rangers, and if Esposito, his neighbor, was Phil, another hockey player.

He told himself to stop wondering and get moving. He opened the door, went to the elevator, pressed the button, waited, saw that the car was already on the ground floor, got in, debated going to three or to five, decided he'd rather walk down than up, pressed five, and rode the elevator up.

The car stopped. Neuman started to get out, then realized he'd neglected to ask the super where 4-B was in relation to the elevator and the stairs, and whether there was a doorway from the main hallway to the service elevator hallway. He thought about going all the way back to the restaurant, then realized he could find out by checking out the fifth floor, got out, checked, found that 5-B was two doors down from the elevator on the left side and that the third door down on the left was the door to the service elevator hallway.

He was not at all pleased with the way his mind was working.

Nor his body, either, for when he started down the stairs to the fourth floor he nearly tripped and went tumbling down to the landing. He got his balance, sat down on a step, let his adrenaline get back to normal, and walked carefully the rest of the way, holding on with both hands, like a child.

Someone on the fourth floor was frying chicken. Someone else was watching television. Someone else was talking loudly—on a tele-

190

phone, Neuman guessed, for there was no audible reply. From inside 4-B he could hear nothing. No light showed under the door.

Neuman went down the hall to the door to the service elevator hallway, opened it as quietly as he could, slipped inside, turned, and nearly fell over a kitchen garbage can brimming with knives. He stood very still for a long time, trying to figure out the meaning of this. He couldn't figure it out.

No light showed under the door from the kitchen. From inside, there was no sound.

Through the hallway window, which opened onto an airshaft, came the wail of a siren.

Fucking Klinger, Neuman thought, then listened more closely and heard that it was an ambulance, headed for St. Luke's perhaps.

The Green Tree. St. Luke's. This apartment building. They were all within a stone's throw of one another. They had been so close, if this was where Ré had been staying, to Ré. He, Neuman, had been so close to Redfield.

Neuman took a deep breath, then another, then pounded twice with the soft part of his hand on the door to the kitchen. "Bobby?"

Inside, someone stirred. A chair scraped.

Neuman moved away from the door, pressing himself against the wall. "Bobby, it's Jake."

The chair scraped again. There was the unmistakable sound of a revolver being cocked.

Neuman put his hand inside his coat and touched the butt of his pistol—a gesture he had had, as a young detective, to teach himself not to make. By reassuring yourself that your gun was there, you alerted everyone else to the fact that you were armed—everyone you didn't want to know, that is.

The lie sounded tinny from the moment Neuman began to speak. "Bobby, we got Ré. We got him down the block. Somebody called nine-one-one to report a suspicious man hanging around the corner. The cops who answered the call recognized his description from the all-points. They frisked him and found that book he'd been reading. What's it called? *Pilgrim on Tinker's Creek*? He told us about the stuff in 'Nam. He told us he's been tracking you, that he saw you

191

come up here with what's-her-name—Linda. So it's in the bag, Bob. Let's go downstairs and wrap this up. Hey, nice work, thinking he'd follow you here. Only thing is"—Neuman laughed and winced at its hollowness—"you should've told somebody else what you were doing."

Water ran in the sink. A glass clinked, burbled as it was filled. The water stopped running.

Neuman took the keys from his pocket and jingled them. "Bobby, I got keys from the super. I'm going to open this door so we can talk better. There's a chain on it, right, so you don't have to worry about me coming in. I'll just open it a crack and we'll be able to talk better. I could use a glass of water myself. It's hotter than hell in this hallway. There must be heat pipes, or hot water pipes, or something, in these walls. . . . Bobby? I'm alone."

Always expect the unexpected. That had been the dictum of Sergeant Hubert L. Stevens, Neuman's most memorable instructor at the Police Academy. "Think about everything that could happen, then figure it won't 'cause that sucker doesn't want you to know what he's going to do. Then think about everything that you can't think of and figure one of them'll happen, 'cause that's the way that sucker's mind's working."

Neuman was caught with his figurative pants down, for all he'd been thinking was that Redfield wouldn't respond until he started unlocking the door with the keys, then would tell him to stop, to back away from the door, to get the fuck out of there.

Instead, when Neuman had unlocked the top lock and then the bottom lock, Redfield, who had used the noise of the locks turning to cover the sound of his slipping the latch and the chain, yanked open the door and pointed his gun at Neuman's head.

Neuman shrugged. "I guess I wanted you to take me. I mean, they say you get what you want. It's like you wanted to get caught—writing notes, pushing your luck by going after these women in public places, leaving things around your apartment so we could find them. Wasn't it you who said that to somebody the other day—that the guy who killed those women wanted to get caught?—Or was it me? I don't know. I forget."

192

Redfield aimed his gun at Neuman's heart. "Take it out real slow, Jake. With two fingers. By the butt."

Neuman did as he was told and held his pistol out to Redfield like a boy showing his mother a dead mouse.

"Toss it out the window," Redfield said, jerking his chin toward the airshaft.

"Hey, Bob. This is a good gun. I mean, it used to be. I haven't fired it in years, except on the range. I don't want to bust it up."

"Come on, Jake. I don't have time for your bullshitting."

Neuman looked sadly at the gun, then at the window, then back at Redfield. "There might be some wino sleeping one off down at the bottom of this thing. I don't want—"

Redfield snatched the gun from Neuman's hand, started to toss it out the window, stopped himself, and slipped it in the back of his pants, under his leather coat. Neuman saw another gun in a hip holster.

Neuman shrugged. "I guess you meant—"

"Get inside," Redfield said, holding the barrel of his gun an inch from Neuman's temple.

Neuman went inside the kitchen, shutting his eyes and clenching them so that when he opened them they would be somewhat accustomed to darkness. The first thing he saw when he opened them was a human form crumpled on the floor beneath the wall phone, whose receiver dangled from its cord. "Oh, no, Bobby. No."

"Sit in the chair, Jake," Redfield said. "Get your cuffs out—you never carry anything else and you better not be carrying now—get your cuffs out, cuff your right wrist, put both hands out behind you, around the back of the chair."

Neuman did as he was told. "Bobby, if she's . . . I mean . . . you should let me call an ambulance."

Redfield slipped the chain of the cuffs through the rung of the chair and back out again before snapping the bracelet on Neuman's left wrist.

For some reason—the workings of his mind were a mystery to him—Neuman thought of the whore, Valentine, and of her dream of going to Arizona. He would have liked to be there with her. He might even have left Maria if he could have been there rather than here. "So, Bob, this isn't a situation I ever expected to be in—me cuffed to a chair and you standing over me packing three guns, at least; maybe you've got—"

"Jake," Redfield said. "It's not going to work. This time, the talking's not going to work."

Neuman laughed. "I guess I didn't really think it would. I mean, out in the hall there I thought it might. I thought if we could have a nice friendly talk, no guns or anything, just you and me on either side of—"

Redfield left the room—to look, Neuman guessed, out the windows of the other rooms.

"You see, Bob?" Neuman called. "Like I said, I'm alone. Just me and my shadow. Nobody knows I'm here. Hey, I was kidding before— about Ré? We didn't bag him. He called us, told us you were here, but we didn't bag him."

Redfield reappeared at the door, a dark silhouette, looking bigger than Neuman remembered. "Called *us*, Jake? Or called you?"

"Oh, hey, no. Me. He called me. Did I say us? You know how it is, you work with somebody a long time you start saying us when you mean me. I mean, it's like being married."

"I wouldn't know," Redfield said.

Neuman could no longer play the clown. "What is it, Bob? What is it with you and women? I guess I can sort of understand a guy like you being pissed off about a woman like Chris Kaiser. I mean, you're the same age, you're smart, you're good-looking—not in the way she was good-looking but good-looking still—and she's making a couple of million bucks a year and you're making thirty grand and not having your picture plastered all over town and having people treat you like some kind of movie star or something. And Keyes—well, I don't know what it was about Keyes. I don't understand women like that, I don't know how their minds work, I wouldn't know what to say to one if I met her at a party. Not that I go to parties, but you know what I mean. It's like they're aliens, from another world. I don't have anything against them—whatever gets you through the night—but I don't understand them. Maybe it's the same with you, hunh? You don't understand them and you don't like them writing books about it, about you. . . .

"In case you're wondering, we found the carbon copy of the manuscript you dumped at the hotel. That wasn't too smart, but I gues you didn't have much choice. Like I said, we found the carbon copy and one of the cops—Mazilli, you know Mazilli; I almost forgot you knew Mazilli—it turns out Mazilli's a whatdoyoucallit—a speed reader. He read the whole book in about five minutes. Told us all about Beau, the private eye with the tattoo on his shoulder. You know, Bob, what if you'd had a partner who was into physical shit, who liked to go to the gym, work out, swim, take a steam bath? You'd've had to keep your shirt on in the shower, or else everybody'd've known about the tattoo. Not that they would've known what it meant, but still. You were lucky you got a fat, lazy fuck like me for a partner. . . .

"You did a lot of dumb things, Bob. You really did want to get caught. Those notes. We haven't searched your place yet, but Klinger's getting a warrant. I'll bet we find the typewriter sitting out on a desk, and maybe the original of the book too. We probably won't find the thirty-eight, you've got that on your belt, and the silencer in your pocket, I guess. Killing Chris Kaiser was dumb when it turned out you knew her, were—what?—lovers for a while. Telling Bloomfield you were going to search the garbage at the hotel was dumb— telling him and then not doing it. If you'd said you'd done it, who the fuck would've known? You wanted to get caught."

"It's not easy, Jake," Redfield said. He had stood silently through all this, looking out the kitchen window, his back to Neuman. "I'll be glad when it's over."

"When did it start, Bob?" Neuman said gently. "When did you start feeling it was something you had to do? I remember you saying about the nurse—what's-her-name, the one Carlos grabbed on the subway?—I remember you saying that ever since 'Nam you couldn't see an Oriental woman without thinking maybe she was packing a grenade that had your name on it. But that doesn't go for all women, does it? Women don't pack grenades, not as a rule, not in my experience."

195

Redfield laughed softly. "In mine, they do—in a manner of speaking."

"They're ballbreakers, you mean?" Neuman said.

Another laugh.

"Well, maybe they are, but so are we, wouldn't you say? I mean, we're whatever the equivalent would be: tit-wringers or whatever you'd call it. I mean, everybody's tough on everybody else; it seems to be human nature. But that's no reason to kill people. . . . This woman here, Linda Walsh, is she, uh . . . ?"

"I sapped her with my gun," Redfield said. "When she screamed into the phone. I can't stand it when women scream. I can't stand women's voices. Screaming when they come. Christ, you should've heard Susannah scream when she came. And then she writes a book saying men don't make it as lovers. Shit."

"You knew her that well, too," Neuman said. "There sure was a lot I didn't know about you, Bobby. Christ, I know more about some of my worst enemies than I knew about you."

Redfield turned away from the window. "Who's downstairs, Jake? Special Services, or just your people?"

"I was trying to hold it to just my people," Neuman said, "but Special Services was on the way when I came up. If I were you, I wouldn't stay around here a minute longer. I'd go over the roof and try to get down through another building. You can go all the way to Broadway on these roofs. You may still have time, but you don't have much."

Redfield turned back to the window. "I've been running a long time, Jake. I don't feel like running anymore. . . . How did Ré make it—make it out of 'Nam? Did he tell you?"

"No," Neuman said. "No, he didn't. . . . You know, Bob, the DA's not going to have much of a case against you at this point. I mean, the word of a known murderer who says he just happened to see you going in and out of various buildings at the time women in them were getting murdered. I mean, unless there's some hard evidence—a typewriter, the kind of paper the notes were written on, the gun—"

"You'll find all that, Jake," Redfield said. "The typewriter's on a

196

desk, like you said, along with a stack of paper. The novel's in a drawer. The gun's on my hip. The silencer's in my coat pocket."

"Shit, Bobby, why? Why, why, why?"

Redfield turned and sat on the windowsill, leaning against the pane.

Neuman wanted to tell him to be careful: the glass might break, a sniper might shoot him in the back. He said nothing.

"Why?" Redfield said. "I've been trying to tell you why. It wasn't just 'Nam. That was part of it, but it's too easy to blame it all on 'Nam. I saw some terrible things there, and did some terrible things, but I survived, and that was what it was all about. It wasn't about winning or losing, it was about living. Coming back was the hard part. You've heard all this, it sounds like bullshit, but it's true. We were treated like outcasts, like killers, rapists, savages—like losers. The people in the neighborhood, my family, they were afraid to look me in the eye, afraid to shake my hand, afraid to give me a hug, a kiss. I was covered with blood, and they didn't want to be contaminated. Women were the worst. They'd fuck their brains out, get off on being with an ex-GI, then they'd curl up in a corner of the bed and moan about how they'd been ruined, letting themselves be touched by a murderer."

"Not all of them, Bob," Neuman said. "It can't have been all of them. You just landed the wrong ones. You didn't give yourself a chance to find the right one."

"What's *all*, Jake? What does it matter if it was one or two or ten or twenty? It was happening. You know and I know that everyone out there isn't a murderer. But we also know that some people are, and that those few're enough to make this city the sewer it is, this country the sewer it is, this world the sewer it is. So what's all? . . . The antiwar types, the ones who marched in marches—Christ, they were smug. 'I told you so, you naughty boy. I told you the war was immoral, illegal, unconstitutional.' Shit. Unconstitutional. I just did what I was told by people I'd been taught to respect: presidents, senators, generals. It hasn't been told yet, Jake—somebody'll write a book about it someday, about how the antiwar movement wasn't what it was cracked up to be. Oh, there were a lot of people, but half of them, two thirds of them, maybe ninety percent of them—they were in it for the sex and the drugs. . . ."

197

Over Redfield's shoulder, Neuman thought he saw a movement on a rooftop across the street. He tried not to look at it, but he had to. A pigeon flew up and away.

Strange, Neuman thought. Pigeons didn't fly at night. Or did they?

"Chris was into that antiwar shit," Redfield went on. "And the feminist shit that went on along with it. She had pictures of herself that had been in newspapers and magazines, her with crowds of other women marching in Los Angeles—that was where she was from— San Francisco, Washington, marching for abortion, marching against something else, marching, marching. In one, she's right up in the front of the march, wearing a cotton blouse, like one of those Indian blouses a lot of women wore in the sixties. You can see her tits. I don't mean you can just sort of see them. You can *see* them. She might as well have not been wearing anything at all. So where's the logic, Jake? 'Don't treat me as a sex object.' 'Here're my tits.' It was the same thing when she got famous. 'I'm a serious professional.' 'If you look fast, you can see my crotch through the slit in my skirt when I cross my legs.' Is there a tradeoff? If a guy makes it big in any business, can he get away with coming to work with his shirt open and pants so tight his balls bulge out? He can't. You ever read any Freud, Jake? He said, 'Anatomy is destiny,' that you are what your sex was meant to be. Women were meant to have children. More than that, they were meant to fuck. They know it. Every last one of them. But they feel guilty about it, so they put on airs. They talk about careers, about feminism, about equality. But all they want to do is fuck, and they can't even keep it a secret. They get a job on television, do they just do the job? They do not; they wear clothes that say fuck me."

Neuman could make out Redfield's eyes in the dark, so it stood to reason that Redfield could make out his and would see him staring at the rooftop across the screen. If there were a sniper there, it was of particular concern to Neuman, because if the sniper missed Redfield, he would hit him. "Bob, I—"

But Redfield got off the windowsill of his own volition. "You read the letters, Jake. I don't need to say more. It's what I feel. You have to act based on how you feel." He went into the living room, then on into the bedroom.

198

Neuman heard water running in the bathroom. He stood as best he could, which wasn't well at all, tried to walk, managed to hop, hopped toward the wall phone, tried to get his chin up to the hook to depress it and get a dial tone, couldn't, nearly pitched forward onto Linda Walsh's body, got his balance, hopped back to where he had been, but, thankfully, less directly in front of the window.

Redfield came out of the bathroom, out of the bedroom, and walked to the living room window.

"Bob, if there're any shooters out there, you're a sitting duck. Those guys have night sights, they can see a spade in a coal mine."

Redfield laughed. "They got to clear the building, Jake. It's s.o.p."

"I wouldn't count on s.o.p. in this case," Neuman said. "I wouldn't count on it at all. . . . What's your plan, Bob? You must have a plan, don't you? . . . You know, even if they convict you, you're not going to get the chair. Even what's-his-name—Berkowitz—he didn't get the chair, and he killed—what?—eight women, nine women? Christ, I read he'll be eligible for parole in a couple of years. A smart guy like you, maybe you'll write a book or something, like what's-his-name, that guy Abbott, Jack Abbott."

"A cop in stir, Jake?" Redfield said. "How long do you think I'd last?"

"Then what's your plan?"

Redfield came to the door. "Where's the key to your cuffs?"

"On my chain."

Redfield pulled the chain from Neuman's pocket, unclipped the chain from his belt, and unlocked the cuffs.

Neuman rubbed his wrists. "What's going on?"

Redfield reached under his coat and took Neuman's gun from the back of his pants and handed it to him. "Hey, Bob, what is this?"

Redfield took his service revolver from his shoulder holster and cocked it. "I want you to shoot me, Jake. Kill me. I can't do it myself. I had the gun in my mouth in the bathroom just now, but I couldn't pull the trigger."

Neuman put his gun on the kitchen table, shaking his hand as if it were hot, laughed nervously, and said, "You crazy fuck."

"Or else I kill you, Jake."

"You crazy fuck. What the fuck do you want to kill me for?"

"I'll get the chair if I kill a cop."

"So kill some other cop, for Christ's sake. Kill McGovern, kill Klinger. Kill fucking Mazilli, he's another reason we got on to you, you dumb fuck, that was another dumb thing you did."

Redfield smiled. "I wanted to get caught, Jake, like you said. You caught me, so I'm going to kill you, unless you kill me first."

"You crazy fuck," Neuman said.

Redfield flexed his left arm and looked at his watch. "I'll give you thirty seconds, Jake."

That's too long, Neuman thought. He doesn't want me to do it. Thank God. "What's to keep me from shooting you in the leg or something?"

"Shoot to kill, Jake, 'cause if you don't I'll kill you. . . . Twenty seconds."

"Or in the balls? I could make a real unhappy guy out of you without killing you."

"Fifteen seconds."

Neuman looked at his gun. "I don't even know if there're any bullets in that. It's been so long since I fired it."

Redfield reached for the gun, lifted it, sprang the clip, closed it, and handed it to Neuman. "Ten seconds."

"You crazy fuck."

"Five seconds."

Neuman hurled the gun at Redfield's head, nicking his temple. He stood, picked up the chair, and hurled it at the knees of the off-balance Redfield, sweeping his feet out from under him. He aimed a foot at Redfield's face but couldn't kick him there, kicking him instead in the shoulder, breaking, he was sure, his big toe.

Redfield rolled under Neuman and knocked him flat, knocking his breath away. He got to his feet and pointed his gun at the chest of Neuman, who had rolled onto his back. "Get up, Jake."

"Shoot me, you crazy fuck," Neuman shouted. "Shoot me, you goddamn fucking coward. You scumbag. You . . . you traitor." And Neuman began to weep.

But the sound of his weeping was swept away by the sound of the

200

semiautomatic rifles in the hands of the three policemen who burst through the apartment's front door and turned Redfield into a snapping, quivering, shaking bag of blood.

The policemen were strangers. And they were specialists: they wore baseball caps, flak jackets over black turtleneck sweaters, black pants, black leather gym shoes. They all had the same face, the face of death.

Neuman knelt over Redfield's body, his fingers confirming what needed no confirmation. He looked up at the cop on the left. "You son of a bitch. You didn't challenge him to drop his gun."

The cop in the middle said, "We heard you yelling, lieutenant: 'Don't shoot, don't shoot!'"

"Then you heard wrong, you stupid fuck."

"Are you all right, sir?" said the cop on the right.

"You stupid fucks." Neuman got up and went into the kitchen, switching on the light as he did. He knelt over Linda Walsh's body and slowly turned her onto her back. There was blood behind her ear from where she had been struck by the gun butt and blood at her nose from her fall to the floor. The blood at her nose burbled. She breathed.

"Thank God," Neuman said. "Oh, no. No, no, no, no, no."

THIRTY - SIX

Neuman put his badge and gun on Deputy Chief Inspector Lou Klinger's desk.

Klinger semaphored his hands at them, as if they were a meal he hadn't ordered. "Come on, Jake. Give me a break."

"It was an execution. I can't work for a department that carries out executions."

Klinger moved a pile of papers between himself and the badge and gun. "He confessed to you, for Christ's sake . . . Didn't he?"

"I can't say that he did," Neuman said. "We talked about it, about how he felt about women, about the world. But I can't say he confessed, no. He never said, 'I killed Chris Kaiser, Susannah Keyes, Martha Wine.'"

Klinger plucked a piece of paper from the top of the pile, flourished it, read from it. "Items found in the apartment of Detective Sergeant Robert Redfield: one Olivetti portable typewriter, pica type, with extrusions—whatever they are—on letters c, k, and l and upper-case W matching those on the letters written by the alleged killer of Chris Kaiser, Susannah Keyes, and Martha Wine. One manuscript of an untitled novel written on an Olivetti Praxis typewriter belonging to Susannah Keyes and identified by Keyes's agent, Zoe Zell, as being a novel written in Keyes's style and containing several spelling and grammatical errors typically committed by Keyes in drafts of her books. Part of a ream of Sphinx twenty-pound bond paper—"

"It was an execution," Neuman interrupted. "And I don't understand why everybody's taken it in stride. If it was a civilian who got blown away that way there sure as hell would be demands for an investigation. Don't cops have civil rights, too, even if they're suspected of being killers?"

"Suspected?" Klinger said. "Suspected? Nobody suspected Bobby, Jake. He took Linda Walsh hostage. He took you hostage. He admitted to you—maybe not in so many words, but he admitted it—that he killed three women in cold blood and sapped a fourth—I just got a call from the hospital, she's off the critical list, there's no brain damage, she'll make it—he pulled a gun on you, he was going to kill you, too."

"No," Neuman said. "He couldn't've done it, no more than I could've killed him, the way he asked me to."

"Because he was your *part*ner?" Klinger said sarcastically.

"Because he was my partner, because he was my friend."

"What kind of friend, Jake? You said yourself you didn't know anything about him, you didn't even know he had a tattoo over half his fucking torso."

"I've never seen you with your shirt off, Lou," Neuman said. "You've never seen me."

Klinger rested his elbows on the desk and interlaced the fingers of his hands. "Let me get this straight, Jake. Are you saying Bobby was innocent? Are you saying this was a case of mistaken identity?"

"No."

Klinger sat back and hooked his thumbs in his belt. "Good. Then that's that."

Neuman pointed at the badge and gun. "And there's my resignation. What do I do—fill out a form, write you a letter?"

Klinger rubbed his eyes with his forefingers. "For Christ's sake, Jake."

"Lou, try and see it my way: my partner was a killer and I didn't know it. I could've known it; the tips were there. He wanted to get caught. He even said he had a theory: the killer was a cop; a cop can go places other people can't, get people to open doors, get in and get out of places without worrying about what he'll do if he's challenged. He'll just show his badge is what he'll do. . . . My partner was a killer and I didn't know it. There must be a million other things I don't know. Who's going to want to work with me? Who's going to trust me?"

"You'll work inside for a while. You'll work downtown. Or at the Academy. I can assign you to the Academy."

"Professor Neuman, who didn't know his partner was a killer? Come on, Lou. Those kids aren't dumb. They're hooked into the grapevine."

Klinger smiled at the irrefutability of what he was about to say. "You quit now, you sacrifice a full pension."

Neuman nodded. "I talked about it with Maria. If it's what I want, it's all right with her. Anyway, the Austin P.D. may apply my pension time to their plan. I could wind up with a full pension anyway, or possibly only three quarters. The commissioner's administrative assistant's going to get back to me on that."

Klinger cocked his head. "Austin?"

"Austin, Texas."

Klinger cocked his head in the other direction. "The Austin, Texas, Police Department?"

"It was one of those things," Neuman said. "I got to talking with Maria—about maybe retiring, about maybe working someplace else, out of New York, someplace where maybe people don't kill each other as regular as they do around here. She said she wouldn't mind living someplace that was warm in the winter. I said I'd been thinking the same thing, I'd been thinking about Arizona—"

"Arizona?" Klinger said.

"—Maria said she read somewhere Arizona had some of the worst air pollution anywhere. I didn't know that. I wouldn't've thought that. But if she read it, it must be so. So I said, Well, that leaves Florida and California, I guess, 'cause I can't see us living in Mississippi or Alabama or one of those states, and Maria said it left Texas, too, which I'd never thought of 'cause when I think of Texas I guess I think of deserts, which are warm enough, but that wasn't what I thought Maria meant when she said she wouldn't mind living someplace warm. Like I said, it was one of those things, 'cause Maria said she'd just been talking to a neighbor, a woman who just moved into the building, and she was from Texas, and Maria said this woman said Texas wasn't just desert at all, that it has a lot of pretty country, in particular around Austin, which this woman said was one of the pret-tiest places she'd ever been, and it turns out she's traveled a lot, to Europe and everywhere. And then that same night, the night Maria and I started talking about all this, Monday night, we turned on Johnny Carson and who was a guest but Willie Nelson—"

"Willie *Nelson?*" Klinger said.

"—who I really like a lot, his music, I mean, and just the way he is, kind of tough and kind at the same time. And he lives in Austin, and's part of a whole country-music scene down there that's not like the scene in Nashville, which, to hear him telling Johnny Carson about it, is all slick and commercial and full of wheeler-dealers who don't care about music as much as about making a buck. The show was a rerun, it turned out, the Best of Carson, but still. . . .

"The next morning, yesterday morning, I was listening to the radio

204

while I was shaving and there was an ad for United Airlines or maybe it was Eastern, anyway, some airline, for flights to Dallas, Houston, and Austin. Like, I said, it was one of those things. Then Maria went to the library and got a book about Texas and another book called The Best Places to Live in the U.S., or something like that, that took about a hundred cities and listed all kinds of information about them—like what's the hottest temperature in the summer and the coldest in the winter and how much an unskilled laborer makes on the average and how much certain kinds of professionals make and how many homicides there are and how much it costs to buy a house or rent an apartment and what the cost of living is, and Austin came out looking pretty good in just about every category, except they have tornadoes there, which I didn't like the sound of. . . .

"So I made a couple of phone calls. I called the Chief of Police and said did they need an experienced homicide detective and he said as a matter of fact they did 'cause one of his best men just had a heart attack, which I didn't think sounded like the best advertisement, but he said it wasn't work-related, that the guy had a lot of family problems plus he ate and drank and smoked too much. I asked him about the pension thing and he said I should talk to the commissioner, so I called his office—I didn't get him, I got his administrative assistant—and he said he'd send me some job application forms and he'd get back to me about the pension thing, but I should fill out the forms as soon as I got them even if I hadn't heard from him yet 'cause he was pretty sure they could work something out. He didn't exactly promise me the job, he said he had to talk to the commissioner and the chief and look over my application when they got it—I'm giving you as a reference, Lou, I hope that's okay, and, well, we'll see. Like I said, it was one of those things, and as Maria says—well, she doesn't really say it, I say it, 'cause I don't know much Spanish even though I'm married to one—a Spanish-speaker, that is, but, well, it's one of the Spanish things I do know, and, well, *que sera, sera*."

Klinger sighed. "I guess you've made up your mind."

"Let's just say I've started the ball rolling," Neuman said.

"And I can't talk you out of it," Klinger said.

"Try and see it my way, Lou."

Another sigh. "I have to tell you, Jake, if they ask me for a recommendation, there's one thing I'm going to have to tell them that they might not like."

"I talk too much?" Neuman said.

"Jesus, Jake. Do you ever talk."

The buzzer rang.

"What the fuck is that?" Neuman said.

"The special number, Jake," McIver said.

"For what case?"

"The Samaritan Killer. It's still open. You want me to take it?"

"I'll take it," Neuman said, and got up and went downstairs and into the communications room.

"Hello, lieutenant," Mazilli said, holding his hand over the mouthpiece of the phone, "it's for you. I think it's what's-his-name—Keller. André Keller. You want me to tape it?"

"It's s.o.p., right?" Neuman said.

"Yes, sir."

"Then tape it."

Mazilli gave Neuman his chair, handed him the phone and hit the RECORD button on the tape recorder.

"Neuman," Neuman said.

"Hello, lieutenant, this is Ré Keller."

"Hello, Ré. Where are you? No. Scratch that. You won't tell me anyway."

"I'm a long way away, lieutenant."

"It sounds like it. It sounds like you're a long way away. It's a good connection, though."

"I'm calling about Linda, lieutenant," Ré said. "The last paper I saw that had a story about . . . about what happened said she was in critical condition."

"She's off the critical list now," Neuman said. "She's going to be fine."

"I was wondering about the hospital bill. I don't know if she has insurance. I wanted to send some money."

"I wouldn't know about that. I could ask her when I see her. I

206

thought I'd go see her late this afternoon and I could ask her. You want to give me a number where— No. Scratch that. You don't want to give me a number."

"I think I'll just send some money anyway. It can't hurt."

"I don't know, Ré. I don't know how she'd feel about that. I don't know how, you know, close you two were. She might feel funny, though. I mean, I feel kind of funny just chatting with you like this like we were old buddies and here you are, a guy who killed three of the citizens I'm supposed to be protecting—or two, anyway, Nassau County's not my jurisdiction.

"You know, Ré, if it's your reputation you're interested in saving, killing people's not the way to go about it. The subway thing you didn't plan, I know, and there's probably not a jury around that'd convict you of murder there, although you might have some problems about the gun, if it's not registered and all. The Nassau County thing I don't know all the details about, but the Harlem thing, what's-his-name, Stearns, I don't think you've got a chance in hell of beating that rap. Dealer or not, you iced him cold and that's against the law. Unless it was self-defense. There were no witnesses, you might be able to say it was self-defense. Was he armed? I don't even remember. Anyway, all I'm saying is, if it's your reputation you're interested in saving, you might be interested in coming back here from wherever it is you are and, well, facing the music. Some people'll probably be inclined to treat you like a hero, and since it sounds like you got a bum rap in 'Nam, well, who knows?"

"I'm pretty well set where I am, lieutenant. If people found out who I was, it would make for difficulties."

"Yeah, well, I guess it's me I was thinking about as much as you. You did what you had to do and you got out of it clean. I'm looking at an open case that I'm going to have to keep open, like it or not. . . . You didn't make any mistakes, did you, Ré?"

"I made one. I let Linda know who I am, who I'm supposed to be."

"Hunh. Funny you telling me that. I could ask her about that when I see her. Or wouldn't she tell me?"

"I'm not sure. She might, she might not."

"Yeah, well, it's funny you telling me that. I guess you want to get caught, too—the way Bobby did."

"I guess Bobby and I both wanted people to know something about what we felt. We both had a lot bottled up inside us."

"Yeah, well, I guess that's true of all of us. . . . Look, Ré, I'm going to get off the phone, I've got a pile of paperwork about six feet high. Now that I think about it a little more, I'm not going to mention the money thing to Linda when I see her. You'll just have to do what you think is right."

"I understand, lieutenant. Would you . . . give her my . . . my best wishes?"

"I don't think I'll do that either, Ré. I mean, technically I'm supposed to be hot on your trail, not be a messenger boy."

"I understand. . . . Well. . . . Goodbye."

"Yeah," Neuman said, and hung up.

McIver came to the door. "They traced the call to the overseas operator. Europe. The operators know the numbers of the callers they put through."

Neuman nodded. "What do you think, Tim?"

"I guess we should forget it."

"Just say the call never came through?"

"Something like that."

"Erase the tape? Like Watergate?"

"I don't know. That's something else, I guess."

"Umm," Neuman said. Then he said, "Why don't you turn your back for a minute, Tim? Or better yet, go get some coffee. Not from the back room; around the corner. Get yourself some too. I'll buy."

"Black, no sugar?" McIver said.

"Oh, what the hell. Have them put a little sugar in it."

"Lieutenant?" Federici said.

"Come on in, Steve," Neuman said. "Pull up a chair. Pull it around the side here. I won't be able to see you if you sit in front of the desk. Look at this pile, and I've already finished about half of it."

Federici sat. "There's a rumor going around. Is it true?"

Neuman laughed. "A rumor already? Well, I guess that doesn't surprise me. Klinger was never very good at keeping a secret. What a lousy poker player he is. You should jump at the chance to play with him if you ever get the opportunity. Every hand's written all over his face."

"It's true, then? You're quitting?"

"Try and see it my way, Steve. I don't think I can be very effective in this town any longer. I think I can still be effective in some other town, so it makes sense I should look for work in some other town. I'm not exactly quitting, I'm just relocating. If everything goes through, of course. It's all very preliminary."

"You'll be around next month, then?"

"Oh, yeah. Sure. Yeah. I mean, I don't see getting arrangements made before Thanksgiving or so. Why? Oh. I know why. Toni."

Federici blushed. "I'd like you to meet her."

"Well, I'd like to meet her. I sure hope you two aren't, you know, disappointed when you finally do meet."

"I couldn't resist, lieutenant," Federici said. "I had to ask one of the guys she works with—a guy I got to know a little bit making calls down there about Sergeant Redfield's outfit—I had to ask him what she, you know, looked like. I mean, was she good-looking or just average or a dog or what? He said she was cute, real cute."

"Cute?" Neuman said.

"Yeah."

"Funny. That's what I told Toni you were when she asked me what you looked like."

"You *did?*"

"Yeah."

"She *asked* you?"

"You were standing right next to me."

"I thought she might be, but I wasn't sure. . . . And you said cute? I didn't hear you say cute."

"Well, maybe *I* didn't say it, maybe *she* said it. I mean, she asked me if you were cute or what. No. She asked me if you were as cute as you sounded on the phone. I said yeah."

"Cute?" Federici said.

"Yeah."

"Thanks, lieutenant."

"Don't mention it."

"And whatever happens, lieutenant, I'd like to stay in touch."

"I'd like that too, Steve."

"Miss Walsh?"

"Lieutenant Neuman. I recognize you from your picture in the paper."

"Yeah, well. I wish they wouldn't do that. There're a lot of people out there I'd rather they didn't know what I look like."

"Are you here to ask me about what happened?" Linda said. "I don't know if I want to talk about it."

"I can understand that, Miss Walsh. And, no, I just came by to see how you were doing. You'll have to talk about it sometime, though. I'm planning to have Lieutenant McIver come and talk to you—maybe tomorrow, maybe the day after, depending on what the docs say. He's a good man, very thorough, and he won't waste a lot of time asking questions that aren't important."

"I feel sorry for you, lieutenant. I mean, your partner and all."

"Yeah, well," Neuman said.

"I never realized . . . I thought Ré . . ."

"Yeah."

"Who is Ré? What did he want?"

"It's a long story, Miss Walsh. I don't think this is the time for it. Maybe Lieutenant McIver can fill you in on some of it when he comes to talk to you."

"Ré killed some people, though—didn't he?"

"He killed some people."

"The boy on the subway?"

"I wouldn't call him a boy. And I hate to say it, but he was no great loss."

"One of the patients on this floor is the nurse he was going to rape, the nurse Ré helped."

"That's a coincidence."

"Ré and I were in the Green Tree one day when you and Sergeant Redfield came in for lunch," Linda said.

210

"That's another."

"Did you catch Ré?" Linda said. "Or do you know where he is?"

"No."

"I know what he calls himself. I think I know who he works for. I mean, he's not a professional killer or anything. He has a job."

"Un hunh," Neuman said.

"Do you want to know what he calls himself?" Linda said.

"Do you want to tell me? Before you answer, let me tell you something you don't know because we haven't told the papers about it yet, maybe never will. . . . Ré called us to tell us Redfield was at your apartment."

"Redfield thought Ré was following him."

"He was following him."

"And he called you?"

"Yeah."

"'Cause he knew Redfield had killed those women?"

"And because he thought you were in danger."

"So he sort of saved my life."

"Sort of. Yeah."

"He cared about me."

"He sends you his best," Neuman said. "His love."

Linda laughed. "He called you, said I was being held captive by a madman, said, 'Send her my love?'"

Neuman laughed. "He said it later. Today. He called me today to find out how you're doing."

"He said to send me his love?"

Neuman nodded.

Linda shook her head. "It's crazy. He kills people. What does he know about love?"

Neuman shook his head. "I don't know. But then, there're a lot of things I don't know. . . . You have insurance, Miss Walsh?"

Linda nodded. "The bartenders union. I'm a bartender. At the Gold Rail."

"Another coincidence," Neuman said. "I used the phone there the other night. . . . There's also something called the Crime Victims Benevolent Fund or something like that. You should know about it.

211

There might be a little money in it for you. I'll tell Lieutenant McIver to give you the info on it."

"Thank you."

Neuman put a hand on Linda's shoulder. "I guess I'll be going. You should get some rest."

"You didn't ask me—"

Neuman touched her lips gently. "Shh. Get some rest."

Like a child, Linda shut her eyes. When she opened them, Neuman was gone.